HARDWIRED

Also by Sally Chapman

Cyberkiss
Love Bytes
Raw Data

HARDWIRED

Sally Chapman

St. Martin's Press ≈ New York

Library of Congress Cataloging-in-Publication Data

Chapman, Sally.
   Hardwired: a Silicon Valley mystery / Sally Chapman. —1st ed.
      p.   cm.
   ISBN 0–312–15542–5
   1. Women detectives—California—Santa Clara County—Fiction.
   2. Computer industry—California—Santa Clara County—Fiction.
   3. Santa Clara County (Calif.)—Fiction.   I. Title.
   PS3553.H295H37   1997
   813'.54—dc21   96–53872

First edition: May 1997

10 9 8 7 6 5 4 3 2 1

To Caroline Lundmark, with lots of love

Acknowledgments

Thank you to the following people who provided me with the help I needed for this book: the people at NASA, Carol Lundmark, Nora Cavin, Linda Allen, Paul and Holly Merrigan, Bob Stull, Scot Malloy, Larry Warnock and Joanne Brattain. A special thanks to Dick Hoffmann for never asking me to work through lunch and to my husband, Jim Osbon, for everything.

1

She was a man killer, plain and simple. I knew it as soon as she set foot in our office. It wasn't just the fact that she looked like a perfect day in the Caribbean—flawless, lightly tanned skin, hair the color of shimmering sand, eyes an aquamarine you only see on postcards from lush, tropical places. None of that mattered. I mean, the girl couldn't help the fact that she was physically perfect. And since we're all sisters under the skin, I would never hold it against her.

No, it was the way she aimed those aquamarine eyes at Vic Paoli, my business partner/*mi amore*, that booted up my defenses. She looked at him the way I look at a dessert tray after a nice dinner; something totally desirable, completely obtainable. Maybe you shouldn't have it. Maybe you don't even really want it because you're stuffed already. But you're smug in the knowledge that it's yours for the taking. It made me glad that I'd whacked her on the head with a basketball.

Still, I jumped out of my chair, gasping, "I'm sorry!" The ball, made of foam rubber, bounced to the floor. Paoli scooped it up, his eyes held fast by the woman in the doorway. Being the optimistic type, I assumed he was transfixed because it had been a month since we had seen a potential client. So much for optimism.

I hurriedly swept the empty frozen yogurt cartons into the trash can, buttoning up the jacket of my serious gray suit as I came around my desk. It had been Paoli who put up the indoor hoop on the inside of the supplies closet door. I had been opposed to it, but during those prolonged stretches of time when we saw absolutely no clients I had managed to develop a pretty good shot, ricocheting the ball off the door and into the basket while sitting at my desk. I had won five dollars off Paoli that week alone.

As she breezed by me I inhaled the faint aroma of pure, fresh roses with just a hint of vanilla, the kind of expensive European perfume I haven't been able to afford since I quit my corporate job and started a computer fraud investigation business with Paoli. Her pale blue suit looked like a St. John knit, the seven-hundred-dollar kind, the kind I've *never* been able to afford.

She glided up to Paoli and kissed him on the lips while I looked on open-mouthed, too astonished to shout "foul!" He squirmed, although not nearly enough for my taste. I was just about ready to go find a garden hose to turn on them when they separated.

"Margo. I can't believe it. It must be . . . " he stammered, clearly as amazed by the liplock as I was. I had never seen him blush before. "I haven't seen you since college."

"Almost ten years," she said, running her finger under his chin. She looked him up and down, taking him all in. He was wearing what I call his Frat Boy clothes—khakis, a white cotton shirt with the sleeves rolled up past his wrists, and tennis shoes. He looked handsome and casual, like he would be more at home in a Gap ad than in an office. But then, he always did.

"You haven't changed a bit," he said, his voice taking on a gooey quality I'd never heard before. He's usually the sarcastic type. I didn't like the feelings of territoriality bubbling up inside me.

Paoli beamed at Margo, oblivious to my annoyance. In fact, he seemed oblivious to my existence in general. He perched on the corner of my desk while she seated herself demurely in front of him in one of our client chairs, tossing her blond hair back and tipping her head slightly as she smiled at him.

I cleared my throat and extended my hand. "I'm Julie Blake." Yes, I'm also here in the room sucking up oxygen.

"Oh," she said without enthusiasm. She unstuck her eyes from Paoli. It looked like it hurt.

"Julie, this is Margo Miller," Paoli said excitedly. "Margo, Julie. Margo and I know each other from college."

"Is that how you describe it?" she said with a little tinkle of a laugh that coincided with a churning in my stomach and a fervent wish that I had done something more attractive with my hair. That morning I had hurriedly pulled it into a ponytail, although it really looks better loose around my face. But I have this Puritan work ethic thing about getting to the office early, even when there's practically no work to do.

Paoli laughed, looking uncomfortable. "Really, Julie, it's been ten years since I've seen her and she looks exactly the same."

I was so happy for her. I stretched my lips into a stingy smile. Margo slowly recrossed her legs, clearly for Paoli's benefit.

"The thing is, Vic, I think you've actually gotten better looking," she said smoothly. She reached over and gave his biceps a playful squeeze. "Nice muscles. You must work out every day."

"Well, almost," he answered, obviously pleased that she had noticed.

I watched the two of them, trying my best to squash the jealousy rumbling inside me. To be honest, it surprised me that Paoli had once dated Margo. Paoli is broad-shouldered, sexy, and baby-faced, but his personality just didn't jibe with this elegant cat-woman. I had always imagined him going out with sassy cocktail waitresses before he met me.

Our new dog Cosmos, recently acquired from the local pound, came over to Margo and shoved his nose up her skirt.

Wagging a finger at him, I said, "Bad dog. Bad Cosmos. Down." He looked at me plaintively. I don't think he liked this woman any more than I did.

Margo patted his black head, raising her eyes to Paoli. "Your dog, I imagine. Handsome men have handsome dogs."

"Actually Cosmos prefers to be called a Canine American," I joked, and she tossed me a weak smile.

Cosmos proceeded to sniff at her open-toed, suede high-heeled shoe which exposed a glimpse of red toenails. Cosmos has had a few problems with office life when it comes to his urinary habits, and normally I take exception to it, but if he was ever going to lift his leg indoors I prayed he would do it right then. Being a gentleman, Cosmos just took a few more sniffs and retreated back to his bed.

Our Silicon Valley office is small, just big enough for our two desks, a couple of file cabinets, and two leatherette client chairs. Almost everything is rented, including the ficus plant.

We had found room for Cosmos' bed in the corner next to one of the file cabinets. Most of the building's other tenants are start-up high-tech firms like us and no one seemed to mind him at all.

"So, Ms. Miller," I said, deciding it was time to steer the conversation away from how absolutely fantastic they both looked. I crossed the room and closed the door to the supplies closet, concealing the basketball hoop. Paoli managed to throw the ball into the closet just before the door shut. He responded to my scolding look with a grin.

"Call me Margo," she said without looking at me.

"So Margo, what brings you to town?" I said with forced cheerfulness. Sitting back down at my desk, I folded my hands primly in front of me.

The smile left her face for a second then flashed on again, but with less wattage. "I have a problem, and I thought Vic might be able to help."

"Of course, I'll help. What is it?" he asked.

She took a breath and held on to it a second. "You know I work for NASA?"

"Sure. Jeff told me about a year ago. Jeff was one of our best friends in college." He said the last part to me then turned back to Margo. "He said things were going great for you."

Margo sighed. "They were." Shifting in her seat, she looked down at her lap for a moment, then cast her eyes back up at him. It was a sexy little maneuver—three hours in front of a mirror and I might be able to do it myself. "But now there's a problem."

I hoped it was that she needed money for a sex change operation.

"I work in Houston, at the Johnson Space Center," she began.

"Isn't that where they do all the astronaut training?" I asked.

She nodded. "I'm in charge of public relations. The Space Center has image problems, and they hired me to help turn things around. I've been there two years, and I've been fairly successful, but about a month ago someone started hacking into the computer system that handles our Mission Control communications."

I could feel my business sensors perking up.

"You mean the computers that actually communicate to the astronauts in flight?" Paoli asked.

"Exactly."

"But what does public relations have to do with the computer system?" I asked her, standing up and going around to the front of my desk again, where I sat down on the edge next to Paoli. All my brain cells were suddenly paying attention to what she was saying now that I'd heard the words *NASA*, *computers*, and *hacking* in the same sentence—and if she made any more grabs for Paoli I wanted to be close enough to swat her hand away.

"Nothing at first," she said. "I knew they had some internal people working on the computer problems, and they thought they had it fixed for a while, but last week it all started up again. It's really a lot more than hacking—whoever is doing this has shut down our most vital software programs. Now the problems are threatening to delay the shuttle mission scheduled for next month. That's how I got involved."

"Technical glitches mean bad publicity," Paoli said.

"Always." She paused, widening her eyes. "I thought of you, Vic. You were such a genius with computers in college.

I had to be in the San Francisco area anyway for a conference, and Jeff had told me you started this computer business. Data9000 Investigations, right? I saw it on the door. Anyway, I told the missions director I'd stop in and see you."

Paoli turned up his palms. "You want advice, technical help, what?"

Standing, she touched his arm again and locked her eyes on his. My pulse quickened.

"I've been authorized to hire you. I want you to come to Houston. I want you to find out who's breaking into the computers and put a stop to it."

I thought cynically that it was like the scene in an old Western where the beautiful school mistress asks the sheriff to run the bad guys out of town. But she said the last words with an urgency that told me she was taking these computer problems personally. For the first time I noticed the real distress in her eyes. Although the smile was fixed on her face there was something troubled behind it, and I wondered if she had more on her mind than computers.

"Tell us more about this hacking. How do you know it's happening?" I asked.

She shifted her gaze to me and took a step back from Paoli. "I've seen it myself. It's strange. Nonsensical. Just a series of numbers that pop up from nowhere. One of the programmers showed it to me. He said he was in the middle of using a software program and all of a sudden these numbers flashed across the screen."

Paoli looked at her inquisitively. "Does it disable the software?"

"Temporarily. But when it comes to NASA software even

a temporary disruption can be critical. If we don't get it fixed soon, the next mission will be delayed. Liftoff is October tenth. We have to meet that date."

It was now the second week in September. I shrugged. "Don't shuttle missions get delayed all the time?"

"Yes, but usually it's weather or a specific mechanical or computer malfunction," she said, an edge creeping into her voice. "We know eventually we'll get a go-ahead. This problem is indefinite, and NASA doesn't like indefinites. This mission has gotten a lot of visibility with Congress because there are biomedical experiments scheduled. We need help, and we need it now."

Paoli shook his head, looking puzzled. "But Margo, this is a breach of government security. Why doesn't NASA go to the NSA or CIA? They have computer experts."

She twisted her fingers together. "Yes, of course, you're right, Vic. But if we ask them for help word about the hacking will spread, and that's the last thing we need. You worked for the National Security Agency. You know how it is."

He nodded. "I remember very well."

"So you understand that we don't want problems like this to be blown out of proportion. That's why we decided to talk to you—you can come in quietly, take care of the problem, then go away. And I knew I could depend on your discretion. We have . . . history together. I can trust you."

She paused, opened her mouth to say something else, then clamped it shut again. A shadow passed over her features.

"You were about to say something," I said. "Please, any information you have could help us."

She tried to make her eyes cheerful, but it wasn't happening. "Nothing. It was nothing." She took a deep breath, directing everything she had at Paoli. "Can I count on you?"

I held up a finger before he could answer.

"Margo, if you'll excuse us for just one moment while we conference," I said.

She looked perplexed but nodded. "Of course. But I have a plane that leaves in an hour and a half," she said, checking her watch. "You know how hectic airports are on Friday afternoons."

"We'll hurry," I told her.

Paoli gave me a curious look as we walked out into the hallway. A six-foot-square area near the water fountain is the real heart of Data9000 Investigations, where most of the critical client decisions are made. We call it Conference Room A, Conference Room B being the table by the window at the Hard Drive Cafe.

Paoli steered me to the wall, backing me up against it.

"So what's to discuss? Of course we're going to take the case. We're talking NASA. Astronauts. Big honking computers crunching mind-bending, life-altering data," he said, gesturing expansively.

I wrapped my arms around myself. "I just thought we should talk about it, that's all. It's going to require some travel." I knew this was lame as soon as the words dribbled out of my mouth, but my frontal lobe was searching madly for negatives, and that was the best it could come up with on short notice.

He began to pace in front of me. "So what? They'll shell out for expenses. Julie, this is the type of case you've been wanting—big, important. We'll be promoting space exploration, for chrissake. You can't get bigger and more important than that."

He was right, of course. Nine months earlier Paoli and I

met when a murder and a data theft wrecked a government defense project at my former job at International Computers, Inc. I had been managing the project. Paoli was sent in by the NSA to find out who was hacking into ICI's computers. Our relationship quickly became more than professional, and after knowing each other only a few weeks, we quit our jobs and started our own computer investigation business, naming the firm after the mainframe computer that had brought us together.

In that short time our few cases had tended to be either mundane or bizarre. This was a project we could sink our teeth into, but something was nagging at me, and it was blond, blue-eyed, and answered to Margo.

I have a lousy poker face, and Paoli can always read me. He stopped pacing, put his hands on my shoulders, and gave me that look of his that makes me want to kiss him for about an hour.

"You're not concerned about Margo and me, are you?" He looked more deeply into my eyes. "You *are* jealous," he said, laughing. "This is great." He pulled me toward him, pressing his lips against my neck and growling playfully. "I find it sexually stimulating."

"You find fire hydrants sexually stimulating. You're titillated by tunnels, turtleneck sweaters, sushi," I said, giggling as he kissed my neck, and I was reminded for the one-thousandth-and-sixty-second time why I'm so crazy about him. He's fun and he keeps me from being so serious. He's also great in bed and a whiz with computers. What else could you ask for in a man?

A door opened and we quickly separated. Mr. Lorenzo from down the hall walked toward us and we straightened up into professional postures and returned his nod. As soon as he disappeared into the men's room Paoli pressed his hand against the wall and leaned in close to me again.

"Listen, kiddo," he said, his face inches from mine. "You don't have to worry about Margo. I dated her in college. That was light-years ago. Besides," he said as he nuzzled my ear, "I don't go for tall blondes anymore. I like brunettes, about five-foot-three, a hundred and five pounds, with gorgeous hazel eyes and an attitude. But I know I'm hard for women to resist, so just in case she's been pining for me all these years, I'll break our client rule and let her in on our secret."

I let him kiss my ear a few moments longer, my confidence temporarily stabilized. Then I put my hand against his chest, pushing him back to nonkissing distance.

"We have to be professional. It's not necessary to—"

"Tell her you're my main squeeze?" Paoli finished for me.

I smiled. "The point is, I'm not the least bit jealous," I said, fibbing beyond all reasonableness. "All she needs to know is that we're business partners."

Paoli shrugged. "If you say so."

He gave me a last quick kiss on the forehead and turned toward the office, but I stopped him.

"Wait a minute. There's something else bothering me."

"What?" he asked.

I closed my eyes a moment, struggling for the right words. "I'm not sure exactly. Somehow I think she's not telling us everything."

His face scrunched up. "Margo? Are you kidding? She's not the type to hold anything back, not from me anyway."

"Then why is NASA hiring outsiders to find this hacker? What if they're the ones who are trying to hide something?"

"What if they are?" he said. "The money we make will be just as green. And you know we need the money. So we take the case, right?"

I was torn. On the one hand, the idea of a case at NASA thrilled me right down to my sensible shoes. On the other hand, there was something about the case that just didn't feel right. Maybe it was the idea of NASA wanting outsiders to handle it. Maybe it was because it would take us beyond the familiar confines of Silicon Valley. Maybe it was the way Margo managed to touch Paoli every chance she got.

The tie-breaker, as usual, was money. We had bills coming up at the end of the month and nothing to pay them with. Since I was the accountant in our relationship, I made a quick pact with myself to be more optimistic.

"With your NSA background and a reference from NASA, we should get a lot of government work after this," I said, feeling a bit more chipper. Paoli hugged me with one arm.

We walked back into the office and found Cosmos at Margo's feet, growling. She'd grabbed a catalogue from Paoli's desk and was slapping at him with it, her brow furrowed.

"He's trying to chew my shoe," she said as we came in.

While she was wearing it. Creative approach. I was really starting to like this dog.

Paoli rushed over and grabbed Cosmos by the collar. "Bad boy." Cosmos just looked at him ruefully. "Sorry about that," Paoli said to Margo, hauling Cosmos back to his bed.

"Well?" Her face was expectant. "Will you take the job?"

Paoli straightened, grinning. "How could we refuse?"

Margo smiled back at him, showing lots of pearly white teeth. Capped, I thought. She fished in her handbag and pulled out an envelope, which she held out to Paoli. "I knew I could count on you. This is a plane ticket to Houston. You need to be there first thing Monday morning."

We both looked at her with astonishment. She was only hiring Paoli? I felt the heat rising in my face. I was usually the one people wanted most when it came to our business. Paoli had moved nine months ago from Washington, D.C.; he was a newcomer, but I was well-known and respected in Silicon Valley. The idea of being pushed aside irked me, not to mention the fact that I wanted to jump up and down and yell out that Paoli was my boyfriend and wasn't going anywhere without me.

"Julie and I work as a team," he told her.

She hesitated a second. "But the purchase requisition is only for one person."

Paoli looked at me, then back at Margo. "Sorry. It's both of us or nothing."

How I loved that man. I made a mental note to break down and finally wear that ridiculous silky-thong-lingerie-type thing he bought me for the Fourth of July.

Margo looked pointedly at me for a few seconds. "All right. Get her a plane ticket and just add the expense to your bill."

I wasn't crazy about being referred to in the third person, but now she was a paying client and to me that made a difference. I'm your basic A-type personality and tend to put work first. Although I didn't much like Margo's showering her attentions on my boyfriend, I couldn't let my possessiveness interfere with work, especially a great job at NASA. At least that was what I told myself.

I held out my hand to her. "Data9000 Investigations has an excellent reputation. I'm sure we'll be successful. We'd like for you to fill out one of our client forms." I pulled one out of the file cabinet and handed it to her. "The second page is our rate sheet."

She looked it over as though it were in a foreign language. "I'll give this to my assistant on Monday." Taking a card out of her purse, she scribbled something on the back and handed it to me. "Call our purchasing department. They'll fill you in how expenses are handled." She tossed a feeble smile at me then glided over to Paoli.

"It'll be fun working together, Vic. I'll pick you up at the airport Monday morning."

I guess I was supposed to take the bus.

"Um, there's something else I should tell you about," Margo said. "It's silly, but you should probably know about it." Suddenly she seemed a lot less sure of herself.

I could feel the clincher coming. "What is it?" I asked warily.

"Some protesters are causing problems at NASA, that's all." She cocked her head and smiled slightly. "You know, wild-eyed types."

"What are they protesting?"

"Anything the fools can think of."

I turned it over in my mind. "Could they be responsible for corrupting NASA's software?"

"It's possible. The reason I'm telling you is that they might harass you. Nothing to worry about, though. Now I must go."

"Wait a minute," I said, my eyes widening. "What do you mean, harass?"

"Sorry, but I absolutely can't miss my plane. Vic, I look forward to seeing you Monday."

"Same here," he said happily. "See you Monday."

"So nice to meet you." Margo tossed the words at me like spare change as she went out the door and bumped into my best friend, Maxine LaCoste.

"Oh, sorry," Max said, giving Margo the once-over.

Somehow, I thought with satisfaction, stunning Margo's icy good looks didn't quite measure up to Max's dark, sensual beauty. Max would run rings around Margo in a Miss Universe contest—and then I silently chided myself for putting such emphasis on physical attributes. I had no right to dislike Margo just because she happened to be Paoli's old girlfriend. After all, who was I to criticize his taste in women?

Her hands on her hips, Max watched with narrowed eyes as Margo cruised back to Paoli and gave him a kiss right on the lips. He didn't exactly fight her off, and the sight of it made everything inside me clench up.

I wanted to shout, "Bad girl! Bad Margo! Down!" but I doubted it would work any better on her than it did on Cosmos.

2

As Margo Miller glided out the door Max gave her a final hard look, inspecting her closely for visible defects. I doubted she found any.

"Who was *that?*" she asked me, her voice steely. Cosmos ran up to her, tail wagging, and she bent down to scratch behind his ears.

"Our new client," I said, a little too atypically perky to be believable.

Max arched one eyebrow. "Clients kiss now?" she asked dryly. "This is Santa Clara, not LA."

Paoli chuckled, oblivious to all the unspoken communicados bouncing between Max and me. "Margo's just an old friend," he said as if that covered the entirety of their relationship, which I knew it didn't. "It's way past lunchtime. Want me to get some sandwiches from the Hard Drive?"

Anxious to get him out of the office so we could talk, we hastily gave him our sandwich orders—turkey on whole wheat for me and a veggie special for Max. Since becoming attached to Cosmos, she refused to eat the flesh of any creature with the cognizance to come if you called it. Paoli trotted off, whistling.

As soon as he was out of earshot, Max turned to me, her body pressed theatrically against the door. "Men are human pustules," she said, her voice temporarily low and throaty. "They're repugnant, maggot-infested road kill." Her point made, she walked over to one of the client chairs and dropped into it, swinging her feet up on my desk.

"Having a problem with Wayne?" I asked.

"You know I am," she said, making a face. "Ever since Wayne started working on this corporate merger, I hardly ever see him."

I'd heard this invective about eight times before, so I decided to multitask.

"You used to complain that you saw him too much," I said as I sat down at my computer. I began typing up a new case file, heading it "NASA."

"Well, I didn't realize I'd miss him," she said petulantly. She patted her lap, and when Cosmos jumped up into it, she proceeded to cuddle him, not caring whether she mussed her white linen jumpsuit.

There was a muffled ring and Max pulled her cellular phone out of her Gucci handbag. "Yes, Wayne," she said into the receiver. "I'm at Julie's office."

That couldn't have been a big surprise to him; lately Max spent almost as much time at our office as I did. When we're between cases, which is most of the time, Paoli and I make phone calls and write letters trying to drum up business. A few weeks earlier Max began dropping by occasionally to help out. Then she started coming more often, sometimes bringing a gourmet lunch for us, sometimes toys for Cosmos; now she was coming every day. Not that we minded. We liked the company, although the past two days she spent most of the time on her cell phone arguing with her new husband.

I concentrated on creating my NASA file while Max and Hansen bickered.

Max and Wayne Hansen had been married a little over a month, and the marriage was already teetering. Hansen, one of Silicon Valley's young, rich, eccentric computer geniuses, hadn't been much more than Max's boy-toy before they married, but the nuptials had induced a manliness in him that I respected. For the first time he wasn't letting Max walk all over him, and he looked good without the Charles Jourdan heel marks. Currently he was negotiating a merger between his company and another high-tech firm, and so he wasn't paying Max the attention she thought she deserved. And she thought she deserved a lot.

With irritation, Max shoved the phone back in her purse. "The creep put me on hold. Why did I marry him in the first place?"

I stopped typing, happy to do a little psychological analysis. "I think you're afraid that because Wayne doesn't have much time for you lately it means he doesn't love you. That's what's really bothering you. But that's irrational. He's just tied up with business right now. It'll pass."

She grimaced as she scratched Cosmos behind the ears. Cosmos was in heaven.

"I'm not so sure, Jules. Men are inferior organisms. They're not like us. They lack depth and consistency, probably because they have almost no estrogen. Cosmos is the only male I trust." Cosmos yawned his appreciation. "And speaking of man problems, it looks like you've got a few of your own."

Having finished entering the NASA case information, I hit the print key and logged off the computer. Then I got up, walked around my desk, and sat down on its edge. "Like what?" I asked, feigning ignorance.

Max nudged Cosmos off her lap and stood up. "Like that Vamp-O-Matic that was just here, and don't pretend you don't know it. I saw the way you looked at her when she gave Vic mouth-to-mouth. And I don't blame you. Vic's lips are your turf."

She was hitting too close to home. I slid off my desk and started tidying it, even though it was already perfectly tidy. "Margo doesn't know that. Paoli and I decided a month ago that we wouldn't let clients know we have a relationship outside the office. We decided it's not professional."

If Max's eyebrow had shot up any farther it would have hit the ceiling. "You're really going to work for her?"

I gave some papers a last couple of riffles just as the printer began printing out the NASA file. "Well, yes. It's a great opportunity. A case at NASA."

Margo slowly shook her head, making a *tsk*ing sound. "My poor, little, naïve compadre. Forget NASA. Forget the case. If you let that woman near Vic for longer than a nanosecond you ought to have your neural pathways Roto-Rootered."

She was expressing my own fears, but at the moment I was up to my eyeballs in denial. "That's silly. I'm not the jealous type."

The edges of Max's mouth curled up, and I knew what she was thinking. Paoli spends most nights at my house, but several months ago, in a frenzy of restraint, I had insisted that we spend a couple of nights each week apart. Except during those nights I found myself miserable. On one of those evenings, being under the mistaken impression that Paoli was with another woman, I had tiptoed through his shrubbery trying to get a peek in his window. It was my bad luck that Paoli had discovered me up to my Calvin Klein-clad rear end in the foliage. I was still embarrassed about it and Max had the good taste not to mention it. Out loud.

I threw up my hands. "Okay, when it comes to Paoli I can be a little jealous, I admit it. But Margo is just an old girlfriend from eons back, and it means nothing."

Max eyed the doorway that Margo had just cruised through. "Don't kid yourself. Everything means something, Jules. That was a very attractive woman dressed to make the most of it."

"The woman was wearing a simple business suit."

"So she's subtle." Max ran her eyes over me and winced. "And look at you. Where'd you get that gray suit? A convent? And your *hair*. It's . . . flat."

"Gee, I forgot to spray it and hang by my ankles this morning," I said sarcastically.

She frowned. "You're a beautiful woman, Jules, but you have to strut your stuff a little. Are you wearing that Wonder Bra I bought you?"

With one finger Max pulled out the neck of my blouse and looked down it. I chuckled and pushed her hands away. Whether she intends to or not, she always makes me laugh, and I knew she had my best interests at heart.

"I appreciate your concern, but you're overreacting. Paoli loves me. He's not interested in Margo," I said, picking up the NASA file.

Max shook a finger at me. "Take some advice from

one who knows. Never be too confident."

"Listen, Margo may be his old girlfriend, but this is strictly business," I told her, checking the document for errors. "We'll spend a few weeks in Houston—"

"You're going to Houston?" she asked, like I'd said Zimbabwe.

I looked up. "Don't worry. We won't be gone long."

Now it was her turn to look uncomfortable. Since she had married Hansen, Max had quit her job at Comtech, not wanting to work at a company where she was married to the boss. She kept saying she was going to find another job, but so far she hadn't. She certainly didn't need the money, but she did need to keep occupied, and with Paoli and me out of town she would have to get creative.

Max put a hand to her neck, a casual gesture, but she almost looked like she was about to strangle herself. "I'm not worried," she said. "It's just that, well . . . I'm concerned about Cosmos. You can't take him with you, so I guess he'll have to stay with me, won't you Cosmos?" Max made kissy noises and Cosmos trotted over, tail wagging. "We're being abandoned, aren't we Cosmos?" she said mournfully, looking up at me. "I still think you're nuts to take a case with She-Devil."

"You hardly met her."

"True. It would help if I knew the woman's intentions."

"I know her intentions. She was here on business."

"Hah. Let me be the judge of that. Was her makeup fresh?"

"I have no idea."

"How high were the heels on her shoes? Over two inches?"

I hesitated. "I don't know. Maybe."

"Could you smell her perfume?"

"Well, yes."

"There you have it. A situation is building."

And a situation *was* building, only not the kind Max meant.

3

A conclusion is sometimes that place where you simply get tired of thinking. After hours of self-analysis I came to the conclusion that Margo's attentions to Paoli didn't really make me jealous after all. Those initial flurries of anguish had been merely temporary hallucinations, a brief fluctuation of hormones that I scolded into submission. ("Down hormones! Bad hormones!")

So when she rested her fingers on my boyfriend's arm as we sped down the Houston freeway, it must have been scientific interest that made me want to bounce my briefcase off her well-coifed head. From an engineering perspective I only wanted to measure its trajectory and record any variances that could be attributed to the application of hair gel. It couldn't have been that I was jealous.

From the moment our plane took off that Monday morning I felt trouble coming, a vague sense of disquiet that sat inside my bones and gnawed at my stomach. Half a dozen worries tugged at me. Was Margo holding back information about the case? Was I crazy to let Paoli near this woman whom Max claimed could probably crack men like walnuts between her thighs. Would Max remember to feed Cosmos?

When certain no one was looking, I slipped out my bottle of Maalox and, like a closet boozer, sneaked two gulps. But it didn't ease my foreboding. My fretting was worsened by the fact that my control-top pantyhose gripped me like a vise, and no amount of shifting or sliding relieved my discomfort.

To impress on NASA my no-nonsense professionalism I wore a navy blue suit with a high-necked blouse, but taking Max's advice, I had on my lavender Wonder Bra underneath. The Wonder Bra was her idea of the heavy artillery required to counter Margo's assault on Paoli. Unaware of the fact that he was the object of this battle and unencumbered by restrictive lingerie, he relaxed comfortably in his seat, wearing the only suit he owned that didn't look permanently rumpled.

We had carried our two bags onto the plane, so we made it to the airport pickup area in record time, where we found Margo leaning casually against her pale blue Mercedes. It was the less expensive model targeted at the yearning upwardly mobile, but it set off her eyes. Paoli started to get in the back, but she made some excuse about how the passenger seat was stuck and there would only be room for him up front, so I was relegated to the back alone.

The drive to the Johnson Space Center took close to an hour, but it seemed longer, with Margo and Paoli waxing incessantly about the fun-filled, drunken revelry of their college days. A couple of times I considered ripping open my blouse, revealing the lavender loveliness of my Wonder Bra, and shouting, "Get a load of this, people!" but I opted instead for sulking, quietly inhaling the smell of the expensive leather upholstery, and looking out the window.

The South Houston scenery was less than inspiring, a

succession of barbecue stands, billboards, and low cinderblock buildings. What I remember most is that the land appeared perfectly flat. I'm used to California, where there are always hills or mountains in the distance, but in Texas it looked like you could roll a bowling ball and it would go until it fell off the earth.

As we got off the freeway the scenery changed to open land, and all my misgivings about the case shrank into insignificance when we turned onto a road marked NASA 1. I sat up straight so I wouldn't miss anything, feeling my excitement rise. I, Julie Blake, was going to NASA, not on some bus tour, but as someone who, at least for a few weeks, belonged there.

"We're here," Margo said cheerily as we turned onto a broad drive. I saw a guard building in front of us, but that was all, because the main gate was obscured by at least fifty angrily shouting protesters carrying signs that read "Money For Schools, Not Shuttles," "Spend Tax $$ Closer To Home," and "Food and Shelter First, Space Last."

The protest surprised me since I couldn't relate to anyone who opposed science. My attitude had always been the more technology the better, which is why I only buy food that can be microwaved. But I realized their reasoning had at least some validity, and I stored the topic away for further attention.

A green sedan was stopped in the middle of the crowd, and we braked about ten yards behind it. I glanced at the rearview mirror and saw the irritation in Margo's eyes as she watched the protesters.

"Who's having the party?" Paoli asked.

"C-CINS," she said, spitting out the word the way she would spoiled fish. "Citizens for Cutbacks in NASA Spend-

ing. See the man in the plaid shirt with the biggest sign?"
Margo pointed to a man standing in the front of the crowd,
shouting through a megaphone. "That's Harvey Lindstrom.
He organized C-CINS six months ago. It started out fairly
tame. Phone calls to the NASA director, letters to the editor of the local paper. But their tactics turned nasty. Now
they're here every day."

We watched the crowd bobbing in front of us waving
their signs and chanting. Although Margo's Mercedes wasn't
far from them, the protesters seemed to focus all their attention on the green sedan.

Paoli turned to Margo. "I see their signs, but what's their
main gripe?"

"They think space exploration is a waste, that the money
should be spent for social welfare projects. But what they
don't understand is that space research *is* for social welfare,"
she answered.

A couple of the protesters who apparently didn't get this
connection between NASA and social welfare began yelling
at the driver of the green sedan. Living in the San Francisco
area, I had seen my fair share of demonstrations, but the
ones I remembered had almost a pep-rally atmosphere, with
a lot of people joining in because of the camaraderie, or perhaps because of some sense of nostalgia for the sixties. These
C-CINS people had a militant air that put me on edge.

I leaned forward between the bucket seats. "These people seem too rabid to be protesting space research. I'd expect
a group this angry outside an abortion clinic," I said to
Margo.

"NASA has been pushing back a little on them, that's
all," she answered with a dismissive fling of her hand, yet
peevish enough that I could tell she felt uncomfortable dis-

cussing it. "We got a court order to have them removed, but then—"

At that moment the driver of the car in front of us leapt out and began waving his arms and shouting angry insults at Harvey Lindstrom. Margo visibly tightened. I couldn't catch all of it because the car windows were rolled up, but I heard a few words, most of them the four-letter variety.

There was an ugly explosiveness between the two men, and the protesters stopped their chanting and watched the confrontation in apprehensive silence. The driver raised his fist in front of Lindstrom's chest. Lindstrom backed away, but his opponent closed the distance between them. I bolted up in my seat, alarmed that no one in the crowd made a move to prevent the possible fight.

"Wait in the car," Paoli said, directing the words at me as he unfastened his seat belt and reached for the door handle. Luckily, just then the guard hustled out, pulled the driver aside and tried to calm him down. From the guard's manner, I got the impression the driver was someone special.

Eventually the driver reluctantly got back in his car and drove through the gate. The protesters yelled and slapped the fenders as he went by.

Margo, Paoli and I sat silently, stunned by the small drama we had witnessed. After a moment Margo said, "Oh," in a small voice, remembered her purpose and pulled her car forward into the throng of protesters. They shouted a few half-hearted insults but without the same zeal.

"Sorry about the delay, folks," the security guard said with a labored smile, only slightly ruffled by what had just happened. With a sweep of his arm, he waved us through the gate as it reopened.

Margo cleared her throat. "Well, as I was saying," she continued, sounding rattled, "the C-CINS people don't understand the value of NASA research. This planet is going to run out of resources in the next century. Shuttle experiments have let us measure the impact of weather changes on water supplies and agriculture. We've been able to study the oceans so that someday we can safely maximize their potential to provide food and energy. And we all know the value of satellites."

I'm sure Paoli was reflecting gratefully on the cable sports channel. I was thinking that Margo sounded like an evangelist, and it made me like her at least a little. I admire people who have a passion for their work.

"What sort of research is planned for the next shuttle mission?" I asked.

Margo was calmer as she pulled her Mercedes past the gate and began to answer my question. "Some ocean observation, but the research is mostly biomedical. Experiments that have to be done in zero gravity. That's why this mission is so important. We're in a tacit competition with the Chinese to see who can get the results first. If the experiments are successful in zero gravity, we'll have them beat. In fact," she said, glancing briefly at me in the rearview mirror, "I have my suspicions about the Chinese and our computer problems."

I raised my eyebrows. "You think the Chinese could be hacking into the NASA computers?"

"It's possible, isn't it?"

Anything was possible. That's what makes life so interesting. We drove through the campus of concrete and glass buildings separated by grassy quadrangles, and the realization that I was actually at NASA made me feel giddy. The day was sunny with a haze in the air that made everything seem a bit out of focus. People dressed in casual summer clothes walked along the sidewalks in twos and threes, and I imagined them discussing quarks, black holes, and the fiery surface of Venus.

NASA looked so commonplace that it was probably difficult for outsiders to believe that this was where we had launched men toward the moon. But not me. The very sight of it gave my nerve endings fresh fire. NASA reminded me of Silicon Valley, everything simple and unremarkable on the outside, when inside, technology that revolutionized the world was at work.

We pulled into a parking lot in front of a six-story building near the south end of the campus.

"This is building four," Margo said after she turned off the ignition. "It's where the astronauts have their offices. The computers are in the data-processing facility on the first floor."

I felt tingly, and like a kid going to the circus, I couldn't wait to get out of the car.

"Will we meet any astronauts?" Paoli asked, and I smiled at him. He obviously felt the same way I did.

"I have a feeling you'll see more of them then you'd like to," Margo answered. "The shuttle crew is very concerned about the mission. They hate delays and they like to get involved in things, especially anything technical."

We stopped at a security office where we filled out half a dozen forms, including three separate confidentiality statements making us swear not to divulge any NASA secrets after our work was over.

"I'm surprised you didn't do background checks on us," I said to Margo after I signed the last of them.

She cut her eyes at me sharply. "I did, on you."

At first her remark annoyed me, but then I was glad she had checked me out, because it meant she knew I graduated from MIT and Stanford and that I had been the youngest vice president at the largest computer company in the world. Now if only I could tell her I had Paoli in my bed almost every night.

After Paoli and I had our pictures taken and received contractor ID badges, we dropped off our luggage in a storage room and took the elevator to the fourth floor. Margo managed to keep Paoli always by her side. I felt like the kid sister nobody wanted to play with, and I had to remind myself over and over again how calm, adult, and completely unjealous I was. Maybe I could get it tattooed somewhere.

We stopped outside a white cube of a room about the right size for Cocker Spaniels. It was furnished with a single gray desk, three chairs, a phone and a computer.

"Here's the office you'll be using while you're here," she said.

It had a window, which was excellent, and there was an unframed map of the solar system pinned to the wall, so in our spare moments we could plot out courses for future space travel. Actually I felt lucky we had an office at all, since Margo probably would have preferred to have Paoli sharing her office. Maybe even in her lap.

I laid my briefcase on the desk and surveyed my new surroundings. "We'd like to get started. We'll need access codes for the computer system, printouts of the software at the source code level, everything you've got on the security system. And we'll need to meet with some of the operations people," I said.

"Of course," Margo replied. "But the SM–15 crew is having lunch together in one of the training rooms and I thought you'd like to meet them." She cast a glance at Paoli. "They'll insist on meeting you anyhow, and this will be convenient because they're all together. I told the commander this morning we'd be coming by."

All my schoolmarm seriousness drained right out of me at the prospect of meeting real live astronauts.

"Well, since we have to meet them anyway," I said, trying hard not to seem too excited. I wondered if I had the nerve to ask for their autographs.

"Good. I have to go check something in my office first. I'll be back in a minute," Margo said.

She went off and Paoli and I started settling in. I took out a new purse-size notebook I had brought to keep track of the case. I had separated it into sections headed "Expenses, Daily Progress, Billable Hours," and "Misc." Under "Billable Hours" I noted what time we arrived at NASA, and under "Expenses" the price of my plane ticket.

Then I turned on the computer terminal. We didn't have the password or access code so we couldn't expect to actually use it, but I just liked having it turned on, being one of those weird people who thinks computers are friendly. There was a knock at the door.

A smallish man in his late twenties was standing there, looking at us nervously. He had wavy, dark blond hair and freckles, and his eyes were the color of gunmetal. He was wearing khakis and a pink golf shirt, both not quite clean and a little too big for him, and his face had a disconcerting unevenness to it, which I realized was because his nose was crooked. The needle on my Geek-O-Meter flapped wildly. He was a techno dweeb.

I can say this because I'm a computer geek myself and I know my own breed. The main difference between me and the guy in the doorway was that a couple of years ago Max took over most aspects of my outward appearance, and now my hair was styled and my clothes matched. Most days.

"Are you the Data9000 people?" the visitor asked.

"You found us," Paoli said with his usual good-natured friendliness. "Come right on in."

He didn't move. "I saw you with Margo," he said with a shy smile. "I'm Michael Jaep. I'm the operations manager for the data center."

"Just the man we need to see," I said encouragingly. "So you have direct responsibility for the computers?"

"That's me."

"Have a seat," I told him. "We've got a lot to talk about."

He waved a hand in front of his chest. "I can't stay. I've got a meeting in two minutes. I won't be much help anyway. I've done my best to figure out how the hacker is getting into the computers, and I haven't come up with anything. Are you guys going to start right now?"

"Margo's going to introduce us to the SM–15 astronauts first," I said.

He looked astonished. "Really? Good luck to you. I was just with them; they phoned and asked me to bring up a report they needed. The meeting's getting stormy."

"What do you mean?" I asked.

Michael got a mischievous look. "I mean that Garza's laying down laws like he's Moses, and the rest of them are spitting mad."

Paoli stopped unloading his briefcase. "Who's Garza?"

"The mission commander, and a great one, except sometimes his people skills are nonexistent. But that's the norm around here." Michael gestured grandly. "We're here to explore new worlds. To go where no man has gone before," he said in a mock announcer voice. "But then you know what NASA really stands for, don't you? Never-A-Straight-Answer."

Paoli and I both laughed and at that moment Margo appeared. She looked miffed, and I knew she had caught part of the conversation.

"So you've met. Good," she said crisply, giving Michael the same look I gave Cosmos when he chewed up my running shoes. "Michael, you'll need to get them set up with computer IDs. We'll be busy for the next hour, but please have them ready to go by four at the latest."

"Yeah, sure," he said, holding his head low as if she might smack him. "Nice to meet you." He gave us a stiff-handed wave and left.

Taking the elevator down to the first floor, we went outside and climbed into a golf cart which Margo drove up to another building, parking in front. She inserted her badge in a card reader and we went through the double glass doors and followed her across a linoleum-floored entry, then through another door.

I gasped as we entered the colossal room on the other side. It was cavernous, four stories high, and almost as long as a football field. An enormous American flag, a Texas flag and a flag with the NASA emblem hung on the side wall. The room and almost everything in it was white, but there was a broad blue stripe painted along the perimeter.

I felt my mouth drop open when I saw the space shuttle at the far end, but after a second I realized it was a full-sized mockup without wings. There were other life-sized models in the room, everything so massive it made me feel I had shrunk, like the man in that old horror movie from the fifties.

Paoli and I looked around us in amazement. There were several dozen people working in the room, some wearing astronaut-type jumpsuits. Most of them worked with the equipment in small groups, while others observed. I was so thrilled my heart pounded.

"Where *are* we?" Paoli asked.

"This is the main training facility for the astronauts. It's where they learn to live in space—to eat, sleep, work, even to use the bathroom. As you can see, we have mockups of different sections of the shuttle, as well as some proposed parts of the Space Station. The SM–15 crew is through here. Come with me."

Paoli and I were so busy looking at everything that Margo had to stop and wait for us a few times as she crossed the training area. We followed her into a long hallway.

We turned a corner about halfway down the hall and the shouting became audible. Margo's steps slowed and I saw the apprehension on her face as we approached a closed door; the angry shouts were coming from behind it. A sign to the left of the doorjamb read "Saturn."

Just then the door swung open and a man burst out. He froze, startled for a second by the sight of us. He was maybe in his early thirties, about five ten, slim and pretty-faced, although at that moment his features were distorted with fury. He pushed past us and stomped down the hall, disappearing around the corner. Margo gave us a taut, apologetic smile.

"Let me tell them you're here," she said, and slipped inside, closing the door firmly behind her. There was sudden silence, and then low conversation.

Paoli nudged me. "Things are a little strained here in NASA-land," he said.

I nodded. "There's an awful lot of yelling going on in this

place, outside and inside. But I'm sure everyone's under a lot of pressure. Probably too much work to do, and no room for mistakes."

In the hallway hung at least fifty photographs of astronauts. While we waited for Margo, Paoli and I looked at them and found a photo of the man we had just seen. Boyish-looking in the picture, grinning sweetly at the camera, he was quite attractive when his face wasn't twisted in ten different directions. There was something in his face I liked. He reminded me of someone.

Paoli draped his arm over my shoulder. "Now, you're not going to get infatuated with these astronaut guys are you?" he said. "I'm not sure I can compete with a space traveler."

"Lots of people call you a space cadet," I told him, turning away from the photograph. The door opened and Margo stuck her head out. Her eyes zoomed in on Paoli's hand still resting on my shoulder.

"Come on in," she said, and we went inside. Three men and one woman sat around an oval table in a small plain conference room. All of them looked to be in their thirties or early forties, and they stared at us with the sort of warmth usually reserved for one's proctologist. The men were dressed casually; the woman wore a dark blue jumpsuit with a NASA emblem above the pocket.

There were half-eaten sandwiches in front of them and raw vegetables cut into bite-sized chunks were piled on a platter in the center of the table, reminding me of how hungry I was. Papers lay scattered in front of everyone and an engineering drawing I couldn't identify was taped to a white board at the front of the room.

There wasn't a lot of extra space, so Paoli and I squeezed between some chairs and the one window, which looked out on some trees and a pond, and remained standing. My control tops had a death grip on my hips, but now was not the time to try to adjust them. Margo stood near the head of the table.

"This is Vic Paoli and Julie . . . "

"Blake," I reminded her with a forced smile.

"Of course. Julie Blake. They're here to work on the computer problems. Vic and Julie, I'd like to introduce you to the SM–15 shuttle crew."

I felt self-conscious as all sets of astronaut eyes scanned us critically.

"What's your background?" asked the fortyish, dark-haired man at the head of the table. After giving him a closer look I recognized him as the driver who had gotten in the fracas with C-CINS. He was a different animal now, more controlled, but he sat rigidly in his chair, inspecting us with sharp-witted eyes. From his position at the head of the table and the fact that there were more papers sitting in front of him than the others, I gathered he was the leader of the group.

"This is John Garza, the SM–15 commander," Margo told us before we had a chance to answer.

All the cool sexual confidence she displayed with Paoli had evaporated. Her face flushed, the pitch of her voice rose girlishly, and she seemed excitable, eager to please, like an over-anxious terrier. It was interesting to see the change in her, but the poor girl was going to have to fetch and roll over, because Garza didn't even give her a glance.

"What are your credentials?" Garza asked again.

Oral exam time, but I knew the drill. I took a breath and held it a second. "Mr. Paoli and I both have extensive computer backgrounds. We've designed mainframe security systems from the ground up and done troubleshooting on installed systems. Mr. Paoli was a senior computer analyst at the NSA, where he specialized in network security. I was a vice-president at International Computers, Incorporated, and I designed their whole system. We specialize in computer fraud and information security."

His eyes remained fixed on mine. "Neither one of you looks old enough to have those credentials."

I wanted to say, "When I smile really big I get little crow's-feet around my eyes," but instead said, "Our assistant can fax you our résumés," and met his gaze directly. "And I have a list of references, if you'd like to see it."

I was exaggerating wildly. We had no assistant, and to date we had merely a handful of references, and only two from sizable companies. I held my breath. Margo was staring at me owl-eyed. I guess I wasn't supposed to speak unless I received her go-ahead. Darn.

Garza was still giving me that hard look. I wondered if I should open my mouth and let him check my teeth.

"That won't be necessary," he finally said, and I breathed easier. "Although credentials are important here at NASA, we like to put the emphasis on action, not resumés." The comment seemed directed more toward the people at the table than at Paoli and me, and from the looks on their faces they didn't much appreciate it.

"I'm sure NASA will give you all the necessary computer access," Garza added, relaxing a little.

"We'll need more than that," Paoli told him. "In cases like this you usually end up investigating people as much as you investigate machines. There are a number of people we'll need to interview."

Garza frowned again, then quickly smiled. He had nice

teeth, and it was a dazzling smile enhanced by an intelligent glimmer in his eyes. It crossed my mind that he was really very sexy. From the vibrations emanating from Margo I got the impression it had crossed her mind, too.

But his smile dimmed as he leaned forward in his chair. "Let me introduce you to the rest of our group. This is Lanie Rogers. She's our engineer."

She bobbed her head at us from the other end of the table. About thirty, she was a petite woman with curly reddish brown hair and a jaunty face that made her look like an exuberant gym teacher. Her eyes were blue, so pale you felt you could see right through them, and they contrasted sharply with the current redness of her face. One of the shouting voices we'd heard earlier had been distinctly female, and she was the only female at the table. She gripped a pencil between two fingers and tapped it nervously on the table, creating an annoying staccato.

"And next to Lanie is Ben Lestat. He's our second-in-command."

Lestat sat stiffly, arms crossed, face grim as he examined us. His eyes darted to Lanie's tapping pencil, and with an irritated grunt he grabbed her hand to make her stop.

There was only one person left to introduce, the most interesting-looking character of all. Tall, massive, he sat with his chair pushed just far enough back to show he didn't consider himself a part of the group. He had a slight smile on his face, and his tranquil expression didn't fit the prevailing mood. His bald head was shiny, with a gray shadow over the ears indicating that he shaved it.

"And this is Harlan McKenzie. He was commander of the SM–13 mission we flew four months ago." Garza cleared his throat. "I think you encountered Gary Olander in the hall. He's our payload specialist."

I made a mental note to find out what that meant.

Garza smiled paternally at the group, shuffling his papers into a neat stack. "I think we're done here for today."

Lanie Rogers rose halfway out of her chair. "We're not finished. We haven't settled anything!" she said, flustered, her fingers clutching that poor pencil so tight her knuckles were white.

"I have another meeting," Garza said, his tone gentle but firm.

Lanie threw the pencil across the conference table and got up. She brushed angrily past me, closing the door behind her a lot harder than she needed to.

Garza emitted a small, mirthless laugh. "There are little spats in the best of families."

McKenzie stood up. "I'll go talk to her."

"I'd appreciate that," Garza told him and McKenzie went out.

"Ben, please remind Lanie when you see her that the two of you are in the WET-F Tuesday at nine. Don't be late. There will be another mandatory lunch meeting tomorrow, same time."

Pushing his chair back noisily, Lestat gathered the papers in front of him, then exited. Margo led Paoli and me out into the hallway. Garza followed, holding a small tape recorder to his mouth and speaking into it in a low voice. I couldn't hear what he was saying, but I assumed he was recording incredibly important astronaut ideas.

He clicked off the recorder and put it in his pocket. "I'd like to talk to you a few minutes," he said to us.

"Of course," Margo replied eagerly. "I've told them both how critical the timeline is on the computer issues."

Their eyes caught for a second before Garza quickly turned to Paoli and me. "Once a shuttle mission gets delayed it causes Washington to get involved, which complicates things around here. Plus the fact that the publicity from a computer security problem could hurt the whole organization."

"You mean, how can you build a complicated space station if you can't handle something relatively simple like computer security?" Paoli asked.

Garza didn't seem to appreciate his insight. "Our budget's already been slashed, and we're still having to fight for every dollar. There are a lot of people gunning for NASA right now. You saw the crowd outside the gate today."

Paoli and I exchanged a look. Not only did we see the crowd, we saw Garza wrestle with them.

"We noticed," Paoli replied.

"This isn't some college student we're looking for. It's much more malevolent. Whoever is doing this is making a deliberate attempt to demolish NASA software. If you're looking for a hacker, you should start with C-CINS. What better way to destroy a mission than to foul up the computer programs?" Garza's voice dripped animosity.

"We'll check out every possible angle," I said.

Garza glanced at Margo. "You have to take them over to see Lisa." He tossed it off casually, but Margo's whole body stiffened.

"Lisa didn't say anything about wanting to meet with them."

"Lisa wants to meet with everybody," Garza said with sarcasm. "She's in her office all afternoon, but you know how her calendar gets. I'd take them over now." He started to leave, but Margo took hold of his elbow.

"Why didn't she call me directly? I have a meeting with a Senate PR person in ten minutes. I don't have time to deal with Lisa," she said heatedly. "And I'm sick of her attitude. There's no reason for her to route things through you."

Garza paused before responding. "I'm the flight commander, and the computer problems are affecting this mission. Therefore, anything associated with them should be routed through me," he said condescendingly, as if he were talking to an irritating child.

Margo's face crumbled.

There was an awkward silence, then Garza turned to me. "I'm very interested in computers. You'll find that a lot of the functionality in the shuttle software is due to my input. If you need any information, just give me a call."

Oozing confidence, he gave me an astronaut smile, uncaring of the misery he was inflicting on Margo. He checked his watch.

"I have another meeting so I've got to go. But take my advice. If you're looking for a hacker, start with C-CINS." Garza then turned and walked away, leaving Margo looking after him like a lost little girl.

4

Men can be jerks. It's a universal truth right up there with gravity, the theory of relativity, and the fact that the price of gasoline goes up during the summer.

Although I fought it, I couldn't help but feel sorry for Margo as I watched her gather up her self-esteem, which was currently spilled all over the floor. I've been trounced a couple of times by men myself, and I don't like seeing it happen to somebody else, especially when there are witnesses.

There was a clumsy silence, which, thankfully, Paoli broke.

"What was all that shouting about before we went in?"

Margo's gaze had been downward, but at the sound of Paoli's voice she lifted her face and pasted on her beauty-queen smile. But it seemed staged, like the smiles on the astronauts' faces in the photographs on the wall behind her.

"There's been some last-minute reshuffling with the crew, and some people are getting short-tempered, that's all," she said, trying to make it sound normal and unimportant. My instincts told me it wasn't.

She straightened. "Well, if we're going to see Lisa Foster,

I'll need to put off that PR person. I'll leave you two in the training area while I make the call. I won't be gone long."

We turned the corner and Margo gestured to the doorway that led back to the training facility. She told us to stay at that side of the room and not wander around.

Once again we entered the enormous training room, which for me was the equivalent of Disney World. Both of us were delighted to get another look at it. Standing on the sidelines, our view was partially obstructed by some of the equipment, but we could see two men in jumpsuits entering the side of the shuttle mockup. Across the room a man carrying a laptop computer led a group of Japanese men in business suits up metal scaffolding to a large, white, square module with spokes coming out of it, which I learned later was a simulation of part of the proposed Space Station.

I heard music playing softly and recognized Gershwin's "Rhapsody In Blue," a piece I've always liked. The idea of Gershwin playing amid all the high-tech space equipment made me smile.

"Aren't those the astronauts we just met?" Paoli asked, pointing to the far side of the room. Lanie Rogers, Ben Lestat, and Gary Olander stood huddled in front of a large drum-shaped object that looked like a huge gyroscope. It sat at an angle, rotating slowly, held about three feet off the ground by metal framing.

Whatever fantastic thing it was, they didn't pay any attention to it. Olander spoke heatedly to Lanie and Lestat as he zipped himself into a blue jumpsuit. I could tell by Lanie's body language that she was trying to console him, and it seemed to work, because he stopped talking and looked upward a moment, as if collecting himself. Then he spotted us. Lanie and Lestat, seeing him distracted, looked for its source.

They seemed disconcerted by our presence.

There was something going on with these people. I wanted to know more about it and wanted just as much to know more about them. I saw the three of them exchange a few words, then to my amazement, Lanie waved us over.

I tugged on Paoli's arm. "Come on, let's go talk to them."

"But Margo told us to stay here."

I gave him a look that let him know what a dumb statement that was, then we crossed the huge room.

The astronauts were reserved when we first said hello, and I wondered why they wanted to talk to us, but immediately began asking questions, the first one about the music. Lanie explained that it was coming from Olander's portable CD player; he had loaned it to her so she could listen to it while she worked.

"What's this?" I asked, pointing to the huge gyroscope behind them.

"A satellite trainer," Olander replied. "It rotates at approximately the same speed as a satellite in space. Lanie's practicing changing a faulty control module."

"The proverbial moving target," Lanie said, and we all laughed. The astronauts seemed more at ease now that we were talking about what they obviously loved. Even Lestat, who was still quiet, didn't seem as rigid as he had in the conference room.

Paoli asked them what their roles would be on the SM–15 mission.

"My main job is to repair the satellite," Lanie answered. "Ben here will be in the cockpit with Garza. And as Garza told you, Gary's our payload specialist."

Apparently it was an unhappy subject. Olander's face

burned, and I could see his anger rising. Lanie's fingers briefly wrapped around his wrist.

"You'll have to translate for me. What's a payload specialist?" I asked.

It was Olander who answered. "A payload specialist works with special projects the shuttle has scheduled. I'm a biomedical specialist and I'm also this mission's photographer. I'll be photographing some new kelp formations off the coasts of Africa and Australia."

"You'll have to excuse my ignorance here, but what for?" Paoli asked good-naturedly.

Olander smiled a little and I studied him. He had a pleasant face when he wasn't furious, yet it occurred to me that there was something lightless behind his eyes, as if much of the human, feeling part of him was closed off.

"Good question. For food," he answered. "We're looking for new sources."

"You should try one of Gary's kelp omelets," Lanie told us.

Lestat made a face. "Ugh, they're terrible. Eggs and seaweed."

We chuckled over this, then I asked Olander about the biomedical experiments.

"We're doing tissue cultures," he said.

"Now it's your turn," Lestat interrupted before Olander could continue. "What exactly will you two be doing to find this hacker?"

He was suddenly very serious, and Olander and Lanie also looked at us intensely, waiting for our answer. Now I knew why they had called us over. They wanted to know exactly what we would be doing.

"We'll approach it a couple of ways," Paoli said. "First we'll run a few special virus scans. Then we'll go through all the communications software, the audit logs and all the programs that have been infiltrated by the hacker."

"Looking for what?" Lanie asked.

"Internal breaks. User IDs that have been used in ways they shouldn't," Paoli answered. "Security weakness where someone from the outside could come into the system. Or places where someone from the inside could break in."

"You mean someone inside NASA?" Olander asked, and Paoli nodded. "That's why you said you'd be investigating people as much as machines."

"That's pretty much the procedure," Paoli told him. "It's not that tough to find out how someone's breaking into a computer system and plug the hole. But we're hired to find out who as well as how. That way there's a better chance it won't happen again."

The astronauts' mood darkened, but I didn't have time to pursue it because just then we heard our names called and we turned to see Margo at the door. Paoli and I said goodbye and started to leave, but Olander stopped us.

"One more thing. I wanted to apologize for what happened earlier," he said, a little bashful. "My storming out of the meeting, I mean. I almost ran the two of you over." He gave us a broad smile, looking more like his photograph in the hallway. I liked him. As an only child, I had fantasized about having a brother, and at that moment Olander fit the picture I had always held in my mind's eye: smiling, intelligent and kind, in contrast to his coldness of a few minutes ago.

"Sorry we strayed off course," Paoli apologized to Margo when we reached her.

"You were never able to follow instructions, Vic," she said, smiling at him. "That's one reason I've always liked you. Come on, Lisa Foster can see us now."

"And exactly who is she?" I asked as we left the training facility.

"The director of the Space Center. Temporarily, until they decide on someone permanent."

"What happened to the last one?"

"He was retired."

Paoli frowned. "Sounds like the retirement wasn't voluntary."

"It wasn't. Not that he did a bad job. But he wasn't popular, and he had to be sacrificed in order to get more funding from Congress."

Now it was my turn to frown. "Sacrificed? NASA has to fire people to make it look like they're making changes?" I asked as we pushed through the double glass doors and went outside.

After the cool air-conditioning inside, the heat came at us like a sock in the face. We got back in the golf cart and Margo drove off back toward Building Four, where our office was.

"It's the federal government's way of doing things," she said when we were on our way, answering my question. "Not NASA's. But if we want funding, we have to play by their rules. Lisa was made director as a transitional measure, but she wants the job permanently. She's military," Margo added, as if that explained something.

"Nice to know the federal government has all the political intrigues of the private sector," Paoli said.

Margo pulled up in front of the building next door to Building Four, an identical concrete-and-glass construction.

We went through the double doors at the entrance and rode the elevator to the top floor. Following Margo down a couple of hallways, we ended up in a small reception area where a young man sat behind a big desk. On the desk was a computer, a pile of manila file folders stacked so the edges were perfectly even, and a nameplate that read "Gerald Conner." The young man wore the only suit and tie I'd seen so far at NASA, and he had a prim, smug look about him, as if he had all of life carefully tabbed and filed.

"We're here to see Lisa," Margo told him.

Gerald Conner looked us over as if he were the dress code patrol. He buzzed his boss and told her we had arrived and then ushered us inside the adjoining office.

It was medium-sized with one window and had a definite military air. The beige carpeting was worn and the walls were hung with photos of former presidents and a smattering of generals.

My own father, who died when I was six, was a lieutenant colonel in the Air Force, and so I have an affection for certain things that are military. The American flag in the corner and the photos of generals on the walls made me think of my dad. There was always a photograph of Eisenhower on the wall of his office. Flags, starched uniforms, and the smell of shoe polish always leave me with a dull, inner ache.

Lisa Foster was sitting with her back to us and it took a couple of seconds before she swirled her chair around and gave us a full frontal, snapping my attention back to the present.

She wasn't what I expected. Foster was in her forties with a head of thick auburn hair that fell to her shoulders, its length and abundance having a lioness effect. Her face was hard; her eyes were small and close together, sitting above a sharp angular nose and full lips that would have been luscious if they hadn't been so pinched. She obviously spent a lot of time on her hair and her makeup, and although she wasn't a pretty woman, she was striking. Rising from her chair she introduced herself and gave our hands rapid, firm shakes before sitting down again.

I guess I'd expected her to be in uniform, but she had forced herself, including most of the fifteen extra pounds she was carrying, into a too-small, bright red suit. The skirt was stretched tight across her stomach and hips and I could almost hear the fabric screaming for mercy. Still, there was a basic, raw vitality lurking just beneath her surface, and I had a feeling that once she got out of her business suit, Ms. Foster might show a very different side.

Foster gestured to two chairs, so we sat. Pulling a chair out from a small table against one wall, Margo took her place beside us. Foster sat with her elbows on her desk and her fingers laced. There was a large cocktail ring on the third finger of her right hand.

"Normally I don't interview contractors," she began. Her voice was raspy. "But this project has particular interest for me."

Paoli leaned forward in his chair. "Margo has explained how important the shuttle mission is. We'll find the hacker."

Foster eyed him. "I'll expect nothing less. NASA likes to deal with a select group of contractors. We normally don't go outside our standard list, but in this case no one was qualified for the job." I found that hard to believe but kept quiet. Foster leaned back in her chair, her hands now gripping the edge of her desk. "A recommendation from Miss Miller is hardly enough to put me in awe of your skills. I want you to know I expect results."

The remark was nasty, and I wondered if Foster and Garza had bet that day on who could make Margo cry first. In the high-tech world of Silicon Valley, public relations people are sometimes looked down upon, but it was obvious that Foster's dislike of Margo went deeper. From the look on Margo's face I knew it was mutual.

"You can count on us to give our best effort," I said, trying to ease the tension.

Foster didn't want the tension eased. "I need more than your best effort. This computer problem could create an extremely damaging mess. I'm the one carrying the load here, and I intend to get the results I need," she said. "And I need them in a week, otherwise the shuttle mission will be delayed. Do you get what I'm saying? Results in a week."

My gut clenched. I wondered if she was going to pull out a flip chart and show us a diagram of what a week looked like. I turned to Margo.

"Did you know about this time limit?" I asked her.

Margo fidgeted in her seat before answering. "Well, yes."

I was furious, but I managed to stay outwardly calm. "And you didn't tell us?"

"I just assumed it wouldn't take you long," she said, stumbling a little on the words. Foster was giving her a dirty look, and Margo's beautiful face showed duress.

Paoli jumped in to save her. "You can count on us, Ms. Foster. If you need this case handled in a week, we can do it. We'd like to have NASA as a reference."

Foster's eyes narrowed to little slits that looked like they might emit death rays. "If you succeed, maybe you'll get a reference. If you don't succeed in one week, which translates to next Monday, I wouldn't count on getting any more work from the government or from any of the companies we contract with."

She said this last part rather casually, but it had the effect of a stink bomb tossed into the room. The threat about losing government work was bad enough, but half the companies in Silicon Valley did contracting for the government. If we screwed this up, we'd be screwed ourselves.

I twisted uncomfortably in my chair. What kind of snarl were we getting into? Maybe Paoli wanted to pass out assurances that we'd find this hacker in a week, but I was more cautious by nature. We had yet to completely assess the problem, so we had no idea how difficult it would be to catch the hacker. Or if we'd even be able to catch him at all. But if we didn't do it—and do it in a week—it could hurt the future of Data9000. I remembered the misgivings I'd felt earlier that day and made a mental note to trust my instincts in the future.

Paoli stood up. "We better get started."

No kidding, I said silently. We said tense good-byes and left Foster's office. Margo stayed behind.

As soon as we were in the hallway I got out my notebook and hastily scribbled in the "Misc." section, *In future, query potential clients closely regarding timelines.* I stuck the notebook back in my purse, glancing at Paoli.

"What a shrew," he said as we headed for the elevator. "I can't believe she did that."

"I'll say. What did she think she'd gain by not telling us about the one-week limit until we got here?"

Paoli came to a halt, looking bewildered. "I didn't mean Margo. I meant Lisa Foster. You're not mad at Margo, are you? Sure, she should have said something about the time limit, but she probably just didn't realize it would cause us trouble."

I glared at him in disbelief. "Paoli, when you worked at the National Security Agency, how long did it normally take you to find any particular hacker?"

He didn't say anything for a few seconds, and I could tell that he was annoyed with me for asking the question, but at the moment I didn't care.

"A month probably," he finally answered.

I pressed my finger into his chest. "It usually took you a month to find a hacker. Now Margo the Model has lured us into a case in which we're supposed to find a hacker in one week, *one week*, or else our reputation will be trashed. I'd call that trouble. I'd call that Trouble El Grande, and she knew about it beforehand and didn't tell us."

I could feel the heat rising between us, and it wasn't the fun kind. I hated arguing with Paoli. It always left me feeling hollow and insecure. We walked silently back to the elevator.

Paoli angrily jabbed at the Down button. "I know you don't like Margo," he said with irritation, "but I think we should give her the benefit of the doubt. She's obviously in a tough situation."

I had a dozen sarcastic replies on the tip of my tongue but wisely decided against using them. After all, I was hoping to sleep with him later.

"Didn't you notice the way Lisa Foster treated her?" Paoli went on. "I guess Foster's really committed to the shuttle mission, but what an attitude that broad has got."

The elevator doors opened and we stepped inside.

"If you ask me, it's not the mission Foster's so concerned about," I said to him, glad to get the conversation off Margo.

"It's her job. She wants the position to be permanent, and it's not going to be if this shuttle mission gets delayed."

Paoli shook his head. "Well, that's typical. Everybody's tuned to radio station WIIFM—What's In It For Me."

I had a sick feeling that what was in it for me was a chance not only to lose our business but the love of my life as well.

5

My life was happening in dog years. In the past nine months I had quit my job as well as my fiancé, started a new life, complete with a new man, a new business, and a new and reduced financial status. Once pretty even-keeled, these days I was emotionally about as stable as plutonium, and now here I was a thousand miles from home, embarking on a case with "disaster" written all over it in DayGlo.

Paoli and I went out into the Texas sun, which beat down upon us mercilessly, a physical reminder of the pressure we were under. I could feel the perspiration on my forehead, under my Wonder Bra and along the length and breadth of my control-top pantyhose. It was at least ninety degrees, hot for September, but the thick humidity made it feel even warmer. I unbuttoned the top two buttons of my blouse.

In front of us was a large, square, grassy area with a sidewalk around its perimeter. The people passing by didn't seem bothered by the heat. I supposed they were used to it. I wondered if they felt the same way about the pressure.

I looked at Paoli, my only ally in this predicament, and touched his hand. I wanted to tell him that I was sorry we had argued and that I adored him beyond all reason, but just then we heard our names called. Paoli and I turned and there was Margo scurrying toward us, her high heels clicking like castanets on the pavement.

"I took the stairs so I could catch you," she panted when she reached us. She pressed her hand to her chest. "You'll have to excuse Lisa Foster. She's never a nice person, but right now her job's on the line."

"It's no excuse for being such an ass. I can understand her venting on outsiders like Julie and me, but not on a coworker," Paoli said.

Margo beamed her appreciation. "You were always sensitive, Vic."

I said a silent ugh and could barely keep myself from revealing the fact that Mr. Sensitivity sometimes refers to male sexual arousal as "making a pup tent."

Margo excused herself, Paoli watching her as she walked away. I tugged on his elbow. "Come on. We only have a week to do this job and day one is more than half over. Let's get to work."

But when we reached our office, I detoured to the ladies room, where I dug around in my purse for my Maalox, unscrewed the top and took a good-sized gulp to help put out the fire that Lisa Foster had lit in my stomach.

When I got back to the office I found Michael Jaep and Paoli huddled in front of the computer terminal, two open bags of Cheetos in front of them. Michael gave me a funny look.

"You have white stuff on your lip," he said.

I wiped it off with my fingers.

Paoli looked up at me. "That's just Maalox. It's Julie's idea of snack food."

"The tablets are easier, aren't they?" Michael asked, obviously familiar with the subject. "Not so messy."

Paoli cocked a thumb in my direction. "She thinks the liquid hits the spot faster. Julie likes things to happen quick."

"Not everything," I said with mock haughtiness. Paoli gave me a sidewise smile and I knew he wasn't mad anymore. That's one of the things I love about him: he never holds a grudge against anybody. I, on the other hand, can let things fester inside me for years. Carbon turns to diamonds before I let go.

He handed me a bag of Cheetos as a sort of peace offering. I took a few and gave it back to him. "Come look at this," he said, pointing to the screen. "Michael was showing me the log-on procedure, and as soon as we got into the software programs, the hacker turned up. I guess we got lucky."

"Actually the past few days the hacker's been popping up a lot," Michael said.

I dragged up a chair, swallowing my Cheetos. Sure enough, a series of numbers flashed on and off the screen, moving from left to right.

"Has this turned up in all the software programs?" I asked.

"All the ones associated with the SM–15 mission. The other software programs are okay."

I gave the numbers a harder look. "That's odd that the hacker is able to pick and choose his programs. And doesn't NASA have a complex encryption code?" An encryption code is what the government and corporations use to make computer data secret.

Michael nodded. "We have a hundred-and-twenty-eight encryption key code."

"Which means it should be pretty much impossible to break," Paoli said.

"But our hacker doesn't care," I explained. "You only need the encryption code if you want to read the data in the software programs. Whoever is doing this just wants to foul up the programs, not read them."

Michael looked distraught. "What's wrong?" I asked.

He turned to me, his eyes full of worry. "Do you think the hacker could be someone here at NASA?"

Paoli gave him a guy-type pat on the shoulder. "Listen, Michael, hackers are frequently somebody inside the company."

"Still, I'd hate to think somebody here would do this. I mean, in the first place, why would they?" he asked, fingering his shirt buttons, a habit that probably caused him to do a lot of sewing. His face was always slightly contorted with nervousness, his anxiety baseline a few levels higher than the rest of us.

"Lots of reasons," Paoli answered. "They could be mad at their boss, ticked off about the health plan."

Michael grimaced. "They did cut back on our dental last year."

I leaned close to the screen. Michael followed suit, and we were head to head for a moment while we studied it. The numbers were grouped in fours and at first glance appeared to be random. Just when I thought I had discerned a pattern, they evaporated, and the normal software appeared on the screen.

"Now you see them, now you don't," Michael said. "Only now the software program will be unusable for an hour or more."

We pushed back our chairs and for the next five minutes Paoli and I asked Michael questions about the computer setup. When we were done he asked us if we had met the

SM–15 crew. I told him we had, and from that point on he seemed more interested in the astronauts than the computer.

"They're a great crew, even though they're on edge right now," Michael said. "Garza's a veteran. Totally committed. If you cut him, he bleeds NASA. He's been on at least six missions, and before that he logged over five thousand hours of flight time with the navy."

"You know a lot about him," I said.

"Yeah, well, everybody here knows the backgrounds of the crew members. Around this place they're like rock stars. And everybody on the SM–15 crew is impressive. You'd be amazed at the things they can do. Garza and Lestat are both able to give in-flight appendectomies."

"You're joking," Paoli said.

"I'm not. If there's a medical emergency they might not be able to get the shuttle down fast enough. Some of these astronauts are as close to supermen as you'll find."

"What about Harlan McKenzie? He seems a little different from the rest," I said.

"You mean Space Monk?" Michael replied with a smile. "He's not going up on this mission. He's the CAPCOM."

I rested my elbow on the desk. "And that is?"

"The Capsule Communicator. There are hundreds of people working on a mission, but Mission Control only allows one person to actually communicate information to the crew."

"Why's that?" Paoli asked.

"To cut down on miscommunication. The CAPCOM is always an astronaut, and McKenzie has the job for the SM–15 mission. I think they're keeping him on the ground because he's gotten so strange."

"Define strange," I said.

Michael reflected on it a moment. Then he got up and shut the door. He sat back down with his hands in his lap and his knees pressed together.

"McKenzie used to be like the rest of them—intense about the work, aggressive, but fairly conservative. But since his last mission he's gotten into this Buddhist thing." Michael lowered his voice even though the door was closed. "That's why people starting calling him Space Monk behind his back. He's like a different person. I'm not knocking him. He's an extraordinary physicist."

"From what you told us, extraordinary is par for the course around here," Paoli said.

"McKenzie's more than that," Michael said earnestly. "He always has been. He goes deeper."

I was intrigued. "How?"

"Well, for instance, I don't think he's married anymore, but I heard he has a kid that's deaf and autistic, and that he started some fundraising organization for autistic children. Most people around here don't feel they have the bandwidth for things like that. Everybody respects McKenzie. People just make jokes about him since he shaved his head. You probably noticed that things are a little straight around here."

"We noticed," Paoli answered.

Michael checked his watch. "It's almost five. I've got some things to finish up so I've got to run, but I'll check back with you tomorrow, okay?"

"One last thing. Do you have a printout of the hacker's message?" Paoli asked.

"Yeah. I got one a couple of weeks ago. I'll go get it and bring it down."

Michael left. Paoli and I pushed our chairs together in

front of the computer screen and started running a sniffer program. A sniffer monitors traffic on a computer network and would help us determine if anyone was coming into NASA's network who shouldn't be there. We were in the middle of it when Margo walked into our office, preceded by her perfume. I guess it's easier than knocking.

"I hate to bother you with this, but they need you to fill out some forms so we can get you on our voice-mail system." She had recovered from her earlier agitation, currently all silky smoothness, like one of those models whose faces adorn Chanel magazine ads. "Do you have time, Vic? I'll take you down to administration."

Obviously a penis and a testosterone surge was required to fill out forms. I popped a Cheeto in my mouth and crunched it savagely. It was so hard not to blurt out, "He's my boyfriend." Every cell in my body wanted to, but I was too proud to let her or Paoli know how much jealousy was building up in me.

Paoli looked at her, then at me. "We've got to have voice mail," he said with a shrug.

I shrugged back. "Great. Go ahead." Was it my imagination, or did Margo give me a little smirk of victory?

The two of them left and I sat there stewing and eating the rest of the Cheetos, feeling shunned and childish and finally very thirsty. I decided to find a soda machine and get something to drink before I tackled the computer system solo. Taking my wallet with me, I roamed the maze of hallways but without any luck, so I found the stairs and went down one flight. I was exploring a doorway when someone said behind me, "Can I help you?"

I turned to find Harlan McKenzie standing a few feet from me. He was wearing dark slacks and a bright red cotton jacket, and the top of his head was so shiny I could have checked my teeth for Cheetos crumbs in the reflection. But I had to admit that McKenzie's baldness made him more attractive rather than less. Towering in front of me, he seemed as large and solid as a modern-day Zeus. I was taken aback for a moment and just stared at him, dumbfounded.

"I'm looking for a soft drink machine," I finally said.

"Soft drinks aren't good for you."

"I stay away from motorcycles and skydiving to cut down my overall risk factors."

His smile widened. "We don't have a soft drink machine on this floor, but there's a lunchroom, and I know for a fact that the refrigerator is stocked with sodas. I'll take you."

We walked together down the hall without speaking. I felt like a schoolgirl, thrilled to be next to him. I wondered what marvels he had seen, what miracles he had witnessed cruising around space.

He led me around a corner to a small kitchen with a table and chairs. The walls were hung with bulletin boards pinned with flyers proclaiming that the U.S. government was an equal opportunity employer, that flu shots would be available through the end of October, and that anyone who left a mess would be strapped to the outside of the shuttle for the next liftoff.

McKenzie opened the refrigerator door and asked me if I wanted regular or sugar-free. I really wanted the kind loaded with fructose and calories, but I'm perpetually trying to lose five pounds, so I opted for sugar-free. I thanked him and turned to leave, surprised when he offered to walk back up with me.

Along the way we chatted about earthquakes, always a hot topic with people outside California. I'm fairly petite and

McKenzie was tall, at least six feet four, and with my usual low-heeled shoes on I had to strain my neck to look up at him.

As we got to the office Michael came trotting down the hall waving a piece of paper. McKenzie and I waited outside the door.

"Got the printout," Michael said. McKenzie said hello to him and Michael returned the greeting with enthusiasm. I could tell he was in awe of Space Monk.

"I've got three of them, all different programs," Michael told me as he and I examined the papers. "I don't have time to tell you much right now, but it's pretty self-explanatory. This first one's a screen print of a navigation program that's got the hacker's stuff right in the middle of it," he said, showing me the offending lines.

I thanked him, and while we arranged a time to meet the next morning, McKenzie took the printouts out of my hand. When Michael walked away I turned to McKenzie and saw him staring at them. He looked more than startled. In fact, he looked shocked.

"What is it?" I asked, concerned he might be ill.

"This printout. The code here in the software," he said slowly, his eyes still stuck to the documents.

"Yes?"

"I've seen it before."

"In another program?"

He looked at me. "No. On the shuttle. During our last mission."

"Well, when you're aboard the shuttle you communicate with the Johnson Space Center computers, right?"

McKenzie shook his head. "This was different. There was a malf. A malfunction," he said, seeing my confusion. "The computers had gone out. There was no communication with Mission Control. Nothing. Then something else happened, something . . . strange. Then the computer screen was blank, and the next thing I knew this showed up on it." He pointed to the numbers that had been infecting the NASA software.

I looked at the numbers, then back at him. "How do you know they're the same?"

"I can't be certain every number is identical, but the groupings are the same and that's enough for me to recognize it. When the computers came back I asked Mission Control if the computer system had gone out. They confirmed that all of the computers had been dead for four minutes. Yet these numbers were on the screen."

His gaze was fixed somewhere over my head. I broke his trance.

"You said something strange happened just before you saw the numbers on the computer screen. What was it?"

His attention snapped back to me. "That's not something I can discuss," he said, suddenly agitated. "We all agreed not to discuss it."

"Who agreed?" I pressed him. "The shuttle crew?"

He looked at me stonily.

"It's your obligation to tell me anything that relates to the hacking. You have to tell me," I insisted.

But McKenzie just walked off. I stood there staring after him, bewildered. Although I didn't understand it, I was sure that what I had seen in his eyes was fear.

6

My weird and aborted conversation with Space Monk lodged itself in my head. I spent the next half hour in our pygmy office studying the hacker's numbers, and then I started on the communications software programs. There were half a dozen of them, and I sifted through them line by line. But McKenzie's words kept echoing through my brain.

In fact when Paoli and Margo breezed back in the office, looking into each other's eyes and laughing, I was so wrapped up thinking about McKenzie I hardly even wanted to hit her.

After a few more magic moments she left, and Paoli dropped into his chair and rolled it over to me.

"We'll have voice mail by tomorrow morning."

"That's nice," I said. "I got the printouts of the numbers that show up in the software programs. Look, the numbers aren't random after all." I stuck the printouts in front of him, having highlighted some of the numbers with a yellow marker. "It took me a while to find it, but there's a pattern. See what I mean?"

He studied them a few seconds, then his face brightened.

"These numbers have to mean something, Julie," he said excitedly. "Why would the hacker use the same series in the same order again and again unless it was some sort of message?"

"But what sort of message?"

The question dangled out there with no answer on the horizon.

Paoli rested his chin on the heel of his hand, looking at the printouts. "I knew some guys in Washington who specialized in breaking codes."

"You think that's what this is?"

"We won't know unless we try to break it. I'll call some of my old friends at the NSA. The Defense Department puts their secret information in codes that change every hour. If these numbers mean anything, the NSA software will figure it out."

He reached for the phone. I put my hand on his arm. "You can't tell them it's connected with NASA. We signed confidentiality forms."

"I won't have to tell them."

"How can you avoid it?"

He smiled. "Creativity, determination and a never-give-up attitude. And if that doesn't work, I'll lie."

He went to work while I continued with the communications software. After twenty minutes, Paoli hit pay dirt when he reached some person at the NSA named Bart he used to play rugby with. After some cajoling and a reference to a long-ago evening featuring two sisters named Lulu and Kiki, Bart agreed to take a look at the hacker's numbers.

I wandered around the halls again until I found a fax machine and faxed the printouts to Washington, and when I got back Paoli was busy with the computer. He looked absorbed, but I managed to tear him away and tell him about my odd conversation with McKenzie.

Paoli reacted the same way I did.

"Computers with no power don't have stuff on the screens," he said, pushing his chair back from the computer. "Maybe old Space Monk wasn't getting enough oxygen to his helmet."

I sat down next to him. "It's off the edge of weird, isn't it?" My tone was somber.

Paoli shrugged, not sharing my gravity. "So Space Monk's not operating on all thrusters. It's still a great case."

"You think so?" I asked. I stood up and began pacing the small office. "I know we're at NASA. I know these are astronauts, America's finest and all that, but there's an undercurrent here of something. I'm not sure, but it's like . . . " I stopped pacing and faced him. "Like malevolence."

He looked at me like I was crazy. "Malevolence? Julie, get a grip on yourself." He shook his head and chuckled.

"Then why is almost everybody we've met here either pissed off or paranoid?" I asked, irritated.

Paoli laughed. "It's the way of the world these days. It comes from urban stress, inhaling Windex, eating vegetables without scrubbing the pesticides off first. People are neurotic and there's not much we can do about it. We can't just pack our toys and go home."

"I know that," I muttered, "but we have to be careful."

"Julie, you're overreacting," he said, rolling his chair over and giving my suit jacket an affectionate tug. "Everything here is fine. They're under a lot of pressure, that's all. They've got computer problems, a bunch of protesters yelling at the gate, and you've read in the papers how NASA is being hit hard by spending cuts. That's all it is."

I put my hands on the arms of his chair and leaned down over him. "It's more than that, I'm sure of it. I've worked on projects with plenty of pressure, but I didn't see all this yelling and whispering and people seeming so upset." I stepped back from him and averted my eyes. "Maybe you're paying so much attention to Margo you're not seeing what's around you."

"I could get angry at that remark. Fortunately for you, I'll let it go because I know you're nervous, this being such a big case and everything."

I felt his eyes following me as I went to my desk, sitting on the edge as he continued.

"You know, Margo likes you. She was just telling me that you're very intelligent. You should try to get to know her better."

I'd rather swallow a lug nut. Paoli looked at his watch, but it wasn't on his wrist. He's always forgetting it. "What time is it?" he asked.

I checked the Seiko that almost never left my arm. "Almost seven thirty. Why?"

"McKenzie may still be here. Let's go talk to him. There's probably an explanation for what he saw on the shuttle, and if we uncover it'll make you feel better."

"We don't know where his office is. He's probably gone home anyway."

"No problem. I remember Margo telling me that all the astronauts have their offices in this building except for him because he had to have a bigger window or something. He's next door. And she said the astronauts stay late."

She was right. We found McKenzie in his office. It was spare and very neat, with a couple of artistic black-and-white family photographs on the walls. I noticed a picture of

McKenzie with a much older woman, two small boys and a couple of dogs. I figured the woman was his mother. Everybody was smiling, including the dogs, except the smaller of the boys, who looked sullenly at the camera, his eyes dull and vacant. I remembered what Michael had said about McKenzie having a deaf and autistic child. It was hard for me to imagine how painful it would be to have a child with a serious problem like that.

It was close to sunset. The overhead fluorescent lights in the office were off and McKenzie had turned on a spherical desk lamp, which gave the room a dreamy glow. He was bent over a large paperback that looked like an engineering manual. On top of the bookcase that stood against one wall were two expensively small stereo speakers and a portable CD player. I recognized the music of Chopin playing softly.

McKenzie closed the book when he saw us. "Can't remember where the soft drinks are?" he asked with a smile.

"We need to talk with you," I said soberly. "About what you told me earlier."

I didn't get the reaction I expected. McKenzie tilted his head very slightly and he gave me a benign look. It was funny, but it crossed my mind that he was looking at me as if I were some sort of inferior life form with whom he was determined to be patient. And somehow I didn't resent it.

"I was planning to speak with you tomorrow. You were right, Julie. I have an obligation to tell you what happened."

I sat down and Paoli stood beside me, his arms crossed. I was learning that with McKenzie nothing happened fast. He took a few seconds to gather his thoughts and then folded his large hands in front of him.

"Four months ago I was on the SM–13 mission along with Garza, Lanie Rogers, Gary Olander and Ben Lestat," he began. "We did a number of experiments with latex spheres, released a probe into orbit, practiced some maintenance routines on the shuttle exterior. All fairly standard. But on the third day strange things started happening. Something malfed the computers, and we lost all of them."

"How many did you have on board?" Paoli asked.

"Five. All identical, though a couple have slightly different programs; if one goes down, another takes its place. Only this time they all went out at once. I first noticed it because we lost a navigation-state vector."

"A what?" I asked.

"It defines the spacecraft's position. That's what drew my attention to the computers. Within thirty seconds they all went black. Garza was talking to mission control and nothing was showing up on the ground."

He had been building momentum as he spoke, but he suddenly stopped, hesitating. "That's when I saw the numbers on the computer screen," he told us. "On all the computer screens."

This wasn't exactly new information, and I wondered what he was getting at. "So the computers came back on," I said.

He shook his head slowly. "No. They were still down." He drew out the statement, emphasizing each word. "The screens were black, but the numbers showed up on them. The same numbers I saw on the printout you gave me."

There was a pause in the music and, as if on cue, a Tchaikovsky piece began playing, with lots of dramatic piano.

Paoli ran his hand through his hair. "Wait a minute. You're really saying the computers had no power, but something showed up on the screen? That's crazy. It's impossible."

"My thoughts exactly, when it happened," McKenzie said. "But the numbers didn't come from the computer. They couldn't have."

I turned up my palms. "Then where did they come from?"

"If you question my sanity, then you can confirm my story with Garza. He saw the numbers, too. Everyone else was in the lab bay, but they came into the cockpit to talk about the power outage. So they witnessed what happened next."

I shifted uneasily in my chair. "Which was?"

There was a long silence. "The light," McKenzie finally said, his voice softening as if he were starting to pray. "The green light. It engulfed the cockpit. It's hard for me to describe it really. Such a brilliant green. It felt like being inside an emerald that was electrically charged." He looked down at his hands as if they held some answer, then looked up again. "It was alive. I'm sure of it."

I felt a shudder run from my scalp to my toes then back again. Paoli and I exchanged a wide-eyed glance.

"How exactly do you mean 'alive'?" Paoli asked cautiously.

"It was a life form. We all felt it. We all knew," McKenzie said with a sudden urgency.

The statement hung in the air, bouncing off Tchaikovsky, and for a moment no one spoke.

"Did the crew tell the folks at Mission Control?" I finally asked him.

McKenzie leaned forward. "No. We hardly mentioned it to each other. It happened so quickly. A few seconds and it was over. The light was gone, the computers powered up, and we all sank back into our separate realities. We refused to acknowledge that what had happened actually did happen."

I held up a finger. "Let me get this straight. This strange thing happened with the computers. You saw the numbers on the screens even though the computers had absolutely no power. Then a big green light that feels like it's alive fills the shuttle and nobody mentions it?" I couldn't keep the sarcasm out of my voice.

McKenzie laughed gently. "You forget that we're all basically scientists. We believe in what is rational, what can be proved. That's the only explanation I can give. But a few weeks ago we did begin discussing it, at least with each other."

"How come?" I asked.

"We had to talk," McKenzie answered. "We were all having the same dream."

I felt Paoli's hand press against my shoulder. Part of me wanted to call the funny farm and have McKenzie hauled off in a straitjacket, but I was too riveted by his story to do anything but listen.

"Tell us about it," Paoli said, pulling up a chair and sitting down.

McKenzie's smile faded. "We've all shared an odd dream. Everyone in the crew. At first no one talked about it. But then one day about a month ago Lanie mentioned the dream to Gary, then Gary to Ben and Ben to Garza. Finally they came to me. We all dream of the green light. And it turns out we have the dream on the same nights."

I cleared my throat nervously. "So in this dream you just relive what happened on the shuttle," I said, trying to find a logical explanation. "That seems reasonable. It was a powerful experience, whatever it was."

McKenzie looked at me with a half smile. "Always hungering for order, aren't you? Even in the midst of chaos. But, you see, the dream is different from what we experienced on the SM–13."

"How so?" Paoli asked.

"I can only tell it from my perspective, but it's the same for each of us. I'm in a stark white room, alone. It's completely silent. There's a door. I open the door and outside I see space, black space with stars and planets so close I can touch them."

McKenzie held his hands in front of him, as if framing the picture he described. "I walk out the door, unafraid, and I'm suspended in space. Then the light comes. It consumes my body, beginning with my brain and then filtering through my arms, torso, and legs. My hands are last," he said, the words hypnotic.

My bewilderment must have shown on my face, because all of a sudden McKenzie reached out and took my hand. He felt dry and warm, his touch reassuring. "It doesn't hurt, Julie. The opposite, really. It consumes my physical self but leaves my consciousness intact, only disembodied. Floating in the same star formation where the shuttle was positioned when we first saw the light."

I was captivated. Feeling his large, strong hand around mine, looking into his keen eyes, for a moment I believed him. His words were like some slow dance I was caught up in, and all I had to do was close my eyes, forget myself, and give in to it. But then, with an unpleasant psychological jolt, I remembered who I was, where I was, and why I was being paid to be there. I slipped my hand out of his.

"You'll have to forgive me, but I'm not understanding any of this," I told him.

"We all talked about it," he said kindly, "and we all agree now that what we felt that day was definitely some form of

intelligence. You see what this means." He looked at us ex-
pectantly.

"No I don't," I said.

"The numbers. The numbers contaminating our NASA
software are the same numbers I saw on the shuttle. It's no
hacker we're looking for. It's a life form. Something or someone is trying to communicate with us."

Just then the music stopped.

7

The room was so quiet you could have heard a pin drop on Pluto. I glanced over at Paoli, wanting to exchange a look of amused disbelief, but I couldn't get his attention. He was too busy staring rapturously at McKenzie. Maybe Paoli believed in the Easter Bunny, too.

"So to summarize," I said to McKenzie, "you think the hacking isn't the work of some computer expert. You think it's being done from outer space by little gray men with huge heads and big black eyes?"

McKenzie tightened up. "If you insist on using the lowest common denominator, then yes."

"And what do they want? Volunteers for medical experiments?" Chuckling nervously, I looked again to Paoli for support but quickly realized there wouldn't be any drifting my way.

Pressing my hands against my knees, I inhaled deeply and considered the fact that I was talking to an astronaut, a man whose experience was much more vast than my own. I was being disrespectful, and that wasn't what I intended.

"I'm sorry, Harlan. I don't mean to insult you, but you have to admit your story is hard to believe."

"What other reason can you give for the light, for the computers displaying information when they were completely without power?" he asked.

Admittedly, I was stumped. "What about sunspots, or a transmission from a satellite?"

McKenzie relaxed again and smiled that half smile of his and shook his head. "Sorry, Julie. Not possible."

"Then maybe the error was Mission Control's. They *thought* the computers lost power but they really didn't."

McKenzie gave another shake of the head. "No. I had the data double-checked. The computers were definitely down."

I gave an exasperated sigh. "You just haven't found the answer yet. There's some reasonable explanation."

McKenzie studied me. "I question your definition of reasonable. You seem like an intelligent and analytical person. Why would you choose to believe something that's outside the laws of physics rather than accept a more reasonable answer just because it doesn't fit your intellectual model?"

Suddenly restless, I got up out of my chair. "Sorry, but my intellectual model doesn't include aliens."

I went over to the window, and Paoli followed. It was almost dark out, and the campus streetlamps were shining, the tree limbs black against the deep purple sky.

"Statistically speaking, the chances of there being life in another solar system are excellent," Paoli said tightly. I could tell he was annoyed with me, but at the moment I didn't care.

"Actually, it's been determined that the chances of there *not* being life in another solar system are infinitesimally small," McKenzie said behind us. "And if there's life out there, why wouldn't it try to communicate?"

He had a point, but I was far from convinced. I turned and faced him. His expression had darkened.

"I have to ask you not to tell anyone we had this conversation, at least no one outside the shuttle crew," he said somberly. "NASA is full of skeptics like yourself, Julie. If it was known that the SM–13 shuttle crew believed they had encountered an unexplained life form, not only would we be laughed at, we could lose any chance for other shuttle missions."

Paoli looked puzzled. "I don't get it. I'd think NASA would be pretty interested if their astronauts came across something like this."

"I mentioned the experience with the green light to Lisa Foster, and as a result I was pulled off the SM–15 crew and relegated to CAPCOM. I can live with that, but I wouldn't want anyone else's career damaged. The only proof we have is a shared experience that the other crew members are reluctant to discuss. But you can confirm what I've said with them. If you speak to them privately, I'm certain they'll back me up."

Even with all the wild things he'd said, it was this last statement that astonished me most. In the back of my mind I guess I'd thought McKenzie didn't really believe this alien-green-light thing, but he had to believe it if he was encouraging us to confirm the story with the other astronauts. They couldn't all be crazy. Here was some data I didn't know how to compute.

"There's one thing I don't understand," Paoli said to McKenzie.

Just one? I thought.

"Julie said that when you saw the numbers on the printout you looked shocked," Paoli went on. "But didn't it occur to you, or to Garza, that the numbers showing up in the

NASA software could be the same ones you saw on the shuttle?"

"You have to understand that for the past few months Garza and I have been working with simulators. We won't see live shuttle software until two weeks before liftoff," McKenzie answered.

"So you never actually saw the numbers interfering with the NASA computers?" I asked.

He nodded. "We only knew there was a problem. We had no idea what it actually looked like. The administrative systems most of us use day-to-day, like e-mail, have never been touched by the hacking."

"But surely after the SM–13 mission you reported what had happened on the shuttle computers?"

"Of course. But I described it only as erratic data showing on the screen."

"And nobody made the connection?"

He laughed softly. "You're persistent, aren't you, Julie? But the simple truth is that different departments here don't always communicate very well with each other. What I wrote in my mission report was never read by our computer staff. They don't even have the security clearance to access it."

I had to admit that sounded all too likely. When I worked for a large corporation it always amazed me how little information flowed between different groups.

There didn't seem to be anything else to say about it, at least not for the time being, so we thanked him for his help and went out. The hallway was empty. In fact, the whole building seemed eerily hollow. As soon as we got on the elevator Paoli started in on me.

"You were rude as hell to McKenzie. He's a brilliant man.

An astronaut," he said, gesturing wildly. It's in the Italian half of his blood. The other half is Polish. "You don't talk to astronauts that way. It's not right."

One of my many flaws is that I don't always take criticism well, especially from Paoli. As usual my first response was to fight back.

"I don't believe in sacred cows and it bothers me that you do. Just because you had the astronaut outfit for your G.I. Joe doll doesn't mean these NASA guys are gods."

Paoli rolled his eyes. "First of all, there was no astronaut outfit for G.I. Joe. Way too sissy for Joe. He was a Marine," he said with sarcasm. "And secondly, I think it takes some huge chutzpah on your part to challenge a guy who's an astronaut and a physicist on the subject of outer space issues. He obviously knows a little more about it than you do."

"On the other hand, just because he's well-educated doesn't mean he's infallible," I said. "And it doesn't mean he can't get carried away with an idea and make an error in judgment."

"So what about the fact that the numbers showed up on the computers when they had no power?"

"I'm going to need corroboration on that before I expend too much energy on it," I said stubbornly. "There are always explanations. Besides, there are plenty of people to suspect for the hacking right here on earth."

We went outside and started across the quadrangle. It was completely dark out. The outdoor lights that cast semicircles of amber light on the ground looked like sinister alien moons. I looked up to see the stars the way I always do, but then McKenzie's tale of the green light popped into my head, and I quickly directed my eyes ahead of me. It seemed safer.

I knew Paoli's mind was churning. As we walked across the campus, our arms sometimes touching, the sound of our footsteps on the sidewalk resounding in the silence, I could feel his agitation. I wanted to agree with him. I wanted us to think along the same lines so there wouldn't be this strain between us, but I couldn't force my mind someplace it didn't want to go, and I would never pretend.

"All right," he said after a few moments. "We know Margo said the Chinese could be responsible for the hacking because they're trying to delay the mission."

I hunched up my shoulders. "I don't like that one. Our hacker has too much information about NASA's computer programs for it to be someone that far on the outside."

"So maybe the Chinese hired someone at NASA to do the hacking for them."

"Possible. But like you said, it could also be an employee with a grudge or even one of the protesters. I say we work with those options before we look outside the earth's atmosphere."

"You really know how to take the fun out of things," Paoli grumbled. "Let's call it a day. We don't how long it'll take us to find our motel."

"I think we should get in another two hours of work. We're on a short timeline, remember?"

"Yeah, you're right. I guess I forgot. All this alien talk."

We went back to our office and started our own homegrown virus scan, keeping at it until ten, but the scan didn't turn up anything so we decided to quit.

I called our motel and got directions. It was farther from NASA than I'd thought, but I realized that was probably why it was so cheap. NASA was giving us a fixed amount for living expenses, and our overall office budget was so tight that

I was trying to have some expense money left over to help pay the rent.

We went back down in the elevator in silence, and I was thinking about the unpleasant fact that I had booked two rooms for us. I had no choice, since we had to turn in receipts and I didn't want NASA to know Paoli and I were working during the day and scrambling the sheets at night. And now things were tense between us, and I hated to think the situation might degenerate into our sleeping in separate rooms. As we walked outside into the warm night air I brushed my hand against Paoli's.

"Listen, I'm sorry if I've been bitchy. I'll apologize to McKenzie." I paused, swallowing hard to get my pride down my throat. "And I'm sure I'm going to grow to like Margo." I tried to say it like I meant it.

Paoli gazed down at me and smiled, his eyes crinkling at the corners. When he smiles his whole face gets into the act, which is just another thing I love about him.

"It's okay," he said, pulling me behind the massive trunk of an oak tree that must have been standing in that spot when people traveled by horse and wagon, not space shuttle. I could hear its leaves trembling as Paoli put his arms around me and kissed me. We dropped our briefcases on the ground. I didn't make my usual argument about his lack of professionalism because one, it was so dark and so late I doubted anyone would see us, and two, I really wanted him to kiss me. We lingered that way, the kiss intensifying until I thought I would melt into my shoes. So why was there a little devil on my shoulder telling me at that moment Paoli might be comparing me to Margo?

But before I had time to analyze it I heard a shout. Jumping apart, we turned to see Lanie Rogers running toward us.

She stumbled into our arms, gasping for breath, her hair tousled from the run, her eyes wild.

"What is it?" Paoli and I asked simultaneously.

"Gary," she blurted, her eyes full of dread and panic. "He's dead."

8

*L*anie was shaking so hard I had to hold her shoulders to steady her. "Where is he?" I asked her.

But she just kept saying, "He's dead! Gary's dead!"

I put my hand against her cheek and forced her to make eye contact with me. "Lanie, listen to me. Where is Gary?"

She bit her lip, closed her eyes and got some control back. "In the trainer," she said shakily.

"Which one? Where?"

"I can't get him down. I tried, but—"

"Lanie, take us to him," I said firmly.

She nodded and together the three of us ran to the training facility where we had met the astronauts earlier in the day. She fumbled with her badge trying to get it in the card reader and finally I had to help her.

We entered the glass double doors, crossed the entryway and followed Lanie into the training room.

More than half the overhead lights were turned off, and the pure white mockups, so stark in the daytime, were ghostly in the dim light. The shuttle trainer loomed in the back of the huge space like a sleeping giant.

"Over here," Lanie said. The activity had calmed her

some, although her voice still shook. She led us to the shuttle trainer, and we followed her up a flight of metal stairs and through the shuttle's side entry. My stomach tightened as we went inside. Maybe it wasn't the real shuttle, but it was close enough for me.

We hurried up a ladder, then into a small, white tunnel Paoli had to duck through, and finally into an area with narrow counters and what appeared to be hundreds of labeled drawers and small storage modules. It looked like a lab.

I saw his legs, but for some reason it was his belt that drew my eyes first. The buckle was silver and had the NASA emblem engraved on it. I lifted my eyes and cried out.

Gary Olander was hanging from the ceiling by a white nylon cord wrapped around his neck.

My throat constricted and horror flooded through my body. The cord was knotted around a handle on the ceiling that would have come in handy when you were floating around in zero gravity. Olander's eyes and mouth gaped open. His face was swollen and blue.

A small metal cabinet about two feet high lay on its side on the floor. Olander must have climbed up on it, put the noose around his neck, and then kicked it out from under him.

For a moment Paoli and I stood paralyzed.

"Lift him up enough to take the pressure off his neck," I said to Paoli, getting my senses back. "I'm going to check his pulse just in case."

Paoli winced. He doesn't have a strong stomach for that sort of thing, and I knew he didn't want to touch Olander, but someone had to help me. Lanie was backed into a corner and shaking uncontrollably.

Paoli took a fortifying breath, wrapped his arms around Olander's thighs and lifted him upward. I guess I knew it was pointless—we all did—but I pressed my fingers against the inside of Olander's wrist. Then I looked at Lanie and shook my head. With a shudder, she sank to the floor and began to cry.

"Take him down," she said through her tears.

I put my hand on her shoulder. "Lanie, I don't think we should. We have to call the police."

"Take him down!" she shouted, stretching her arms toward Olander's legs.

Kneeling, I wrapped my arms around her and held her a moment, rocking her like a baby. She buried her face against my shoulder.

"He was my friend," she said, sobbing.

"Let's get you out of here, Lanie," I said softly, stroking her hair. "I don't think it's good for you to be here. We'll take care of things."

Paoli said he would make the call to the police. We helped Lanie up and I followed them out. After he took her out of the training room, I stayed close to the shuttle, but I kept my back to it. I couldn't look at it without seeing Gary Olander inside.

I sat down on the floor, wrapped my arms around my knees, and tried to get the image of Olander out of my mind. I wondered if he had a wife and kids, and how it would feel to learn that your dad had killed himself. I was lost inside myself, enveloped in depressing thoughts, when suddenly the rest of the lights jolted on, one row after another. I squinted into the glare.

Then I heard footsteps. I got warily to my feet, searching the room. A NASA security guard came running toward me, his keys jangling. He was fairly hefty and his face was red and glistening with perspiration from the sprint. He stopped and bent down, his hands on his knees, gasping for breath. For a second I thought I might have two corpses to watch over.

"He's in there," I told him, pointing to the shuttle trainer. The guard hustled up the stairs and into the trainer. He was still inside when the police and the paramedics arrived a few minutes later. After another couple of minutes Paoli returned, and with him beside me, I breathed a little easier. He told me the police were questioning Lanie in the foyer.

One of the policemen approached us and asked for our account of what had happened, and we told him what we could. Genetic predispositioning usually compels me to provide authority figures with all sorts of unrequested assistance and advice, but I was too shaken up to start telling the policemen how to handle things. I had never known anyone, even a casual acquaintance, who had killed himself, and I found the idea unfathomable. The policeman gave me a card with the station phone number in case later we remembered anything important, and I stuck it in my purse.

We were about to leave when Margo dashed in. She was wearing a pink jogging suit and her hair pulled into a haphazard ponytail, my own hairstyle of choice, but for her it had to be an aberration. I wondered who had called her at home to tell her about Olander. Probably security. She scanned the room, making for Paoli when she saw him.

"Vic, I'm glad you're here. This is all so terrible. Can you wait for me?" she asked, her eyes all soft and gooey. He said he would, so we waited by the mock satellite, taking in the scene in front of us. Margo spent a few minutes with the police and then came straight back to Paoli and threw her arms around him octopus style and put her head on his shoulder.

He murmured the appropriate consoling words, and gave me a what-can-I-do? look. I had a few suggestions but kept them to myself.

"Does Olander have a family?" I asked her when she finally peeled herself from my lover.

"A wife. The police called her," she answered. I would have felt better if someone from NASA had broken the awful news, but then it wasn't my decision.

By the time Margo left, Paoli and I were both exhausted. Paoli told me that Margo had reserved a government fleet car for us earlier that day and already had someone put our luggage in the trunk, and for that kindness I was grateful. We had to go back and find our briefcases under the oak tree, where we'd left them when Lanie appeared, and then we went out to the parking lot and checked license plates until we found the Chevy sedan assigned to us.

The car was long and roomy, larger than my apartment in graduate school, the kind of automobile my mother always insisted upon. Paoli drove. We turned out of the main gate onto NASA 1, and then a few miles down, took a left on to a two-lane road that looked like it didn't go anywhere desirable.

Switching on the radio, I played with the dial but couldn't find anything I felt like listening to, so I turned it off. Paoli stared straight ahead at the road, gripping the steering wheel, the other arm resting on the edge of the open window. He looked upset.

The faint odor of salt water and the strong one of a skunk that never made it across the road mingled in the night air. I closed my eyes and homesickness for California washed over me. California was eccentric, full of promise and doom and bright sunshine that illuminated things more clearly than the hazy Texas version. The thick, slow Texas air seemed stagnant to me; in California there was always a breeze blowing. I missed my dog, my friends, the industrial-strength coffee hawked on every street corner. But I would go home soon enough, I told myself.

"You hungry?" I asked Paoli when the silence between us began to bother me.

He made a strangled sound. "Are you kidding? After seeing Olander's face I won't eat for a week." He hit the steering wheel with his hand. "Why did Olander kill himself?" he asked angrily. "He had everything. He was an astronaut, for chrissakes. A space traveler. He got as close to living out *Star Trek* as you can get in this century." Paoli was shouting; he gestured wildly.

"Watch the road!" I warned him as we skidded around the corner, and he put both hands back on the wheel.

He was reflective a moment. "I just don't get it. The guy got to fly in the space shuttle. Isn't that enough to live for?"

"Apparently not," was all I could think of to say.

We drove on a few minutes, neither of us talking. "I want a drink," Paoli said with feeling. "A tall, stiff one. And we should probably get some food."

I agreed wholeheartedly since we had to have something to eat. We pulled in at the first place we saw, a dive called the Countdown. It was small and insignificant looking. We wouldn't have noticed it except for the neon sign that depicted a martini complete with olives.

The swinging front door revealed a dark, smoky room the size of a large storage locker, smelling of cheap whiskey and sour bar rags. A jukebox against one wall was playing a country western song. At one side of it a dirty-looking guy with shoulder-length hair and dead eyes had pulled a chair close and slapped his blue-jeaned thighs to the rhythm. Behind the bar a fat woman with hair bleached to the color and consistency of cotton candy languidly wiped down the counter.

We walked inside.

"It looks like we could catch germs in here," I said in a low voice.

Putting his hand on the small of my back, Paoli pushed me forward. "Don't worry. The liquor will kill them."

We sat on stools at the bar and ordered two shots of tequila. I munched some stale pretzels from the plastic bowl the bartender put in front of us. The tequila slid down warmly and the place started looking a little better.

"Ya'll from out of town?" the bartender asked. She was wearing a dark red jersey top with red sequins sewn on it in the shape of a rocket, or maybe a penis. I wasn't about to ask. The plastic name tag pinned to the jersey read Sister Teresa.

"Yeah. California. Two more tequilas," Paoli said. I shook my head. "One more." Sister Teresa filled his glass.

"They get earthquakes in California," she told us, like it might be a surprise. "Ever been in one?"

Been in one? Lately it felt like my whole life was an earthquake. I ran through my usual repertoire of quake stories guaranteed to thrill and amaze non-Californians. Leaning her elbows on the bar, she clutched her rag in her hand and listened intently, her mouth a horrified "oh" as I embellished every tale.

My stories told, Paoli and I ordered turkey sandwiches which came swaddled in a yard of Saran Wrap. We inhaled them, since we had hardly eaten all day. Patsy Cline crooned "Crazy" on the jukebox.

"Let's dance," Paoli said.

"I don't think—"

"Come on. Life's short."

After pulling me onto the floor, he shoved away a table, and we began dancing, but not the way we usually did, with ear nibbling and a lot of giggling. This was a solemn ritual, the jukebox's blue-and-yellow lights playing on our faces as we swayed to the music. We held onto each other tightly, as if clinging together on a dance floor would make life more comprehensible. It didn't, but at least for the moment the world felt safer.

He gently twirled me away from him, pulled me back again, and as the song ended, dipped me backwards and kissed me. The long-haired guy clapped.

"You Californians. I just love ya'll," Sister Teresa said loudly, then ended up charging us double for the tequilas.

After we left the Countdown it took another five minutes to get to the Seaview Lodge. There was no sea view. It was a one-story, L-shaped motel, aged and frayed around the edges with a minimum of frills. All the rooms faced the parking lot. Ah, the glamorous life of an entrepreneur. I yearned for my corporate days when I stayed at shiny clean Hiltons with room service, bellmen and complementary little bottles of shampoo and bubble bath.

The motel office was locked and dark, so we fiercely rang the outside bell until the lights came on and a man in a T-shirt and Bermuda shorts groggily opened the door. An Oilers baseball cap was perched high on his head—did he sleep in it? I wondered. Yawning and scratching his belly, he slid a check-in card across the Formica-topped counter.

"Businesspeople?" he asked.

"Yes," I replied.

He nodded his approval, his face breaking into a smile. He had several gold teeth. "We encourage business clientele," he said as he gave us our room keys.

It was midnight when we made it to our rooms. We checked out both of them and carried all the bags into the one that looked the cleanest.

The air conditioner was an old window unit. It shook and coughed to life and then settled down into a low, desperate growl, but at least cold air came out of it. The room smelled like douche, and the brown carpet looked as if a whole parallel universe of dust mites and crawly things dwelled in its nylon forest.

Aging wallpaper clung to the walls, peeling near the ceiling. The best I could tell, the pattern was a western motif, with brown lassos and spurs. At least that's what I hoped they were. I eyed it a few seconds to make sure nothing moved. After giving the room a closer inspection I decided it looked clean enough and sat down on the bed.

Sinking into the pillows, I looked around, feeling vacant and worn out. Paoli stripped off his clothes and headed for the shower in his underwear.

Tossing aside the bedspread, I lay back, reached for the phone and dialed Max, telling myself it was time to check on the dog.

"Cosmos is fine. He's right here on the couch next to me eating Rice Krispies," Max said.

"Rice Krispies?"

"He wanted Captain Crunch, but I thought the sugar would be bad for him."

"Is Wayne home?"

"No, he's off at some business dinner." There was a pause on the line. "It's awfully late there for you to be calling. You don't sound good. What's wrong?" I told her about finding a corpse in the shuttle trainer our first day on the case. "How *horrible.* It wasn't Margo was it?" she asked, followed by a, "Down Cosmos. Bad doggie."

"Don't be mean," I said.

"But he's humping my leg."

"I mean about Margo."

"Is she all over Paoli?"

"Of course not." I stopped and took a breath. "She's just upset about things, naturally."

"I knew it. You're worried, Jules. I can hear it in your voice. Do you need me there with you? I can be there to-morrow."

"I'm fine. Really, I am."

"Listen Jules, you don't have to pull that 'I am woman, hear me roar' act with me. If you want me out there, just say so." There was another pause. "I'd like to come."

"Maybe I'm the one who should be worried about you," I said.

"I'm okay. I saw three movies today."

"It wouldn't be fun for you here, Max. You'd never see us. We'll be putting in sixteen-hour days on this case."

We assured each other we were fine, but neither of us sounded like she meant it.

Paoli spent half an hour in the bathroom flossing and brushing his teeth, which meant he was still upset. Too both-ered to sleep myself, I got out of my work clothes and slipped on one of Paoli's old T-shirts, tossing my Wonder Bra in a drawer. I made a mental note to inform Max that the uplift to my bosom had been less than effective in keeping Paoli away from Margo.

I got a description of the NASA computer security sys-tem out of my briefcase and sat down on the bed to exam-ine it, thinking that working would get my mind off Olander. It didn't. The sight of his bluish, lifeless body hanging in the shuttle trainer kept intruding into my thoughts.

I forced myself to focus harder on the software printout in front of me. As far as I could tell, the system had all the right security levels and backup to make it as close to foolproof as computers get. Computers, like people, are always fallible, although in a contest between a computer and a human I would always put my money on the machine.

Paoli came out of the bathroom still wearing his tightiewhitie underwear and the sight of him was enough to take my mind off computers and suicide, if only for a moment. Paoli has a great physique.

"There's something we have to do tomorrow," I said.

"Other than solve the case, what?" he asked, stretching.

"We need to talk to Garza and see if he corroborates McKenzie's story."

"And if he does, will you accept the fact that there might be an explanation for this hacking that's less than ordinary?"

"I suppose," I said, not in the mood to be argumentative.

Paoli sat down on the bed and pressed me into a lying position. His face was close to mine; I could feel his breath on my skin, and affection for him washed over me.

"You were right about this case, Julie. It's weird. It doesn't feel right. Half of me wants to bolt right out of here. I don't like the protesters. I don't like all the shouting going on around NASA. And I especially don't like finding dead guys."

I ran my finger across his cheek. "We can't quit. Foster would ruin us if we did," I said, although I was glad he wasn't liking this case. How attached could he be to Margo if he was willing to dump the job she had given us?

He rolled onto his back. "I wouldn't consider quitting,"

he said. "Foster or no Foster. We couldn't leave Margo alone in this mess. She needs us now more than ever."

My heart did a tumble. I reached over and turned off the light, and Paoli cuddled up beside me, but he made no move to make love. To be honest, I didn't feel like it either—I was too worn out and upset. But I wanted *him* to feel like it.

He fell asleep right away, but I wasn't that lucky. I lay there in the dark, thinking about aliens, Gary Olander hanging from a rope, and the possibility that Paoli was dreaming about Margo.

Finally I got out of bed and pulled one of the two chairs over to the window. Opening the blinds, I looked out at the parking lot. There were a dozen vehicles there, most of them trucks. I wondered what other fools would stay at the Seaview Lodge.

I also wondered why Gary Olander had wanted to kill himself and why he chose to do it the day we arrived. Was he afraid of our investigation, of what we would find out?

Figuring that sleep wouldn't be coming for me for a while, I got my notebook and went into the bathroom, turning on the light after I closed the door. I put down the toilet lid and sat down on it to work.

I'm as big a computer geek as anyone on the planet, but I've noticed—since I can't afford a laptop—that it feels good to work manually sometimes, that I enjoy the tactile sensation of pen on paper. I uncapped my ballpoint, and in the "Progress" section of my notebook I wrote, *Began analysis of software. Nothing solid yet. Determined that contaminating numbers are repeated at forty-eight-digit intervals.*

In the "Misc." section I wrote, *Found corpse.*

9

Day two," I announced with foreboding the next morning as we drove past the crowd of protesters and on through NASA's main gate. The security guard checked our badges and waved us through, but with less gusto than he had the previous day. I wondered if he knew about Olander. He was short and pleasantly tubby, with a pink cheerful face as round as a full moon, and his badge said his name was Zack.

Paoli was off locating coffee and I was sitting at my desk working with the computer when Margo breezed into our office looking spiffy in a navy pantsuit, her blond hair swept up into a French twist with bangs and tendrils framing her face. I've seen mannequins in store windows that were less well groomed. Her perfume fingered the air toward me and I wondered if I could get up the nerve to ask what it was so I could splurge on a bottle.

But her face was pale and when I looked at her more closely I could see that her eyes were slightly swollen.

"How are you holding up?" I asked.

"As well as can be."

"Why don't you sit a minute?"

Politely dismissing the offer, she remained standing.

"Where's Vic?"

"Getting coffee," I told her. "Or as he now calls it, space java."

Her face brightened a little. "He was always fun to be around. You can't help but love him."

The remark stung. Maybe the previous night had left my emotions raw, or maybe it was just the pressure building up in me, but suddenly I was almost desperate to tell her he was my boyfriend. My mouth had just opened to blurt out the words when the object of my adoration, the fire beneath my lust and so forth, cruised into the office holding two mugs of coffee. He handed me one, giving me something risk-aversive to do with my lips. I belted some back and then mouthed an "ouch" when it burned my tongue.

"From the hallway conversation I gather everyone's heard about Olander," Paoli said, sitting.

"Yes, everyone knows," Margo replied.

My curiosity about Olander helped squelch the impulse to tell Margo about Paoli and me. "Do you have any idea why Olander did it?" I asked, patting my tongue consolingly with my finger. "Was he depressed, upset? Was he in counseling?"

"To be honest, I hardly knew him," she answered.

The response surprised me. She said it matter-of-factly, but if she wasn't emotionally wrought over Olander's death, then why did she look like she had spent the night crying her eyes out?

Margo pulled a chair close to Paoli and sat down.

"I know you're busy, Vic, but Lisa Foster wants a preliminary report on how we're going to handle the hacking problems. She asked me to write it, but I need your help. Could you meet with me for an hour?"

"Julie and I've got a meeting with Michael in ten minutes.

Besides, you should get Julie's input, too. We work as a team, remember?" Paoli told her, rather gallantly I thought.

Remembering an old Chinese proverb, something about giving a bird its freedom in order to keep it, I decided to show Paoli how nonjealous I could be.

"I can meet with Michael by myself. Go work on the report and I'll take a look at it later," I said, waving him out with my most self-assured smile.

Paoli shrugged and stood up. "Okay. I'll be back in an hour."

After my bird flew off I took a few deep breaths to remind myself how incredibly self-confident and calm I was, and then I took off for the computer room to ask Michael some questions about the communications software. I found him sitting at his desk in a corner cubicle eating a Danish and staring at a monitor.

Unlike most computer people I knew, he kept his desk and the area around it perfectly neat—manuals in straight stacks, pencils in a cup, his desktop unmarred by the usual pen marks and coffee rings. The only ornamentation was a large photo of a golden retriever.

I squeezed a chair into the small area next to his desk and we shared the anticipated conversation about Olander's suicide. It turned out that Michael knew Olander even less than Margo did. If I was going to get any real information about Olander I would have to dig for it.

We worked together for over an hour going through my questions. I made him show me how everything worked. I was looking for unauthorized access, illegitimate user IDs or IDs accessing computer files they weren't supposed to. From where I sat, it seemed solid. But it wasn't, because someone was managing to break into it.

Since I was temporarily stymied on the how side, I decided to delve into the why. The hacking was aimed at the SM–15 mission, so I figured I'd better get some more background on what it was all about.

"Margo said the SM–15 was especially important because of the biological experiments," I said to Michael. "Do you know anything about them?"

"Sure. They'll be working with a bioreactor and then they're going to do tissue cultures," he answered.

"You'll have to educate me. What's a bioreactor?"

He smiled. "A machine that uses rotation and liquid to separate cells. They've used bioreactors on the ground for years, but they discovered the process works much better in zero gravity. They've already separated cells, like liver cells from pancreatic cells, in space. But this time they'll try to grow them. That's what a tissue culture is."

"You mean you can take a few liver cells and grow them into an actual liver?" The idea amazed me.

"Yes, if the experiment works in zero gravity the way they think it will," Michael answered.

"So if you had a damaged liver and needed a new one, instead of having to find a donor, they could take cells from your current liver and grow you a new one?"

He nodded. "Right. The patient isn't nearly as likely to reject an organ that came from his own cells. It would be a real breakthrough—the kind of breakthrough NASA needs right now."

I mulled it over for a second. "So the Chinese are also after the research. I guess there would be a lot of money in growing organs."

"Money and scientific prestige. We're pretty sure the Chinese stole the initial technology from us. You'd be amazed at the lengths other countries go to in order to get U.S. technology. It would really be a slap in the face if they were successful with the final research before we were."

We spent a few more minutes discussing the security system and then I took off to see if Paoli was back. He wasn't, so I decided to look for Garza and see if he would confirm McKenzie's story. Garza was out. According to the schedule pinned to his door he was in the training facility.

It's funny how much your attitude can change in twenty-four hours. This training facility that had thrilled me yesterday now made me queasy, but I told myself that even though someone had died in that room, eventually I'd have to go back into it. After all, I had a job to do, and only six-point-whatever days left to do it.

With fresh resolve, I marched over to the training facility, slid my badge into the card reader, and walked through the foyer and into the main room. It was bright and bustling with activity, very different from the night before. People huddled around the mockups, some working with them, others observing and taking notes. I was beginning to distinguish the astronauts from the other NASA-ites, even though the astronauts didn't always wear the jumpsuit uniforms. There was something in their bearing. They stood straighter than the others, looked more fit and they had an aura of confidence about them.

I walked around and asked a couple of people if they had seen Garza, but no one had.

My attention kept being drawn toward the shuttle trainer at the far end of the training room standing like a huge, white mausoleum.

Okay, you're a big girl, I told myself. Inanimate objects don't scare you. It only made sense to look for Garza in the trainer. I walked quickly toward it, but the closer I came, the slower my steps got. I stopped a few yards away from the metal stairs that led to the side entry. I was building up nerve to go in when a voice behind me said "He's not in there."

I jumped and spun around to find McKenzie in his NASA jumpsuit. The dark outfit seemed to make him look even larger. At first I was too flustered to speak.

"John's not here," he repeated.

"How—how did you know I was looking for him?"

"Billy told me." He gestured to the other end of the room, indicating one of the men I had talked to when I came in. "He sent me to fetch you. They don't like unauthorized people wandering around."

"Sorry. I just wanted to talk to Garza."

"You can find him in the WET-F in half an hour."

"Then I'll catch him there." I headed toward the exit.

"Please, wait," I heard him say. I turned back to him. "You were looking at the trainer. Would you like to see the inside?" As soon as he said it he caught himself. "I'm sorry. You saw it last night. Lanie told me."

My gaze went to the trainer. Being so close to it made me feel slightly nauseated. Images of Olander flashed through my head, but I forced them out. I wanted to see the inside of the trainer again, to study it more closely, guided by an astronaut. I would never get such a chance again.

"It seems odd that everyone's working today, considering that a coworker hanged himself in here last night," I said.

"We can't afford to lose a day," he answered. "Lisa Foster had security up until the wee hours of the morning finishing up the investigation so the training schedule wouldn't be affected. Gary wouldn't have wanted us to delay the mission."

If that were true, I wondered why he hadn't killed himself someplace else.

"Let me show you around," McKenzie said.

Wavering at first, I said yes, feeling a flutter in my stomach as we mounted the stairs. I wished Paoli were with me so he could have seen it, too. We went inside and I followed McKenzie into a cramped area that looked like living quarters. This time I had the chance to examine my surroundings; it all looked startlingly real.

"This is the middeck," McKenzie said. "It's where the astronauts sleep and eat." Along one wall were what looked like storage lockers, and the adjoining wall was lined with wide shelves. He pointed to them. "Those are sleep stations."

"But one of them is vertical. You'd have to sleep standing up," I said.

He laughed. "In zero gravity there is no up and down the way we think of it. In fact, once we're in flight, the horizontal bunks actually face the floor, so you're sleeping on the ceiling. But you don't know the difference."

He went on to show me the galley, which looked like a single cupboard. You opened the doors and there were trays, an oven and a hand-washing station, which was a big plastic bubble that you stuck your hands inside of so the water wouldn't float out.

We climbed a ladder to the upper deck and the cockpit, which looked similar to the cockpit of a commercial jet, with hundreds of switches and readouts. I noticed several computer screens and keyboards. It was all fascinating, but my mind kept fixing on Olander. I remembered him smiling in that photograph and wondered where he was now—gray and empty, lying on a slab somewhere.

"Do you want to see the lab area?" McKenzie asked, and I jumped.

"Sure," I said. Actually, I wasn't sure at all, but I followed him down the ladder and through the tunnel-like space we'd gone through the night before to get to the lab. It was a Maalox moment, but I had left my bottle in the office with my purse.

It looked different to me. I'd been so focused on Olander the first time I'd been there that seeing the lab now was a fresh experience. The equipment and storage modules were mounted not only on the walls but on the ceiling as well, since in zero gravity you could float around and reach anything. The lab was larger than the rest of the shuttle, about twenty feet long and fifteen feet wide.

McKenzie pointed to various objects and named them for me. "Here we have primate cages and small vertebrate cages. These are the refrigerators for storing bio samples. We call this a glove box." He pointed to a white container with a clear top. One side had two openings with gloves sewn into them so you could reach in and manipulate what was inside without it floating off.

McKenzie's eyes drifted toward the ceiling. "He hung himself from up there, didn't he?"

I nodded. Neither of us spoke for a few moments. Something lodged in my throat. I felt as if Olander was still in there, hanging from the ceiling, his eyes open and staring.

"It seems a strange place to kill yourself," I said, thinking that conversation would make me feel better. "So claustrophobic. There's hardly enough room."

"Olander had been on two missions. He had learned to

use the limited shuttle space effectively," McKenzie said. The words came out cold, but his face was full of feeling.

Over McKenzie's shoulder I noticed that the handle of one of the drawers lining the wall was broken and hanging loose from one end. It was just above eye level and not far from where Olander had hung himself. It seemed incongruous when everything else in the shuttle was so well maintained. I hadn't noticed it the night before.

"I keep thinking of the light," McKenzie said. "I've been wondering the past few days if it didn't have something to do with Gary taking his life."

I looked at him. "What do you mean?"

"I told you that in the dream we feel detached from our physical selves. Maybe the dreams had left him disoriented."

A shiver ran through me. It was hard for me to believe that Olander's suicide was motivated by something so ethereal. I thought about Olander's last moments, imagined him tying the cord to the handle on the ceiling, putting the noose around his neck and kicking out the cabinet from beneath his feet. I couldn't imagine a dream motivating him to commit such an act.

The broken drawer handle bothered me. Whatever had motivated Olander, had he changed his mind at the last moment and grappled for a foothold?

Then a terrible thought struck me. Maybe he hadn't killed himself at all. I wrapped my arms around myself and wondered how you would hang someone if they weren't in the mood to be hanged. The idea of it gave me the creeps.

"What are you thinking about?" McKenzie asked.

"I was thinking that Olander didn't seem troubled to me," I said quickly.

"You barely knew him."

"I know, but I guess it's hard for me to accept that someone who accomplished so much would take his own life. I'd think that leaving the earth's atmosphere would give you a healthy perspective on your troubles," I said.

McKenzie looked at me thoughtfully. "It gives you a different perspective, yes. But is it healthy? I'm not so sure."

"What do you mean?"

"The Soviets have had more experience than we have with extended stays in space. They've found that it can induce depression."

"Because of the close quarters?"

"Sometimes. But there are a dozen other reasons an outsider wouldn't think of."

"Like what?" I asked, intrigued.

"Gravity, for one thing. You live in a weightless environment. You're lighter than air for weeks, maybe months. When you get back to earth the weight of gravity is oppressive. This huge burden bearing down on you, pressing you into the earth."

"I can't see someone killing themselves over gravity."

McKenzie smiled. "Maybe not. But the experience of space changes you in ways you don't expect. I did an EVA a year ago—an extravehicular activity," he said, seeing my puzzlement. "A space walk. There I was, tethered by my feet to the shuttle, dangling upside down in space, in a blackness darker than you can imagine."

"Sounds frightening."

A cloud passed over his features. "But you see, it wasn't. That's what was so disturbing. It made me realize that it's the black space inside us that's truly frightening. The void of space is mild in comparison."

There was a pain in his eyes that I could almost feel inside myself, his desperation jumping to me like an electrical charge. My eyes moved once again to the broken handle. It shouldn't be there, I thought. There was something wrong in this room, something terribly wrong.

Suddenly the walls of the trainer seemed to close in on me.

"Let's get out of here," I said. "I've got work to do."

10

When I got back to the office, I found Paoli leaning back in his chair, his hands behind his head, his feet propped on the desk—his best thinking posture or so he tells me. I told him in a gush of words about the broken drawer handle in the lab where Olander had killed himself.

"It might have happened when the police took Olander's body down," he said after he'd considered it a minute. "There were a dozen people in that lab last night. Any one of them could have broken it."

"Possible. But I think I should tell the police about it."

He swung his feet off the desk. "Yes, Julie, it's quite likely they won't be able to do their job without your assistance," he said so good-naturedly it didn't annoy me nearly as much as it should have.

Fishing around in my handbag for the card the policeman had given me the night before, I dialed the number written on it and told the officer who answered that I had information regarding Olander's suicide. She transferred me to another officer, and when I told him about the broken drawer handle in the shuttle trainer he didn't react with the rapt interest I'd expected.

"The broken handle was at approximately the level of Olander's feet. He could have been struggling for a foothold, trying to save himself," I explained.

The policeman thanked me for my information and that was that. I couldn't help feeling slighted.

Next I called Margo about getting into the WET-F, which she explained was the Weightless Environment Training Facility. My heart soared when she said we could go in, my spirits only slightly dampened by her insistence that she come with us. There was a training scheduled for that morning, but she said it didn't start for twenty minutes, so we had just enough time to catch Garza. Margo said she'd walk us over to the WET-F building.

"It's basically just an oversized pool," she said as we crossed the quadrangle. I still felt some uneasiness from my shuttle tour and it felt good to stretch my legs. "The astronauts put on a waterproof version of their space suits and use the pool to practice some of the maneuvers they'll be doing on the mission."

"Being underwater is the only way they can experience weightlessness?" Paoli asked.

"For practicing EVAs, yes. They also go up in a jet that flies in parabolic curves. That creates weightlessness, but only for about thirty seconds. Working underwater gives them a neutrally buoyant condition for an extended period of time. That means you're neither rising nor falling, which is like conditions in space."

The WET-F was a round building, sort of a hub in the middle of the NASA campus. There was an ambulance parked outside and I immediately thought of Olander's suicide.

"Something must have happened," I said anxiously, hastening my steps. I heard Margo's laughter behind me.

"Don't worry. They always park an ambulance outside the WET-F when there's a training. We've never had a serious accident, but they do it just in case."

I was embarrassed but relieved. When we reached the door Margo slid her badge into the badge reader and the door clicked open. We followed her inside.

We entered a room the size of a high school gymnasium. Almost two-thirds was taken up by the pool, which was unlike any I had ever seen. It was enormous, at least seventy feet long and fifty feet wide and deep enough, according to Margo, to sink a two-story house in. But most remarkable was its color, a deep blue-green, the numerous underwater lights giving it a beautiful and eerie glow. Large, oddly shaped, wire-mesh objects took up most of the rest of the space. Paoli asked Margo what they were.

"They're mockups of the equipment the astronauts will actually use on the mission. They're made of wire mesh so they can be gotten in and out of the water easily. See that one?" Margo pointed to a barrel-shaped object that was being lowered into the pool by a small mobile crane. "That's a mockup of an orbital refueling system."

I was excited as a child, dazzled by everything. The moist warm air, the blue of the pool reflecting on the walls, made the place seem surreal.

A couple of men in skin-diving suits sat on the edge of the pool, then farther down someone was wriggling into a space suit, assisted by two other people. The suit was white and bulky, the torso made of what looked like plastic. When the person in the suit turned around, I recognized Lanie. When she saw us she raised her hand and I waved back. I wondered how hard it was for her to work after what had happened the night before, but maybe she was like me and found her work restorative.

Just then John Garza entered the room with a purposeful stride, talking nonstop into his little tape recorder. He was wearing dark slacks and a blue short-sleeved shirt. Everyone looked up and took note of his arrival. He went to a rack where the torso portions of four spacesuits were hanging, and a man with a clipboard quickly trotted over to him. Garza pointed to one spacesuit torso, jabbing at it with his finger, his irritation obvious. The man jotted down notes while Garza spoke into his tape recorder.

Margo managed to get Garza's attention and we walked over to him. "Do you have a few minutes before you start your work?" I asked. "We'd like to ask you a few questions."

Garza's expression was grim. "I'm very busy. We're having trouble with the practice equipment." He seemed about to say more but took a breath, hesitating, as if weighing the pros and cons, and apparently he changed his mind. "All right. I can spare a few minutes before I suit up," he said, nodding his head toward a door just beyond us. "We can go in here."

Paoli started after Garza. Margo made a move to join them, but I stopped her.

"I think it's better if we talk to him alone," I said. She gave me a funny look but acquiesced. I wasn't trying to snub her. It was just that I thought Garza wouldn't talk about any strange happenings on the SM–13 shuttle mission if NASA ears were listening in.

I followed Garza and Paoli into a small room where several television monitors were mounted on the wall, with two rows of chairs in front of them. The monitors were powered on and it looked to me like they were showing an under-water view of the pool.

"The pool is equipped with underwater video cameras. That's how we observe WET-F maneuvers," he said when he noticed me inspecting them. "I only have a minute so let's get started."

We all sat down and Paoli pulled his chair around so he faced Garza.

"There's no way to build up to this gently," Paoli said. "There are some things that McKenzie told us about the last shuttle mission. Unusual things. We want to talk them over with you."

Garza set himself more firmly in his chair. "What exactly did McKenzie say?" His voice was low and controlled. I sensed he knew what was coming.

Paoli told him the story the same way he had gotten it from McKenzie, the computers powering off, the green light in the cockpit, the numbers showing up. I half expected Garza to laugh at us, but he didn't. He had been all edges and sharp angles, but now his eyes grew mellow and he visibly relaxed. He seemed glad we knew about it.

"Right after the computers went down we heard some-thing hit the window. It was bizarre, disconcerting, like some-one knocking at the door," he said with a small laugh. He seemed more human, not so much the inaccessible astronaut-machine. It must have been this side of him that got Margo's blood stirring. "It had to have been a meteorite, because when I went over to check it out I saw some dark scratches on the window."

"We want to know about the computers," I told him.

"I can't tell you much. I still don't understand what could

have happened. We checked and all the computers were down, yet the rest of the power in the cockpit was on. That was when Harlan and I saw the numbers on the screens. Lanie, Ben and Gary came in, and then we all saw the light." He paused. "*Saw* isn't the right word—I *felt* it. It seemed to flow right through me, as if it had replaced the blood in my veins."

Goose bumps hoisted up the tiny hairs on my arms, my sense of reality catapulted into a new zip code. I had never really expected him to corroborate McKenzie's crazy story. If I knew anything about people, Garza was a grounded and pragmatic person. He didn't seem the type to let his imagination get away from him.

Nobody said anything for a few seconds. Garza was looking at the wall, transfixed by something, perhaps the memory of what had happened that day on the shuttle.

"So only you and McKenzie saw the numbers on the computer screens?" Paoli finally asked. There was something in his voice, so slight that only I would have noticed, but I knew that Garza's confirmation of the green light had thrown him.

Garza nodded. "I think so. Lanie, Ben and Gary walked in right when the light entered the cockpit. After that nobody was thinking much about the computers."

"And the dream?" I asked. "McKenzie said you were all having this weird dream."

Garza sighed with resignation. "So Harlan told you everything," he said. "We didn't realize it until only recently. None of us had talked to each other about what had happened."

"I don't get that," I said.

He shook his head like he didn't really get it himself. "It

wasn't that we didn't want to. I think it was more that it was such a personal experience that we were each afraid we had hallucinated. It can happen in space, although it's only been documented on longer flights."

"So what happens in the dream?" I asked, wanting to see if his version matched up with McKenzie's, and it did, right down to the green light consuming the parts of his body in exactly the same order.

While he was telling us, Paoli gave me a look that said, *I told you so.* I had wanted confirmation and now I had it. Garza had repeated McKenzie's story down to the last bizarre detail.

"McKenzie thinks the hacking could be the work of . . . " I tried to think of a way to put it that didn't sound crazy.

"Alien life forms?" Garza finished for me. "Harlan has shared his theories with me and with Lisa Foster. I'm not sure what happened that day during the mission. I can't explain it; I can't comprehend it. I don't know why it has affected us the way it has. Harlan's a brilliant, well-intentioned man, but I'm not ready to believe his wild theory. I think the C-CINS pack is a much more believable choice."

I felt more comfortable now that the conversation was taking a more terrestrial turn, and there was a change in Garza, too. At the very mention of C-CINS, his face lost its dreamy look. I told him we were planning to talk to Lindstrom.

Garza sat up rigidly. "He'll tell you that he and I got into a fight. But he initiated it, and at the time I felt I had to defend myself. The lawsuit he filed against me is a nuisance, but nothing I can't handle."

"Lindstrom's suing you?" Paoli asked, as surprised as I was.

"I broke the baby's nose," Garza answered with a detectable trace of pride. "Lindstrom's a fanatic. He'll stop at nothing to discredit NASA. If you're looking for a hacker, you should start and stop with him. He's got a motive and the knowledge." His tone was full of anger. His fists clenched. It was funny how the conversation had plummeted so quickly from the stars down to earth.

"I understand his motive, but what makes you say he has the knowledge?" I asked.

"He works for a software firm that develops some type of Internet software," Garza said. "I think he does something with finance, but he would certainly have access to people with computer skills."

There was a knock at the door and a woman came in and asked to talk to him. He spoke to her privately for a few seconds, and when she left, he told us he had to end the discussion. He started after her but then stopped, turning to face us.

"Please be careful how you deal with this information. None of the astronauts on the SM–13 want to be labeled the way McKenzie has been. It can be fatal to a career."

We assured him we would be careful. Garza turned again in the doorway. "In any ecosystem there are always bottom feeders. Focus your attentions on Harvey Lindstrom," he said, and left.

When Paoli and I walked back into the WET-F I saw Lanie in her spacesuit being dropped into the pool by means of a portable, boxlike crane. I asked one of the skin divers why the crane was needed.

"The suits are heavy, especially when they're wet," he answered.

I was eager to see more, but we were shepherded out by a security guard who firmly told us that no visitors were allowed in the area during a training session.

"I'd do almost anything to spend some more time in the WET-F," I said to Paoli when we were outside in the hot sunshine.

"I'll work on getting us back in there," he said.

I gave him a suspicious look. "How?"

"Don't worry, I'll figure it out. You're avoiding the important subject."

"Which is?"

"That you've now got corroboration out the yinyang for what McKenzie told us," Paoli said as we walked along the sidewalk back to our office, the cement shiny as water in the heat.

"Can you define 'out the yinyang'?"

"You know what I mean. Garza is a respected astronaut. People around here defer to him like he's the pope. And we've got his confirmation that what McKenzie said is true. So do you believe it now?"

"Garza also said he thinks McKenzie's theory about the hacking is crazy. Although I'm not so sure I like his C-CINS theory any better."

"Why's that?"

"It just seems to me that Garza is spending too much time trying to pin this hacking on Lindstrom. You have to admit that Garza has a good motive for trying to frame him. Lindstrom's lawsuit could damage Garza's career. And you saw Garza react to Lindstrom that first day at the main gate. Garza doesn't look like the kind of man who likes to be crossed."

I said it all matter-of-factly, as if my thoughts about the case were nicely organized, but the truth was, they were anything but. I'd learned a lot at MIT and Stanford, but nothing I'd been taught had prepared me for dealing with extraterrestials.

11

If you ask me, the alien theory makes just as much sense as pointing the finger at Lindstrom does," Paoli said, lowering his voice as we went back inside Building Four. "After going through the communications software I doubt that an outsider could be the one destroying the NASA computer programs."

I raised an eyebrow. "You don't call an alien an outsider?"

"Aliens are so far out they're in," he joked. We were silent as a man carrying a stack of papers walked down the hall toward us.

"On the communications software, I agree with you. If our hacker was an outsider we would have detected it already, so it has to be somebody on the inside. Maybe Lindstrom has paid someone at NASA to have it done," I said after the man had passed us and turned the corner. "If he couldn't finance it himself he could be getting donations or something. Let's ask Margo. She seems to know a lot about what C-CINS is up to."

"Okay, I'll go find her," Paoli said, a little too eagerly for comfort. The elevator opened just as we approached it and we dashed in. In our brief time at NASA we had discovered that the elevators were annoyingly slow. It's not an original thought, but if they could put men on the moon, why couldn't NASA install elevators that moved faster than the speed of smell?

"I've got a better idea. Why don't I go talk to her while you get back to the computer," I said after the doors closed.

Paoli gave me a sly smile. "How come I get the computer work and you get to talk to Margo? Still jealous?"

"I'm simply maximizing resources. With our short time frame on this case, we can't afford to double-team on anything. Your background in finding hackers is much stronger than mine, so it's more efficient to have you working with the computer. I'm simply being professional."

The elevator doors opened and we stepped out.

"Yeah, sure. I'd kiss you now, but it's not professional."

I smiled. "Save it for later."

Actually I had more than one reason for tracking down Margo myself. Sure, I wanted to keep her and her perfume away from Paoli as much as possible, but I also wanted to check some personnel files on Garza, and since I wasn't too sure I'd find what I was looking for, I didn't want Paoli to know just yet.

Paoli went off down the hall and I set out to find Margo. She was in her office, a standard ten-by-ten room that she had softened with framed Monet posters, a ceramic lamp and a vase of fresh flowers on her desk. She sat with her back to me, staring out the window. I could see just a glimpse of her profile.

"Hi," I said.

She turned around, looking embarrassed that I had caught her in a moment of repose, which was silly, since I spend a lot of time just sitting and thinking myself. Actually, staring off into space is often how I do my best work.

Getting right to the point, I asked her whether C-CINS got any hefty donations.

"I doubt it. As far as I know they're funded by the C-CINS members themselves," she said. "The operation is pretty much run on a shoestring. They never spend more than what it takes to produce signs and flyers."

That meant Lindstrom probably didn't have a convenient pile of money to bribe potential hackers with.

I was going to have to liven up my interrogation skills, learn to throw in a few jokes between questions since I could tell I was boring her. There was a case of PC diskettes on the desk in front of her, and she flipped through them distractedly as she spoke, occasionally sipping from a mug of coffee. When we got the C-CINS part of the conversation over with, I asked her if I could have access to NASA personnel records.

"I suppose so. Whose record do you want to see?" she asked.

"John Garza's."

Bull's-eye. Jerking upright in her chair, she knocked over the half-full mug of coffee in front of her. She jumped up and I grabbed a newspaper from her file cabinet and mopped up what I could. I hoped she had already read the comics. Brown rivulets dripped down the front of her pants and I heard her utter the kind of expletive you don't expect from someone who looks so much like Grace Kelly. I took some Kleenex out of my purse and handed it to her.

"Blot as much of it as you can. You need help?" I asked, standing by and feeling useless as she pressed the Kleenex against her pants.

"No. No, it's okay," she said, completely frazzled. "I've

been such a klutz lately. Dropping things, spilling things." I handed her the rest of my purse pack of Kleenex. "It's just that I'm swamped with work and there's so much going on with the computer problems and the prospect of a mission delay and—"

She clamped her mouth shut, shaking her head.

"I'm a klutz all the time," I said, going for the empathy angle. We both concentrated on blotting in order to fill the awkward silence. We managed to get out most of the coffee, and since her pants were navy, it didn't show much. I assured her that no one would notice.

"So what are you looking for in Garza's records?" Margo asked as we gathered up the used Kleenex.

"Nothing specific. I'm just trying to get some background," I answered. "Eventually I'll check on everybody associated with the case. You never know what kind of information you're going to need, and since we've interviewed Garza, I thought I'd look at his record first."

I was bluffing, of course. I wanted to look at Garza's record because I had suspicions about him. But Margo must have bought what I was selling because she agreed to take me over to building eight, where the personnel department was located.

It was a long walk, so Margo commandeered a golf cart in the parking lot. She drove us over in silence, absorbed in whatever was going on inside her head. I imagined finely tuned gears, little gold circuit boards and a lot of pink fluffy stuff inside her cerebrum. Inside building eight we passed through a bullpen of cubicles to an office in the back.

A large woman with short gray hair stood in front of a tall file cabinet, her brown caftan-type dress draped like a Bedouin tent over her. Upon seeing us she closed the file drawer protectively. Margo explained that I wanted to see one of the files, and the woman looked at us like we had asked to inspect her underwear, but Margo was insistent and she finally backed down. She made Margo fill out a card saying whose file we wanted, then she went to her computer and typed in a couple of commands.

"I've given you access only to Garza's file," she said, proud of the Godlike power she wielded in her tiny part of the planet.

I thanked her, and Margo and I went to a vacant cubicle. I sat down in front of the computer, with Margo pulling up a chair next to me. My contractor status didn't give me access to personnel information, so she logged onto the system with her ID. After she pulled up Garza's data, I expected her to go back to her office to deal with all that work she was supposedly swamped with, but she sat there right beside me, her eyes glued to the screen.

If I'd thought before that she had more than a passing interest in Garza, her fascination with his record confirmed it. Since the personnel manager had to give you access for each specific record, Margo couldn't have accessed Garza's file on the sly. My taking a look at it must have been a golden opportunity for some heavy-duty snooping.

There was a mass of information on him, including records of his schooling and his stint as a Navy pilot. As I scrolled through the data, she asked me a few times to stop so she could read something over.

It was during one of her intense data scans that I found what I was looking for. To keep Margo from knowing what I was zeroing in on, I played a little game, scrolling back and forth like I was having trouble finding anything worthwhile but managing to get a little more information each time.

Listed in Garza's college curriculum were three computer courses, including a class on computer networks. A check of his birthdate confirmed my guess that his college days were twenty years back. Not much of that knowledge would transfer to today's technology if he hadn't kept up his skills, but he'd also had extensive computer experience in the navy.

I managed to refrain from jumping up and shouting, "Bingo!" My hunch about Garza had been correct, and now I had my first real lead, however small. This was one of the many things I liked about my new career combining computers and investigation. You sift through the muck, you prowl around, basically getting nowhere, then all of a sudden you hit upon some really vital information that makes your brain light up like a Christmas tree.

I scrolled around a few minutes longer and then told Margo I was finished. We went out and golf-carted back to building four.

When I walked in the office, Paoli was hunched up with Michael in front of the computer screen. A collection of computer manuals lay open and spread out on the desk, a half dozen more on the floor. My eagle eye spotted the cellophane wrappers from vending-machine packs of Oreos on my chair. The Oreos themselves were sadly missing. I looked longingly at the crumbs scattered on the manuals, wishing Paoli had saved me one.

"I need to talk to you," I said to him, putting the emphasis on *need*. "I checked the voice mail at our office and we have some client issues that have come up."

Paoli gave me a quizzical look. "What client?" He knew quite well we didn't have any other clients. Michael was absorbed in whatever was on the screen, so I wiggled my eyebrows meaningfully at Paoli. He asked Michael if they could finish up later and Michael left.

"I have several pieces of fascinating information," I told him eagerly. "Number one, your girlfriend Margo definitely has more than a passing interest in John Garza."

Paoli emitted a derogatory *humph*. "You just figured that out? On most things you're sharp, but there are life areas where you're a hopeless slug." He reached into his shirt pocket and brought out an Oreo, handing it to me. I silently asked God to bless him. "What else?"

I accepted the Oreo with a grateful smile and sat down next to him. "Garza has a strong computer background. Over the years he's taken multiple courses in networking and programming."

"How'd you find that out? Also, Margo's not my girlfriend. You are."

"Checked his personnel file. Thanks, by the way. Garza tried to point the finger at Lindstrom by telling us about Lindstrom's computer skills, but he neglected to mention his own computer background. If someone as smart and focused as Garza applied himself, he might be able to figure out how to hack into NASA's computers. It would be much easier for him than an outsider, since he has the ID and password and can get on the system."

"Okay, he's got the computer skills to hack into the NASA computers, but what's his motive? Why would he want to screw up a mission that he's commanding?"

I turned up my palms. "What am I, psychic?"

The phone rang. Paoli picked up, said, "Sure" a few times and hung up.

"Lisa Foster wants to see us. Now."

"Why?"

"She says she wants an update on our progress."

I made a face. "We haven't made a lot of progress."

"So we fake it."

This was the part I didn't like. Some people think that you can tinker around a few minutes with a computer and come up with all the answers, but it's far from true. Hacking is sometimes referred to as a virus, but it's really more like a cancer. Cancers have to be located and completely removed, and as far as this surgery was concerned, we had just opened up the patient and were still poking around in its innards. I reminded myself that we had only a few days left to find the hacker, and the idea left me queasy. I had Paoli check my lips for Oreo crumbs, then we took off.

When we reached Foster's office Gerald was sitting at his desk with the phone receiver cradled between his ear and shoulder, jotting down something on a yellow legal pad. Seeing us, he pointed his pen at Foster's doorway.

She was sitting bent over her desk, her eyes directed at a document she held in front of her. She was wearing reading glasses, and as soon as she saw us, she quickly took them off like she was embarrassed by them, which I thought was silly. Being farsighted myself, I could see nothing wrong with reading glasses. In fact, Paoli always implied that he found glasses sexually stimulating. But then, that's Paoli.

"Sit," she said, like we were dogs. When she noticed we remained standing, she gave us a disgruntled look and stood up, I suppose so she could be at eye level. She was wearing a severe black suit with a jacket belted at the waist that made her hips look like they should be wearing a "Wide Load" sign.

"I just got a call from Washington and they want a confirmation on the SM–15 liftoff date by the end of the day. Are you going to have our hacker by five?"

My eyes widened. "We can't give you anything that definite," I told her. She leaned over her desk and gave me a look that would freeze Hades.

"Why the hell not? Margo said you were experts. This is NASA. We expect results here."

The fact that she had raised her voice relaxed me. Barking dogs aren't that scary. It's the quiet ones you ought to be afraid of. I leveled my eyes at her, giving her my best quiet-dog stare. "You'll get results," I said, my tone calm. "We've made progress."

"What kind of progress?" she snapped.

"We've come up with some possibilities about who could be doing the hacking," Paoli said, deciding it was time he jumped in. I appreciated his assistance, but I would have preferred it if he hadn't brought up that particular subject. I had my reasons for trying to keep the conversation general.

Foster stiffened. "Who are you investigating?"

"We're checking out one of the C-CINS protesters," Paoli said.

Foster nodded, liking it. "Who else?"

He paused. I tried to tell him with a glance not to say what I feared he was going to say, but I couldn't catch his eyes. My only option was to slam my hand over his mouth, and I was considering it, but alas, it was too late.

"I know it sounds off the wall, but Harlan McKenzie thinks it could be an alien intelligence breaking into the computer system," Paoli told her.

I closed my eyes and said a big silent *uh-oh*. When I opened them again things hadn't improved. Foster's mouth was set in a grim line, then twisted into a sneer that was going to cause nasty wrinkles if she did it too often. I supposed just then wasn't the best time to tell her. She stomped over to the door, shut it, then turned on us like nothing would make her happier than to smack us around a little right there and then.

"McKenzie's a Zen-spitting idiot," she said, her voice hostile. "He's told me his little theory and it's a pile of horse crap. We're not paying you to waste your time investigating make-believe space invaders." She went back behind her desk and glared at us, daring us to say something else she considered incredibly stupid.

"McKenzie's theory is just one of the things we're looking at," I said, in an attempt at damage control.

She put her hands on her desk and leaned toward us. "You're going to be looking at your butts out the door."

"Now wait a minute," Paoli said, losing his normal good humor. "I know the alien thing sounds, uh, extraordinary, but if one of the astronauts gives us a lead we have to look into it. We're having a former coworker of mine at the NSA run the hacker's code through a decoding software program. It could be a message from somebody, somewhere."

"I don't care if it's a message from Elvis," she said. "I don't want this business about aliens discussed any further with anyone—especially the NSA. Do you understand me? We're all going to look like fools."

"Come on," I said to Paoli. "Let's get back to work."

Foster moved her hands to her hips. "I'm not sure whether the two of you should continue working or not. You've made no progress and you're running around spouting science fiction."

Right about this time I started really getting angry. "We've been doing an excellent job," I said heatedly. "Anyone with experience would use the same approach. We didn't say aliens were responsible; we only felt obligated to mention—"

"This meeting is over," she spat. "You can stay on the job while I consider this matter. I'll be getting back to you. Now you may leave."

Paoli started to say something, but I looked at him and mouthed a *don't* and we left her office.

The whole disgusting scene reminded me of the time I had been sent to the principal's office in junior high school. The principal had been a woman. She even looked a little like Lisa Foster, and I remembered her as having the same arrogant scowl. I had been doing an experiment with baking soda that had taken out one of the overhead light fixtures, and my science teacher had been unappreciative of my scholastic zeal.

I felt the same with Foster as I had back then—wronged, misunderstood, and horribly embarrassed. I guess the only difference was that at least now I had a handsome man by my side, which is one thing I had never had during my school years. I was grateful. But then, it was lover boy who had gotten me into this mess.

When we walked out of Foster's office, Gerald was still sitting at his desk with the phone receiver cradled between his ear and shoulder.

"Good meeting?" he asked. I guess the walls were thin.

"Just dandy," I said tightly. Gerald gave me a sympathetic look. His encounters with Foster probably weren't much better.

Paoli and I walked down the hall to the elevator in silence and I pressed the Down button. Once the doors were closed Paoli put his arm around my shoulders.

"Okay, Julie, I know you're ticked off and if we get fired I'll take full responsibility. But when I brought up the alien thing I didn't expect her to be so narrow-minded."

I held up a finger. "First of all, in my opinion her reaction wasn't narrow-minded, it was rational. Although that's no excuse for her belligerent behavior. Secondly, you can save your breath. I'm too mad at Foster to have any hostility left over for you. Naturally I would have preferred that you not bring up aliens, but I think our main problem is that Foster's looking for a scapegoat to blame at least part of this mess on, and we're an easy target since we aren't NASA employees. Besides, we're not fired yet."

"Technically no, but we're wet-cigarette-paper close."

His lack of enthusiasm bothered me, since he was the one who had been so upbeat about this case. Suddenly I was in the role of cheerleader. I flung out my hand, dismissing his concern as nonsense. "I've never been fired from a job and I'm not ever going to be." I checked to make sure no one was looking and then gave him a quick, encouraging hug. "Let's get back to work. Maybe we'll find the hacker this afternoon."

"Yeah, and maybe they'll let us go up in the next space shuttle," Paoli muttered.

12

*L*ife is tough. It's tougher when you're stupid. I didn't blame Paoli for telling Foster about McKenzie's alien theory because it was my fault as much as his. We should have strategized before we traipsed into her office, done some planning on what we would say to her. It was a misfire that would be hard to correct.

For punishment we spent the rest of the afternoon in solitary confinement in our office with the door closed, doing basic brain labor at the computer until our backs ached and our necks were stiff, going through the communications software again just in case we had missed something. If we had, we were still missing it.

Around five I was thinking it was time to take a break when the break suddenly took us. The door flew open, spewing forth a whole new Margo, the peeved and petulant version, screeching like a toy poodle after you've just stepped on its foot. She didn't waste time on niceties.

"You came close to blowing it with Foster," she said, her voice shrill and sharp. She was red in the face and so flustered she forgot to bat her eyelashes at Paoli.

"Gee, was Mom mad?" he asked.

To say the look Margo gave him was hostile is an understatement.

Paoli sighed and raised his hands in surrender. "Okay, the truth is I was a little out of line, but Foster overreacted. If she fires us she's the one in trouble, because if Julie and I can't solve this hacking problem, my bet is nobody can."

Good going, I thought to myself. He always comes through when I need him.

Every blond hair on Margo's head bristled. I opened my mouth to say something conciliatory but decided against it. I was enjoying their little spat. Who knew? Maybe they would start throwing things. I considered pushing the stapler within Margo's reach.

She took a few seconds and got control of herself. "Fortunately I smoothed things over for you. She's not firing you, but you can't talk anymore about aliens or anything remotely associated. I'm the one that recommended you. It's my livelihood as well as yours if you screw up again."

Paoli stood up and bent at the waist. "Whatever Her Majesty desires."

Setting her shoulders back and lifting her chin, she turned and walked out, her high heels clicking out a Morse Code message that said "Screw you."

Paoli closed the door after her, seeming a little chafed himself. He cocked his thumb toward the hallway.

"This is why I stopped dating her in college. She's such a princess."

I gave him a questioning look. "*You* stopped dating *her?*"

"Well, maybe it was the other way around." He dropped into his chair. "You want to hear the story?"

Did the earth rotate on its axis? I leaned back in my chair and crossed my arms. "I suppose," I said casually.

Paoli swung his feet on the desk, which I immediately pushed off since you could never tell who was going to walk in.

"Well, we were at this Cinco de Mayo picnic and my pal Fred took some refried beans and patted and rolled them until they looked sort of like a dog turd, and then he put them on her plate next to her hot dog when she wasn't looking. When she saw it, she screamed. Then Fred picked up the beans and pushed them into his mouth. She went ballistic. No sense of humor."

I tried to think how I would have reacted if I thought someone had put dog excrement on my lunch plate and then ate it. The vision I conjured up was similar to Margo's reaction, but it was not the time to admit this.

We got back to the software and by seven we were starved, so I went for food, leaving Paoli alone to work. There was a lunchroom on the first floor with a cluster of vending machines. I checked them all out, finally making a managerial decision on K2, which was the pimento cheese sandwich, the only one that looked under a week old. I got two of them, then hit D5 for a cherry fried pie. After getting two Diet Cokes from the soda machine, I put the pie in my handbag and the sandwiches under my arm, and then I headed back to the office, a can of soda in each hand.

The building was quiet. I read the name plaques on the office doors I passed, stopping when I saw Gary Olander's. Nosiness is in my genetic structure, and I especially wanted a look at his office. As if something on his desk or one of the pictures on his wall might tell me why—and if—he had killed himself.

I had only glanced around when a very pretty young woman with short strawberry blond hair popped up from behind the desk. She was wearing tight blue jeans and a Chanel T-shirt and seemed to be in her late twenties. Heavy gold rings dangled from her ears and they were trembling.

"Who are you?" she asked in a loud startled voice.

"Julie Blake. Sorry," I said, awkwardly putting the sandwiches and soda down on a file cabinet that stood by the door. "I'm always getting lost." I waited for her to introduce herself. "And you are?" I said when she didn't.

"Sally Olander." She hesitated. "Gary's wife." She said it like she was ashamed.

Suddenly I felt surprised and sad and awkward all at the same time. I stumbled around for words and finally came out with, "I'm sorry about your husband."

She had heard it a couple of hundred times already. "Yeah. Thanks," she muttered, looking down at her shoes. Her eyelashes were long and so heavily coated with mascara they looked like spiders crawling down her cheeks. She glanced back up at me. "I just didn't see it coming, you know what I mean? It came totally out of the blue."

I'm no expert on relationships, but Paoli and I had known each other for less than a year and I already know his moods. I can tell if the Celtics had won or lost, if he's feeling discouraged about our lack of clients, or if his battered Porsche is having a problem with its pistons. Somehow I think I'd know if he was upset enough to kill himself.

"Was Gary depressed?" I asked.

She looked away again. "I guess he was, at least sometimes. I mean he was up and down."

"What about a note? Did he leave one?"

She went rigid.

"What is this, an inquisition?" she asked, her eyes flashing. "I don't even know you."

"I'm sorry. Please forgive me. I feel close to all of this because I was one of the people who found him."

She ran her hand through her short hair, her face contorting with discomfort. "Oh."

I stepped closer to her. "Sally, I know it's not my business, but the reason I'm interested in the note is that I noticed something in the shuttle trainer. It was a small thing really, but there was something about it." I grappled for the right words.

"What are you talking about?" she asked.

"It's just that, you see, I'm not one hundred percent sure he killed himself."

As soon as I blurted it out I wished I hadn't. It was too abrupt and it wasn't the time or the place.

Her breathing quickened and the gold earrings began trembling again. "It was hardly an accident."

I took a deep breath, swearing silently at myself. "I'm not saying it was. I'm not sure what I'm saying. It's just that I think his death should be looked into."

She started picking things up off the desk randomly—papers, pencils—and stuffing them into her purse. "You're right. It's none of your business. And what you think doesn't mean shit." She glared at me, her eyes piercing. "I'm here getting his personal things, so if you don't mind."

I gathered up my groceries and left, thinking one, I should learn to keep my mouth shut, and two, that Sally Olander's reaction seemed odd to me. If it had been *my* husband I'm sure I would have been vitally interested in any hint that his death might not have been a suicide.

When I got back to the office Paoli and I ate our sandwiches and shared our cherry pie as we continued working. I didn't mention my conversation with Sally Olander to him because, to be honest, I was embarrassed about it.

At ten I was ready to call it quits, but Paoli had other ideas.

"Want to get another look at the WET-F?" Paoli asked.

"Sure, but how?"

Paoli held up his contractor's security badge. "While I was looking at the NASA security software, I typed in a couple of extra programming lines and gave us access. Interested?"

I snatched the badge out of his hand.

"Paoli, you can't make unauthorized security changes, especially to your own file. Change it back."

"Don't be such a Girl Scout. I'll change it back tomorrow. You're the one who said you'd do anything to get back in."

"The exact quote was 'almost anything.' "

"All we're going to do is take another quick look around. You're dying to see it. You're aching to. So let's go. Five minutes, that's all. No one will ever know."

He took back his badge and got up from his chair. "Are you coming?"

I grabbed my purse and went with him. I couldn't help myself.

The NASA campus was quiet as we crossed the quadrangle to the WET-F building. The night air was balmy, the crickets were singing, and a brilliant full moon turned the sidewalks to ribbons of silver.

"What we're doing is not only wrong, it's unprofessional," I muttered as we walked.

"Stop worrying." Paoli reached out and took my hand, which had a soothing effect on me.

"Five minutes, right?" I said.

"Five minutes."

When we reached the door Paoli slid his badge into the card reader and the door clicked open. I followed him in.

"Security is going to know we were in here," I said.

"So what? We're authorized. Their software will only flag unauthorized entries."

Most of the lights had been turned off, and the room was dim, with the underwater lights giving everything an unworldly blue-greenish glow. There were a couple of equipment mockups in the water in preparation for the next day's training. I saw several spacesuits hanging on the wall, shining eerily in the light reflecting off the pool, making them look like high-tech angels. Although I would never admit it to Paoli, I was thrilled to be there, and the fact that we weren't supposed to be only made it better.

"I'd like to get a closer look at those mockups," I said. "You can't see much from here."

"Why don't we go into that room that had the television monitors? We can see them in there."

I looked at him. "But we really shouldn't touch anything."

"Well, we shouldn't *move* anything, but just turning on the monitors won't hurt."

His reasoning was pretty shaky, but I was so eager to take a look that I decided to go with him. The door to the conference room was dark and we went in.

"I don't see how it could attract any attention to turn on the light in here. There aren't any windows, so no one will see," I said.

Feeling around, I found the panel and three switches. I flicked one and turned on a single row of overhead fixtures, which half lit up the room. It was arranged as it had been that day, with eight simple upholstered chairs in two rows. The three monitors were mounted on the wall about eight feet up. I found the power control on a table at the front of the room, along with a control unit with three joystick-type levers that I assumed repositioned the underwater cameras.

I pressed the power button. All the monitors simultaneously buzzed to life, the screens flickering a few seconds before stabilizing into fields of quivering, dazzling blue-green, the screens casting their hue into the dim light of the room. The monitors appeared to show three separate views of the interior of the pool. I stared at the screen closest to me, hypnotized by the glow.

"If only we had popcorn," Paoli said as he settled into a chair. Carrying the remote control with me, I sat down next to him. "Adjust the cameras, Julie. They aren't aimed at anything."

I pushed one of the three joysticks to the right and the view on the right-hand monitor moved. The water was so still that movement was barely discernible at first, but variations in the blue indicated that the camera was moving.

I tried another joystick, moving it firmly to the left. The picture on the middle monitor moved slowly and the edge of an object crept into the lower left corner of the screen.

"You got something," Paoli said excitedly. Once more I pushed the joystick to the left, jiggling it upward, then to the right until I got the object in view.

"It looks like a mockup of some sort of mechanical arm. They probably use it to retrieve things in space. Margo said they use the WET-F to practice retrieving and repairing satellites." I felt Paoli's lips on my neck. I smiled and tilted my chin.

"Don't get me wrong. As far as the general concept goes, I like what you're doing and would hate to discourage it. It's just that the time and place seem a little off," I said.

His lips traveled to my ear, sending shivers through all my favorite body parts.

"That's where you're wrong," he murmured between kisses. "This is exactly the right time and place. The lighting in here is very romantic."

His hand slipped up my skirt, and I could feel my resolve weakening. To make love right there in the NASA WET-F was unthinkable, yet I had never done anything like that in my life, and the idea was exciting. Before I met Paoli I had led such a puritanical existence. Not that I hadn't wanted to explore my sexuality. It's just that I had spent my entire adult life working with computers sixteen hours a day and it hadn't left much time for anything else. I mean I love computers, but they aren't all that cuddly.

I closed my eyes, beginning to give in to Paoli's advances, but then my Girl Scout-librarian-schoolmarm side took over.

"Stop it. What if someone walked in?"

"They won't. Don't worry so much."

"You promised we'd only be five minutes."

"I'll be fast."

His fingers undid the top two buttons on my blouse and I quickly rebuttoned them. He undid them again. I rebuttoned them again.

"This is ridiculous. We can't do this. We're here on a case. We can't have sex on a client's premises. It's unprofessional."

"Relax. We're taxpayers and we're on government property."

I giggled and continued adjusting the joystick to get the retrieval arm in better view.

"As much as I'd like to maximize my tax dollar for a change, right now I want to see more of these space toys. We'll never get another chance to do this."

"Yeah, well, I'm planning for this experience to be fairly unique, too." His hand slipped inside my blouse and I started to push it away, but then something caught my eye on the monitor.

"Paoli, something moved."

"Three guesses as to what."

"No, I mean on the screen."

Paoli's attention remained on my chest. "It's probably just a water filter. You know, this would be twice as fun as a team effort."

"No, it was something else. Like a fish or something."

"Now that would be a good joke. Put a flounder in the WET-F. Reminds me of college. Mmmm. Have I ever told you I love your perfume?"

I pushed the joystick left, then right, then I got it. Something was wedged between the satellite and retrieval arm mockups. Pushing the lever a little farther, something large and white came into view.

"Is there a focus on this thing?" I asked, holding up the control box. There was a round dial on one side. "I think this is it." I turned it and the white object became first blurry and then clear. Then I screamed.

Filling the screen was the chalk-white face of John Garza.

13

I don't remember jumping up, but suddenly I was standing over Paoli, who was sprawled on the floor, his chair on top of him. I stumbled over his legs, almost dropping the control box, bouncing it in my hands like a hot potato until I finally got a grip on it.

Dazed, Paoli sat up, rubbing his knee. "What the hell?"

I pointed to the screen with a wobbly finger. Paoli turned to look and let out a yell.

Garza's face appeared oddly large and luminous against the water's iridescent blue-green. His lips were parted, his dark hair floated upward, and his eyes stared straight ahead. He looked mildly surprised to find himself in such a pitiable condition.

I froze, my thoughts swirling crazily, and it even flashed through my mind that it was some sort of trick.

"We have to get him out," I said frantically, and I sprang toward the door. I ran to the pool, pulled off my flats, and dived in, swimming down to Garza. He was wearing the torso part of his space suit with no helmet. I tugged on his arm, but he wouldn't come and I saw that his foot was stuck in one of the mesh mockups. He must have kicked hard, struggling upward and gotten his foot caught. Panic rose in my chest. I saw bubbles and felt Paoli behind me. He grabbed Garza's shoulder and motioned toward the surface. I swam up, gulped some air, then dived back down. Paoli had Garza freed.

I swam to the side and scrambled out of the pool. Paoli surfaced and swam over with Garza in tow, and I grabbed Garza's arm and tried my best to haul him out of the water, but he was so heavy in the wet space suit that I couldn't handle him. While I hung on to Garza's arm, Paoli got out of the pool, and together we managed to haul Garza out. We laid him flat on his back on the cement.

I know CPR, so I told Paoli to call an ambulance, and though I was out of breath myself, I pinched Garza's nostrils with one hand, held his mouth open with the other, and breathed into him. Garza's lips were like ice and it didn't take me long to feel like I was breathing into a dead man. Still I kept working on him, breathing into him again and again. After a while Paoli took over. But Garza remained perfectly still.

Choking back tears, I sat on my heels and looked at Garza's lifeless face. There was a red mark high up on his forehead just below his hairline. It was horizontal, about an inch long, slightly curved. I stood up, walked a few yards away, and sat down shivering on the wet cement.

Paoli looked ashen, and we sat together, dripping wet, both of us shaken and out of breath, although not quite as out of breath as poor John Garza.

Paoli kept his head turned so he wouldn't have to look at the gruesome sight. My beloved is a tough guy when he needs to be, but he's never at his best around corpses.

It crossed my mind that we should call a security guard,

but at that moment I felt too unnerved to do much of anything. The guard at the front gate would figure things out when the ambulance arrived.

Paoli held his head in his hands. "Tell me this didn't happen, Julie."

But it had happened. Garza was lying wet and very dead by the side of the pool, broad rivulets of water snaking out around him. As I stroked Paoli's wet hair, I heard sirens in the distance, and within moments the paramedics arrived along with two security guards. One of the guards stood over the paramedics while they went to work on Garza. The other one grilled Paoli and me on what we were doing in the WET-F and how we happened to find him.

Paoli tap-danced a while, but he came up with a believable story about our coming into the WET-F to check the personal computers in one of the offices to see if they were part of the NASA network. He said our sniffer program had turned up an ID coming in from one of the WET-F PCs that looked suspicious, so we had decided to check it out.

I hadn't even noticed those computers and I silently thanked Paoli for his powers of observation. He threw in enough confusing technical jargon to get us off the hook with the guard, and I felt pretty sure it would work with Margo and Lisa Foster as well.

I kept one eye on the paramedics laboring over Garza. I noticed they didn't spend much time trying to resuscitate him. When the guard was finished asking us questions I went over to them. The memory of Garza's cold lips against mine sent waves of nausea through me. I shuddered involuntarily, and felt for a moment I'd be sick.

"How long has he been dead?" I asked one of the paramedics. He looked young, early twenties, much too young to be so casual in the face of death. But I guess that comes with the job. As for me, I was close to throwing up.

"Can't tell, ma'am. You know him?"

At any other time the "ma'am" thing would have bothered me. "We met just recently," I answered. I took a few deep breaths and went back over to Paoli, who was talking to the guards.

"You better tell the paramedics not to move the body. The police will want to examine it," I said to them. "With luck the badge reader outside will tell you who was with him."

One of the guards, a large burly man with thick dirty blond hair and a wide face, put his hands on his hips and glared at me. His badge bore the name "Schmidt."

"You telling me you think this could be a homicide?" he said. He was pretty shaken up and I didn't blame him. NASA security guards probably didn't expect to deal with dead bodies, especially on a nightly basis.

"It's possible. There's no way he would put on his WET-F suit and get in the pool by himself," I told the guard. "The astronauts have to be lowered in by a crane. So there had to be somebody else here."

Suddenly the guard was all over his walkie-talkie like he had dialed up a sex-chat nine hundred number.

In the next few minutes controlled chaos struck. First the police arrived followed by a couple of guys in slacks and jackets who had the unmistakable look of upper-rank government security. I had come across the type when I worked on a secret government project at my old job. One of the policemen started to interview Paoli and me, but when one of the government types wanted us, the cop backed off. It was obvious who had the clout.

Dave Kane was six feet tall, a little paunchy, neatly dressed in linen slacks, a shirt and a sport coat. He refrained from giving his exact job title, but he spoke with the calm, educated assurance of a man with seniority and a fat paycheck. He was much less interested in how we got in the WET-F than with why.

They must have been fresh out of personality the day they made him, and the fact that he had about as much warmth as an icicle had probably come up in his performance reviews, because when I called him Mr. Kane, he quickly insisted that I call him Dave. I guess he thought that made him seem like the kind of guy you really wanted to open up to. It didn't, but it least he was trying.

He took us into the conference room with the monitors, eyeing the overturned chair with distrust. It occurred to me that he thought there had been a struggle and there had been, only not the kind he was thinking of. Paoli gave him a cleaned-up version of how the chair had been turned over, leaving out the part about his hand being down my blouse.

"I think Garza's death has something to do with the SM–13 and SM–15 missions," I told Dave vigorously. Now that I was answering questions, I had recovered some of my equilibrium. "The hacking is definitely connected to them. It's too much of a coincidence that two astronauts associated with both missions turn up dead." Dave's eyes flashed when I said "two astronauts." "We've got the hacking covered, so I think you should pay some attention to Gary Olander's suicide—apparent suicide."

I told him about the broken drawer handle I had seen in the shuttle trainer. "You should find out if Olander left a suicide note," I added. "We didn't see one when we found him, and Olander's wife reacted oddly when I asked her about it. You should look into it."

What Dave looked at was me with cold annoyance. "Thanks for the tip. Now let's focus on what happened tonight."

I sighed. We all sat down and then we went through the chronology of events again, Paoli talking sometimes, me at others, both of us tending to talk at once, which I could see was causing Dave some irritation. He didn't write down any of our answers like a policeman would have. He just sat stiffly in his chair, listening intently, his brain a computer tracking all the data and filing it appropriately.

"There's one suggestion I'd like to make," I said to Dave, although I had already made about five. "If I were you I'd check Garza's voice mail right away."

"I got my training a long time ago," he answered.

I leaned forward, my elbows on my knees. "But you see, you won't be able to do it directly from the phone system because I'm sure he had a voice-mail password, and it will take too long to contact the administrator. It would be better to get the messages straight off the computer. And did you notice the cut on Garza's head?"

"He could have hit it on something in the pool," Dave said.

I frowned. "I'm not so sure. It's so high up on his head, and it was in the front. I mean, how did it happen?" Dave looked at me with new interest. Paoli looked at me with his face all pinched up. "Could someone have hit him on the head and shoved him in?"

Dave's expression didn't alter. "I did examine the cut on his head. We won't know for sure until the autopsy, but the paramedic said it didn't look like it was deep enough of a blow to have stunned him. And you just said that his foot was caught in one of the mockups indicating he had been struggling upward, so he couldn't have been stunned at the time."

"Then how did it happen?" I asked.

"We don't know yet."

"I think Garza might have been murdered."

"Your reason for that conclusion?" Dave asked.

Paoli threw his hands in the air. "Ah, jeezus, we don't actually know anybody was murdered," he interrupted. "She thinks everything is murder. She's just that way. You could die choking on a fish bone and she'd swear the salmon stuffed it down your throat on purpose. Garza could have had a heart attack and fell into the pool and drowned. Simple as that."

Normally I would have been insulted by such a lack of confidence, but given the circumstances, I let it slide.

"That doesn't seem too likely," I told him gently. "Garza is—was—an astronaut. He had to have been in good physical condition. He was only in his forties."

"So maybe his heart trouble was congenital. Or maybe he had a seizure or something," Paoli said stubbornly.

I pressed my finger against his chest. "Or maybe someone bashed him on the head and pushed him into the water."

Paoli stood up. "Don't jump to conclusions, Julie. We don't know anything for sure."

Dave just watched us.

I rose. "You're wrong," I said to Paoli, and then turned to Dave. "Computer hacking, an apparent suicide, and another death, the cause of which hasn't been determined, have all occurred within a short period of time. Each is related in some way to two specific shuttle missions. Something must have happened on the SM–13 mission to make somebody want to keep the SM–15 mission on the ground."

Dave didn't say anything. Paoli did.

"On the other hand, Garza could have just slipped and fallen into the pool," he told me. "His suit was so heavy he couldn't get back out and he drowned."

"Possible," I said. "But how did he get the suit on? When I saw Lanie being suited up this morning she had people helping her."

"Yes, but she's small. Besides, Garza was only wearing the top part. He could have gotten that on himself," Paoli said.

I opened my mouth to continue the argument, but Dave interrupted.

"I have what I need," he said quickly. "I'll be in touch."

The party was over and it was time to go home, only I wasn't ready. I followed him to the door.

"If this is a murder, those voice-mail messages could be important," I said to his back. "I'd check his e-mail, too. Trust me, John Garza met someone here tonight."

Dave turned and stared at me as if getting rid of me would take an antibacterial ointment. I get that look a lot. Sometimes I care and sometimes I don't, and in this instance it was the latter. I asked for Dave's phone number, saying we needed it in case Paoli or I remembered anything else, but I really wanted it so I could call him and check up on the status of the case. He probably wouldn't tell me much, but he'd have access to all the important information and it wouldn't hurt to try.

Paoli drove us back to our motel. I rolled down the window, put my head back against the seat and breathed in the smell of yet another dead skunk.

"Is anything wrong?" I asked after the first few minutes of uncomfortable silence.

He tossed me a disgusted glance. "Is anything wrong, she

asks. Yes, there's something wrong. We just found a dead person. Again. We find dead people frequently, Julie. When we started this business I didn't know that I was joining the Corpse of the Month Club. It's starting to get to me. And it bugs me when I see that it doesn't bother you."

The remark stung. I sat up straight. "That's unfair. It bothers me a lot. But rather than dwell on how upset I am, I prefer to concentrate on a solution."

"Garza's a little past the solution stage, Julie."

"I mean finding his killer."

"We're not being *paid* to find a killer. We're being paid to find a hacker."

"But what if the hacker and the killer are the same person?"

"Don't even talk like that. We don't have any proof there is a killer."

"We can't blind ourselves to what's in front of us."

"And what were you thinking, telling that Dave guy to investigate Olander's suicide?"

"I'm not sure it was suicide."

Paoli shook his finger in the air. "Let me remind you that Data9000 Investigations investigates computers," he said. "You remember computers, don't you, Julie? You know, the square things about the size of a minibar made out of silicon chips and circuits with little blinking lights on the outside? Them. That's what we investigate. Not murders. Not suicides."

We stopped talking. Paoli rolled down his window, and the air whipped through the car. I turned up Hank Williams on the radio. Half the radio stations in Houston played country music. Not that I minded. I leaned my head back against the seat again, closed my eyes, and tried to clear my head.

I didn't agree with Paoli, but I understood his frustration. I had naïvely thought that the job at NASA was finally going to be the kind of straightforward computer investigative work we had been looking for. And here we were once again in the middle of a case that didn't involve computers nearly as much as it involved the murky side of the human psyche.

14

We dragged into our motel room feeling as bleak and tired as the decor around us. I flopped facedown, sprawled spread-eagle on the bed as if I had landed there by leaping from a tall building. Paoli collapsed into a chair. We groaned in unison.

"I'm sorry if I was a jerk in the car," he said, his voice soft with fatigue.

I was ready to wholeheartedly forgive him but delayed my response, considering whether or not I had the physical and spiritual strength to strip off my clothes and throw myself on him. The scales were tipped in favor of it, but there was a knock at the door.

Paoli let out another groan.

"Who's answering it? You or me?" I asked him, lifting my head two inches to speak.

"I'll play you for it," he said. "Loser answers. Okay, I'm thinking of a number between one and—"

I swore out loud and slid off the bed as the knocking resumed with more urgency.

"I'm coming, okay?" I opened the door, and there, to my amazement, I found Max and Cosmos. Max looked disdainful, Cosmos looked blissful. He wagged his tail energetically.

"I know you're trying to save money, Jules, but there's a cockroach in my room that's big enough to dance with."

I threw my arms around her, and Cosmos jumped up on me yelping with delight. I'd never been so glad to see them. Paoli vaulted out of his chair, saying hi to Max as he knelt down to scratch Cosmos behind his ears.

"I can't believe you're here. What happened? Why did you come?" I asked in a rush when I was done hugging her.

Dressed in a tight white skirt, a short-sleeved turtleneck and strappy sandals, she walked into the room, dropping her Gucci handbag on the bed.

"Cosmos was stuck in a dangerous state of ennui. He was sleeping too much. Was completely off his Rice Krispies. So I took him to a pet therapist in Marin County. Her name's Shana Aurora. Wonderful woman. Really has insight into the animal mind. I'm thinking of taking Wayne to her, although he doesn't have the strong inner core to work with that Cosmos has. Anyway, Shana said Cosmos was missing you, so we caught a flight out immediately."

"I'm glad you did. And of course I'll pay you back for the flight and his cage," I said.

"Cage?" Max arched an eyebrow and looked at Cosmos. "Pretend you didn't hear that, Cosmos. As if you would ever submit to such degradation."

Cosmos was currently lying on his back, his spotted belly exposed, rapidly kicking his hind leg while Paoli rubbed his tummy. He didn't look very indignant.

"I tried to buy him a first-class seat on United, but the reservations woman refused," Max said. "She actually wanted to put him in the baggage compartment."

"So how did you get here?" Paoli asked. He was on his back now with Cosmos licking his face.

"I told Wayne I was going to rent a car and drive here, and it made him so crazy with worry that he hired a Lear jet. Cosmos loved looking out the window."

I envisioned Cosmos riding in private-jet comfort while Paoli and I had traveled crammed in coach.

"Jules, honey, let's go to the john," Max said.

She grabbed her purse and pulled me into the tiny bathroom, closing the door. No bigger than an inadequate closet, it barely had enough room for two people. I sat down on the toilet lid and pulled my knees to my chest to save space.

"Okay, enough bull," I said before she had a chance to talk. "Why are you really here?"

She bit her lip and her eyes filled with tears. "Oh, Jules, I was crawling the walls, I was so bored and lonely. Wayne's out of town until tomorrow. I just couldn't take it anymore, so I thought I'd spend some time with you. Let him see how he likes being in that huge house all by himself. I know you're going to say it was the wrong thing to do."

"I'm not. I'm glad you're here," I said, really meaning it. "I tell you, Max, this case isn't turning out at all like I expected. I could use a friend."

She put her hands on my shoulders and locked eyes with me. "That's the other reason I came. Last night you sounded terrible. If that Margo tramp is trying to steal Vic away—"

"She's not."

"Don't try to bluff me, Jules. You're worried. I can hear it in your voice. Nobody knows better than me how much you need Vic. He's a man, so naturally he's flawed, but he loosens you up. Keeps you from worrying your brains to a pulp."

She pulled something black and lacy out of her handbag and dangled it in front of me. "The doctor has brought medicine. I also bought you new shoes. High heels. You've heard of them. Flats with polelike projections bracing up the rear." She looked at my feet. "Yours look like the kind birdwatchers wear for field work."

"Somehow I don't think my footwear is the problem."

"Honey, admit it, you need me here, especially after finding that poor man who hung himself."

I told her about Garza, the most recent poor man we had found dead.

I had trouble sleeping that night. I kept thinking about Garza, and about Olander, and pretty soon I was too worked up even to keep my eyes closed. I got up, and in the darkness I pretended I was Garza standing at the edge of the pool; I tried to figure out how he might have fallen in. I imagined him falling in backwards, forwards, and sideways, but regardless of the angle, I just couldn't see how he could have hit the top of his forehead by falling into the pool.

I managed a few hours of restless sleep and awoke the next morning to a sunny Texas day. Huge cumulus clouds floated in the bright sky, the fluffy kind that start to look like faces and animals and monsters if you lie on the ground and stare at them long enough. At least they did when I was a kid.

Unfortunately Paoli and I weren't looking as chipper as the weather. I felt sickened by what had happened the night before, despite Max's arrival, and I could tell Paoli felt just as bad as I did.

While he was getting dressed I got out my notebook and jotted down the previous day's expenses, then under

"Progress" I wrote, *Day two: No new progress on software. Investigating C-CINS and NASA employees as hacking suspects.* Under "Misc.," I wrote, *Found John Garza dead.*

Using the extra key Max had given us, I quietly slipped Cosmos into her room, managing not to wake her, and then left a message for her at the front desk saying we'd be home around ten that night. Paoli and I picked up coffee at the local 7-Eleven and drove in silence to NASA, our spirits low.

"Day three," I muttered as we drove up to the main gate. There was a noticeable absence of protesters. Paoli asked Zack, the guard, why C-CINS had called off the party that day. He shrugged sadly, leaning down to rest his plump arm on the edge of the open car window.

"Must have heard about what happened to poor John Garza," he said, shaking his head. "What can you say about a thing like that? God works in crazy ways sometimes, to take a smart, good man that way."

We expressed our condolences, but somehow I had a feeling Garza's death didn't fall in the *deus ex machina* category.

"The NASA grapevine works fast, doesn't it?" Paoli said to me as he drove through the gate and into a parking space. "Though I guess the security guards would be the first to hear about a death."

"What I'm wondering is who told the protesters?" I said, getting out of the car. "Makes me think there's a mole at NASA giving information to C-CINS."

Paoli gave me a sideways glance. "I love it when we get into spy talk."

For the exercise we hiked up the stairs to the third floor. Paoli hadn't been getting his workouts since we had come to Houston, and he was the one who suggested we skip the elevator. As for me, my favorite aerobic activity is lifting my coffee mug to my lips. As we came down the hallway to our office, me breathing hard, we saw Lanie Rogers standing there studying something on a clipboard. We said hello and she looked at us with tired eyes.

"I'm sorry about Garza," I said.

She nodded woodenly. "They still don't know what happened."

"Any guesses?" Paoli asked.

"Just that maybe it was some sort of freak accident. It's terrible." Her gaze drifted off a few seconds, then came back. "I've got to go. I've got to be in the WET-F in ten minutes."

Paoli looked surprised. "You mean they're going to use it so soon after Garza's death?"

"We're on a tight schedule," she muttered, and walked quickly away. I wondered who would be Garza's replacement.

"See, Julie? They think it was an accident," Paoli said when Lanie was gone. We had continued on our way to our office.

"Ridiculous. Forget about the cut on his head, what was Garza doing so close to the pool? The suits and helmets were by the wall," I whispered as we walked. "If Garza wasn't going into the water, say he just wanted to check something on the suit, then why go over by the pool to do it?" Paoli didn't have an answer. "I'll tell you why," I said. "Garza never intended to go into the pool. Somebody shoved him in."

We reached into our office, and while Paoli went off to find more coffee I got the computer running.

I was waiting for it to boot up when Margo walked past our doorway. I assumed if there was any new information about Garza she might have it, so I bolted out the door and called her name. She stopped, waiting a moment before turning to face me.

When she did it was a shock. She looked wasted, her eyes so red and puffy she barely resembled herself. She wore no makeup except for some lipstick, and her hair looked straggly, like she hadn't washed it. She looked so demolished that I forgot my petty jealousy. I went up to her and took her hand, pressing it into mine.

"I'm sorry, Margo," I said.

Then the tears came. At first there was just a trickle, but after a few seconds the dam burst and she was sobbing. Putting my arm around her, I shepherded her into the ladies room.

"Do you have any Kleenex?" I asked her, since she seemed unaware she needed one. She dug through her Dooney and Bourke handbag. It was cream-colored with tan trim, so expensive and sturdy you'd expect it to produce a Kleenex, but it didn't.

I didn't have my purse with me, so I went into a stall and grabbed some toilet paper. Margo didn't seem a blow-your-nose-on-toilet-paper type of woman, but she accepted it and went to work on her streaming face. After a few minutes the sobs quieted to occasional shudders.

"I'm sorry," she blubbered. "You always seem to catch me at my worst."

"Then your worst isn't very bad," I said with a smile. "You were involved with Garza?"

She blew her nose and looked at me over the wad of toilet paper. "Was it that obvious?" Her voice was muffled by the tissue.

"Things like that usually fly right over my head, so if I

caught on, you can be sure everybody did."

She scrunched up the toilet paper in her fist. "I loved him. He loved me. We were going to get married," she said emphatically.

Garza had never looked at Margo like she was the love of his life. He looked at her more like she was something messy that needed cleaning up.

"Do they know what happened to him?" I asked.

Twisting the toilet paper into a knot, she shook her head. "No. I can't find out anything. Someone suggested he could have had a heart attack or something, but I don't believe it. Astronauts get complete physicals before every mission. John was in perfect health. But what was he doing in the WET-F at night?"

I remembered Garza pointing to the WET-F suit and speaking angrily about it the day before. "He seemed to think there was some problem with the suits when we were there yesterday. Could it have something to do with that?" I asked.

She nodded, blowing her nose again. "It's possible. After the practice yesterday he told me he was worried about them. They'd been redesigned and he thought there was a safety hazard—something about the oxygen components. John could be like a kick in the teeth when something went wrong with the equipment."

She got some fresh toilet paper, held it under the cold water and dabbed at her eyes.

"I've got to get back. Thanks for listening to me," she said, then turned quickly and went out.

Walking back to our office, I thought about what she said, about Garza getting angry about malfunctioning equipment. I couldn't blame him; people's lives depended on it.

But he must have been hard to work with. Like a kick in the teeth, Margo had said.

My footsteps came to a halt. I closed my eyes and conjured up the vision of Garza falling into the pool once more, but this time let the tape run a little longer. Opening my eyes I stood there for a good half a minute. Then I flew into our office, slamming the door behind me.

"What happened?" Paoli said, jumping up from his chair.

I didn't answer him. I was too busy spelunking through my purse for Dave Kane's card.

"What's going on with you?" Paoli asked over my shoulder, his tone perplexed. "Listen, Julie, I can't have a crisis today. My schedule's already full."

I found the card and dialed the number written on it. When Kane answered I put him on the speaker phone, Paoli glaring at me the whole time like I had taken leave of my senses.

"Dave, did the badge reader show that anyone else was in the WET-F?"

There was a pause. "I can't answer that."

"Look, I think I know how Garza got the cut on his head. There *had* to have been another person there with him."

"What happened?" Paoli said.

"Okay, here it is," I said to Paoli, and to Kane on the speaker phone. "Let's say Garza was pushed into the pool. He was a strong man and in good shape. Even with the top part of his WET-F suit on he might have been able to grab on to the side of the pool."

"What are you getting at?" Kane asked.

"That he came up out of the water trying to save himself, and somebody kicked him in the head. That mark on his forehead is from the heel of a shoe."

15

*T*he Information Highway isn't always a two-way street. I'd given Dave Kane what I considered to be a primo theory on the Garza case, but he refused to tell me whether the WET-F badge reader showed that another person had been in the building the night Garza was murdered.

Taking another pass over the target, I pressed him on the issue of Olander's suicide note, but again he told me nothing.

After striking out with Kane, Paoli and I got back to work at the computer. An hour later, my back stiff from sitting and staring at the screen, I got up and walked to the window. Right below I saw a man in dark pants and a sports jacket talking to Margo. I waved Paoli over.

"I'm sure I saw that guy with Dave Kane at the WET-F last night," I told Paoli. "He's got to be high-level security. He could be telling Margo something about Garza."

Paoli gave him a closer look. "From the look on her face I don't think he's asking her for a date."

"So let's go see if he told her anything."

Paoli came along without argument, happy for an excuse to stretch his legs. When we got outside Margo was still talking to Kane's cohort and she didn't look happy. Listening to him without speaking, her face was solemn. When he finished with her, she started across the quadrangle. We caught up with her.

"Margo, what did that guy say to you?" Paoli asked.

She kept on walking, her head down, not wanting to talk about it. We fell into step next to her.

"We might be able to help," he said.

She came to a halt and faced us, her eyes still puffy from crying. "They think I might have killed John."

Paoli blinked. "Why?"

"I don't know. They haven't actually accused me, not yet. But they want to formally question me. I worked late last night, so I suppose that makes me a suspect."

"Probably lots of people worked late," I said. "Why focus on you?"

Her eyes connected with mine and I remembered our conversation in the ladies' room.

"It's not so bad," she said, her tone ironic. "I heard they want to question Ben Lestat, too. Apparently someone saw him with John last night."

We mulled that one over a second, then Paoli asked if she had heard anything new about what happened to Garza, but she shook her head. "Have they checked the badge reader?" he asked.

This time she nodded. "The rumor is that it didn't show anyone coming into the WET-F except Garza and you two. But more than one person can get in on a badge, so it doesn't mean anything."

But she was wrong. It did mean something. It meant that Garza walked into the WET-F together with his killer.

She pressed her lips together, fighting off tears. "Look,

I'm sorry, but I've got to get out of here." She started to leave, but I put my hand on her arm.

"Is there anything I can do to help you?" I asked.

She smiled weakly at me. "No, but thanks. You've been a friend."

She walked off, her narrow three-inch heels tapping on the sidewalk. The mark on Garza's head hadn't been made by a heel like that. But then I remembered she had been wearing a pants suit the day before, and probably a lower heel. I tried to remember what sort of shoes she'd been wearing, but couldn't.

Paoli gave me a puzzled look. "What was that just now between you and Margo? Some sort of girl thing where you communicate with your eyes?"

I debated whether I should tell him. "I don't think it's going to be a secret for long anyway. I think they're questioning Margo about Garza's death because she and Garza had a thing," I said, raising my eyebrows meaningfully.

"I thought it was just a flirtation. You mean Margo was fishing off the company pier?" he asked, and I nodded. He frowned and watched Margo disappear around the corner. "Poor girl. Not only is her boyfriend murdered, but they think she did it."

"Well, like she said, they haven't actually accused her yet."

"You saw the look on her face. She's terrified. We have to help her," he said, his gaze still off in the distance.

I watched him looking after her for a moment.

"Paoli, I know she's your old college friend, but what if she *did* have something to do with Garza's murder?"

His head snapped in my direction. "Margo? Are you kidding? She would never go to any violent movies in college because it upset her to see fake blood. Trust me, she wouldn't hurt anyone."

I hoped he was right. Although Margo wasn't exactly my favorite person, she didn't seem like the murderer type to me. I mean, in the process of murdering somebody, a girl could break a nail or snag her nylons.

Brain cramp. It hit me without warning, descending ruthlessly upon my frontal lobes, slamming my synaptic connections to a dead halt. I sat at the computer cajoling myself into some productive work, but nothing even remotely productive was happening.

Paoli and I had been back in the office for two hours, but we hadn't got much work done. I was too antsy and Paoli sat staring glumly at the computer screen, occasionally pecking at a few keys. I could tell he was worrying about Margo.

Restless, I got up. The office was so small that I only had two options for walking: to the window, or out the door. I usually chose the window. I craned my neck and got a peek at the main gate, where I saw a television news van with its satellite dish on the roof. I also saw a couple of C-CINS signs moving around.

I turned to Paoli. "Let's go talk to Harvey Lindstrom," I said.

He looked up at me. "You think Lindstrom's the murderer?"

"I doubt it. He couldn't even get inside the gate, much less the door to the WET-F. But he might have something to do with the hacking. He isn't a big fan of NASA, that's for sure. Besides, we've gone through the NASA software backwards, forwards and sideways, and we've come up with zilch. Meanwhile the clock is ticking. So let's go directly after the people with motives. Garza was my first choice, and maybe he was the hacker—"

"He wasn't," Paoli said, leaning back in his chair.

"How do you know?"

"Look at this." He pointed to the screen. "The hacker's numbers just showed up in the software I was working with."

I looked and the numbers were there, dancing across the screen, mocking us.

"We already scanned the computers for viruses yesterday and didn't find any," he said. "That means our hacker has to be alive and kicking, which unfortunately Garza isn't."

"That's an even better reason to work on the protesters."

"But Julie, we can't waste time interviewing every protester. There are probably dozens of them out there by now."

"That's why we go after Lindstrom. He's their leader. We start with him and see where it leads. There's a TV crew outside the gates right now. Apparently C-CINS has decided to take advantage of the extra publicity. I'm sure Lindstrom is out there."

Paoli looked unconvinced. "Even if he is, we can't go blabbing about the hacking. NASA wants it kept quiet. If it turns out that Lindstrom isn't the hacker and he finds out we're looking for one, you know he'll tell the press. The media is already going to go crazy with a homicide coming on the heels of a suicide."

"Apparent suicide," I emphasized. "Okay, so let's make up something. Let's tell him we're doing a magazine story and that we're interested in finding out about why they're protesting."

Paoli groaned. "Too transparent. Lies are easier if they have half-truths in them. How about we say we're consultants working on improving security? We'll tell him some equipment was stolen and we want to know if any C-CINS people saw anything."

"He'll think we're accusing him."

"We'll convince him we're not. Besides, the threatening aspect of it will give our story credibility."

We decided against walking out to the front gate. We'd only call attention to ourselves, and we didn't want to have to answer a lot of inquiries about why we were chatting up the protesters. So we took the Chevy, drove through the gate and parked around the corner at a polite distance. I was surprised that there was only one TV van. Lindstrom was talking to a reporter while a cameraman filmed the interview.

He was an average-looking guy, about five ten with a receding hairline and glasses, dressed in black slacks and a slightly wrinkled cotton shirt. But watching him talk to a reporter you could see the fire inside him.

I couldn't hear what he was saying, but his body language was emphatic; he leaned forward, slicing the air with his hand as he made his point. Did Lindstrom believe in his cause so much that he would stoop to hacking to cause trouble for NASA? I was getting ahead of myself.

Paoli and I got out of the car and stood leaning against the trunk, watching the TV interview. With the length of the average TV news offering I assumed the interview wouldn't take long and I was right. After a few minutes the reporter walked away. When the TV van took off, Paoli and I approached the protesters. Lindstrom stood in the middle of them, being heartily congratulated by his compatriots for whatever he had said to the reporter. Paoli called out his name and Lindstrom turned, his self-satisfied smile evaporating when he saw us. We introduced ourselves and told him we were working for NASA.

"Lapdogs of the fascist bureaucrats," Lindstrom replied with disgust. "Did they hire you to harass me? To find out some dirty little secret they could use to damage me? Well, you won't find anything. You—"

Paoli held up a hand to stop the diatribe. "Now wait a minute. We're not here to cause any trouble, but I don't like the attitude you're taking."

Lindstrom turned bright pink as if he was building up steam to punch somebody. The rest of the protesters started to circle around us, a couple of the large males glaring at us menacingly. The females gave us some pretty threatening looks as well, and the word "lynching" came to my mind. I decided to try a conciliatory approach.

"Excuse me, Mr. Lindstrom, but we're not taking sides. And we're not investigating you directly." I addressed the last part to the crowd in general to stave off possible tarring and feathering, cognizant of the fact that after my dive into the WET-F pool I only had one presentable suit left.

I told Lindstrom our little story about the equipment thefts from the parking lot.

"So what do you think we had to do with it?" he demanded.

"Nothing, of course," I said. "But you're out here every day. You see all the cars that come in and out."

He jabbed a finger in the air. "I don't remember NASA ever doing me any favors." There was a rumble of agreement from the crowd. "I try to set up meetings with them to talk about issues and they refuse. So why should I help you?"

His words came out in a fevered rush and he had a funny way of making little wet inhalations between phrases.

"Because you know how it feels when someone refuses to have a simple discussion about something," I said amiably.

"We're not NASA employees. We're just contractors trying to make a living, and we want to ask you a couple of questions. Couldn't we go somewhere and talk in private?"

My line about just trying to make a living got to him, plus the fact that there's a definite Girl Scout aura about me. People tend to trust me.

Lindstrom's face turned a less vivid color. "We can talk over here," he said, tilting his head toward a row of cars parked on the road's shoulder. We followed him over to a small and battered silver Honda Accord. "We'll sit inside."

He unlocked the driver's side door and got in, unlocking the other doors for us. I slid in front next to him and Paoli got in the back. It wasn't as easy as it sounds, since Lindstrom's car was piled with protest flyers and magazines and an assortment of kids toys. Paoli let out an "ouch" as he sat down and pulled a plastic Power Ranger out from under him.

"How many children do you have, Mr. Lindstrom?" I asked.

"Two." His stern expression melted at the very mention of his offspring, but he quickly got it back in place. "So what exactly do you want? Make it fast. I've got a radio interview in a half hour."

Paoli leaned forward between the two front seats and asked Lindstrom a few starter questions about whether the protesters had noticed anything strange going on in the parking lot. Lindstrom immediately got huffy. Paoli assured him that none of the protesters were being accused, but Lindstrom remained tense. It didn't help matters that the car was stifling hot, even with the windows down.

"Listen, I can't vouch for everyone in the group. We get some people outside the official C-CINS organization that are protesting for the fun of it. Don't get me wrong. I like extra bodies bulking up the ranks, but they're not true believers. Protesting is their hobby, you know what I mean?" The words started to come out rapidly, his head bobbing forward with each syllable.

A car passed and the air thickened with dust. "For all I know one of them could have sneaked into the campus and broken into somebody's truck," Lindstrom continued. "Like, sort of a harassment thing."

"Is it possible to sneak inside the campus?" I asked.

Lindstrom cackled. "Of course. These NASA types are basically dealing with old technology most of the time, including some of their security. They're not gods. Do you have any idea how much money they waste on sending that damn shuttle up? Billions every year."

"I get your point, but you have to admit they do some worthwhile research," I said.

"Hah. More worthwhile than education for our children or getting homeless people off the street?" he asked. He took a long breath. "Listen, ethical issues are important to me," he said more calmly. "That's why if anyone in our group is stealing, I'd like to know about it. We don't want to associate with people like that. Even if the government hasn't any standards, C-CINS does." He put his hands to his head, as if the conversation was giving him a headache. "The interview is over now. I've got to go."

I tried to think of a way to keep the conversation going, but Lindstrom saved me the trouble. He closed his eyes a second, collecting himself.

"Wait a minute," he said. "I don't want to be a cold jerk. I want you to know that I'm sorry about John Garza. It was a heart attack?"

Now I knew why there had been only one television van. NASA had apparently released information that Garza had died of natural causes. Or else Lindstrom was pretending not to know any more than that. I told him we didn't know for sure what had happened to Garza, which was the truth.

"Listen, Garza and I had our problems," Lindstrom said. "When I heard he might get kicked out of the shuttle program I admit I was glad, but I never wished something like this on him."

"Garza might have gotten kicked out of the program. Why?" I asked.

Lindstrom stiffened. "Because he slugged me. I'm suing him and NASA for damages." He rubbed his forehead. "I guess I'm just suing NASA now. Garza deviated my septum." He put special emphasis on *septum*. "And I heard that Garza was reprimanded by Lisa Foster for attacking me, that she was thinking about kicking him out of the shuttle program for what he did."

"Heard from whom?" Paoli asked.

The corners of Lindstrom's mouth turned up. "I have my sources."

"Someone at NASA told you?" I asked.

Lindstrom checked his watch. "I have my radio interview," he said tightly. He started the car engine and took off the parking brake. Being intuitive people, we took that as an invitation to get out of the car.

Lindstrom drove off, raising a cloud of dust. Paoli and I stood on the shoulder and watched his car sputter and pop its way into the distance.

16

*I*f Garza's job was on the line because of Lindstrom, he could have been mad enough to frame Lindstrom for the hacking," I said to Paoli as we walked back to our car. Hot and sticky and covered with dust, I felt like we had at least accomplished something.

"You're saying that Garza did the hacking to make it look like Lindstrom's work?" he asked.

"We needed a motive for Garza. Now we have one."

Paoli kicked a rock down the street, skipping it yards across the pavement, and he eyed its progress with satisfaction. Giving him a sideways look, I contemplated what it was that made him want to do such a thing. I don't kick rocks because it would scuff my shoes and shoes are expensive, and it made me wonder if rock-kicking sprang from sex-linked genes. It probably hadn't been researched. I turned my attention back to Lindstrom and the case.

"The next logical conclusion then is that Lindstrom found out what Garza was doing and murdered him for it," Paoli said.

I shook my head. "I still don't see how he could have gotten inside."

We stopped at our car. I looked over and saw the C-CINS people building up momentum, marching in a circle and singing a song I thought I remembered as an old Peter, Paul and Mary tune.

Paoli fished through his pockets for his keys. "You're forgetting something," he said. "Lindstrom has a contact within NASA helping him. He admitted it."

I went around to the passenger door. "So that person let Lindstrom in the WET-F to kill Garza?" I asked him over the car's roof. "But the badge reader didn't show anyone going to the WET-F last night except us and Garza. And I doubt that Garza would have let Lindstrom walk in with him."

Paoli unlocked the car and we got in. "Maybe Lindstrom got in with someone earlier in the day and then hid and waited for Garza." He started the engine.

I took off my shoe and shook gravel out. "But how did he know Garza would be there?"

"The same way he gets his other information. From his spy."

Paoli pulled onto the road, made a U-turn and drove around the corner and back through the NASA gate. I was sure Lindstrom fit into the picture, but for the life of me I couldn't figure out exactly how.

When we got back to the office, Paoli sat down at the computer and I started going through a short list of commercial software packages that NASA used, looking for products that had known security bugs. The process wasn't going to take long because NASA wrote almost all its own software.

I was starting to worry that the crack investigation firm of Data9000 had met its match in the NASA hacker. Paoli and I had gone through all our normal procedures and hadn't found anything suspicious in the computer network. We were at the point where Paoli was trying to break into the software himself, testing areas that could be weak spots. When it came to hacking, Paoli's skills were better than mine, so after I finished my task with the commercial software list, I decided to concentrate on investigating the human element.

My first step was to find out more about Garza. There had to be fresh gossip floating around. Maybe Margo was too far down the NASA information food chain. I figured an astronaut would be more likely to hear essential information, so I phoned McKenzie and told him I wanted to talk. He didn't ask about what. I think he knew. He said I should meet him in his office in thirty minutes, so I sat back in my chair and ruminated on Garza while Paoli worked at the computer.

"Do you think you could hack into the NASA voice-mail system?" I said after a contemplative silence. "We should take a look at Garza's phone messages."

Paoli looked up and grinned. Hacking into computers when he isn't supposed to is one of his favorite things, right up there with sports and me. At the NSA, part of his job was tracking down hackers, and in the process he had become a good hacker himself. As a rule he doesn't use his skills, since hacking is less than legal, but he isn't above a little computer breaking and entering when we're on a case.

"As long as their voice-mail computer is here on the premises, it shouldn't be too hard," he said. "Just look up Garza's extension for me while I call Michael to get access to the phone system computers."

"How are you going to talk him into it?"

"I'll just tell him I think the hacker may be getting in through the phone system."

I got Garza's extension from a NASA phone directory. Paoli called Michael, and then we went to the computer room down on the first floor. We told one of the systems operators that we were working on the hacking problems and wanted direct access to the computer that handled their phone system.

After the systems operator, a big-boned girl with a long, blond ponytail and a Susan B. Anthony T-shirt, called Michael and got his okay, she sat us at a desk with a computer terminal in the corner. We both politely declined her offer of coffee or a soft drink and she left.

"Can you get the voice-mail messages that Garza erased as well as the ones he saved?" I whispered in Paoli's ear.

There were at least half a dozen people working around us at desks and terminals, most of them eyeing us warily. Computer geeks are naturally suspicious of outsiders.

"I can try," Paoli whispered out of the corner of his mouth. "It depends if any new messages were written over the old deleted ones. With some luck the deleted ones will still be there. Those are the ones we want."

Paoli looked at the computer screen a moment, his eyes narrowed in thought. He pecked at a few keys, glanced guiltily around the room, then resumed typing, slowly at first, then faster, until his fingers were prancing across the keyboard. It was only a matter of time before NASA's voice-mail system would be at our disposal.

I watched him a few minutes, then got fidgety. I'm a certified computer lover, but there's nothing as boring as watching somebody else programming one. It's a lot like watching someone read a book.

There was a phone on the desk, so while Paoli infiltrated NASA's voice mail, I checked our messages at the Data9000 office. There was only one call, and it was from my mother.

"I've been trying to reach you for two days," she said in a vexed tone. "Why aren't you answering the phone at your office? I'm worried. And how's that sweet Vic? If I don't hear from you today I'm filing a missing persons report." I knew from experience that she wasn't kidding.

I should have called her back right then, but didn't because I didn't want Paoli to hear any part of our mother/daughter chats. I suspect my mother's doctor had increased her hormone dosage because recently she had started asking me detailed questions about my relationship with Paoli, including our sex life.

Next I checked our NASA voice mail and found a new message.

"This is weird," I said when I hung up.

"Don't bug me. I'm concentrating," he said, his eyes on the screen.

"But we just got a message that went out to all NASA employees involved with the SM–15 project. There's an emergency meeting in half an hour. Everyone is supposed to be there."

"Good. That means there will be fewer people in the computer room looking over my shoulder. I'll stay here and keep at this. You go to the meeting," he said, his voice low, his eyes never leaving the computer screen.

I decided to skip the elevator and take the stairs, kidding myself that racing up a couple of flights would make a dent in the junk food I had been subsisting on. My sense of direction is awful, and even though Paoli and I had taken the stairs the day before, I somehow took a wrong turn and found myself in an empty hallway that seemed to be used for ad hoc storage. Stacks of boxes lined the walls, along with some complicated-looking equipment I couldn't identify. Suddenly a medium crash came from behind a closed door followed by several smaller ones.

Afraid someone might have been hurt, I leapt for the door and pulled it open to find Ben Lestat staring angrily at a wall, his face red, his body tensed, fists clenched. There was a depression in the plaster wall, a lot of scratches and a broken marble pen stand on the floor.

"What happened?" I asked. He jerked around in my direction. I don't think he'd been aware that he had company.

"Show's over," he said rudely. "Now get out."

I said, "No problem," and quickly closed the door, wondering what had made him throw the tantrum. When I got to McKenzie's office he wasn't there, so I asked around until I found the Apollo conference room, where the meeting was being held, across the quadrangle. I set off, hoping all the walking back and forth between buildings was firming my thighs, and when I saw people filing into building one I followed them.

The Apollo room was large with space for about one hundred people. There was a tall podium in the front with an American flag on one side and a framed photograph of the president on the other.

Margo was sitting near the front of the room, but I decided to stay in the back where I wouldn't be noticed. I had a feeling our phone number had gotten on some distribution list by mistake and Paoli and I weren't really supposed to be in the meeting. I didn't want to be tossed out and miss whatever happened.

A small, dark-haired, perky young woman in a pantsuit sat down next to me. She smiled, introduced herself as Janet and asked me if I was new to NASA. When I told her I was doing consulting in the computer department, she asked what I was working on, but just then heads started turning toward the front of the room.

Lisa Foster marched up to the podium and the room quieted, not so much out of respect, but because everyone was anxious to know what was going on.

Foster looked grim. Her jaw was set tightly, her footsteps to the podium an irritated stomp. In spite of all this, her mane of unruly hair was arranged in a lacquered coiffure that must have taken an hour to wash, set, scrunch and spray. The vanity of it made me smile.

Foster leaned forward slightly and gripped the edges of the podium looking around the hushed room. "SM–15 has been delayed indefinitely," she said abruptly, not bothering with any polite introductory remarks. There were a few gasps and a groan of disapproval that rumbled through the crowd.

Foster pressed her lips together. "The decision came from Washington," she continued. "We haven't been able to schedule a suitable replacement for John Garza, so the decision is a correct one. We have to pick up and move on. You'll get your reassignments by the end of next week. The crew has been informed and they accepted the decision gracefully, as we all have to."

Not all the astronauts had accepted it that gracefully, I thought. No wonder Lestat had thrown the fit. He would have been second-in-command on the SM–15 mission.

"That's basically it," Foster said. She briskly exited the room. People sat in stunned silence a moment and then began moving toward the doors. I looked at Janet and saw the disappointment on her face.

"Will anyone get laid off?" I asked.

"No, just moved to other missions."

"So why does everybody look so dejected?"

She shrugged slightly. "People get emotionally attached to a mission. You're working with a specific crew, you have a specific payload and specific objectives. There's a launch date set and everyone gets excited. You feel like you have a stake in it. It's like a family. Any delay is a disappointment, but this sounds like a cancellation. It's a big letdown."

We wished each other luck and Janet followed the others out. I stood there a minute, wondering about my own job security. Would Foster give Paoli and me the ax along with the SM–15?

I went back to the computer room and found Paoli hard at work. He looked at me with a happy expression.

"Got them," he whispered. "All of Garza's messages. You've got to listen to this one. It's juicy."

He punched in some numbers then handed me the receiver. I put it to my ear and heard an angry male voice say, "I have to talk to you. Don't put me off."

I looked at Paoli. "Sounds like Lestat."

He looked surprised. "How can you be so sure?"

"I just spoke to him half an hour ago. It's the same voice."

"I thought it might be him. I tried to trace the extension, but I couldn't. His voice is pretty distinctive, though."

"You think the police and Dave Kane have this message, too?"

Paoli lifted his shoulders. "I'll turn it over to them just in case."

As we went out into the hall, I heard Paoli mutter, "Speak of the devil." Lestat was coming directly toward us, his stride brisk.

"Can I speak with you?" he asked me, then glanced at Paoli. "Alone?"

Paoli gave Lestat a mildly threatening look.

I touched his arm. "It's okay," I told him. "You go make those calls. I'll meet you back at the office."

But Paoli didn't like it. "Excuse us," he said and pulled me a few yards away. "Julie, for all we know he could be a murderer," he whispered.

"If Lestat wants to talk to me, then I have to hear him out," I whispered back. "It could be important. Besides, he's not going to kill me in broad daylight with people everywhere. He knows you know I'm with him."

Paoli argued with me for a few more minutes, but I finally won, and he went off, leaving me with Lestat.

"Let's go somewhere where we can talk," Lestat said when Paoli had gone.

"Can't we talk here?"

Lestat glanced around him. "I'd rather talk in private. Please."

I hesitantly agreed, feeling less certain about being alone with him. Lestat led me away from building four and around a corner. He walked at a good clip and I struggled to keep up. We didn't talk. He took me to a small, windowless, two-story concrete building set apart from the others.

"I don't think I have clearance for this building," I told him uneasily.

"It's okay. We only need one badge." He slipped his into

the reader, the door clicked open and we walked into a small foyer. "This is where they study moon rocks."

"You mean they're still studying the samples they got from the sixties?" I asked. Lestat nodded. "And what have they learned? Are they growing man-eating spores?" I joked nervously. He didn't crack a smile.

"I couldn't say. They don't tell the astronauts much." He opened a metal door. "We can talk in here." Inside it was pitch black.

"No," I protested. Fear shot through me.

He laughed. "It's all right," he said, gripping my arm. How would I get away from him? The first thing I thought was to kick him in the groin, the problem being finding his groin in that blackness, and feeling around for it might give the wrong impression.

My mind raced with possibilities for escape. There were none. I was about to scream for help when half the room burst into iridescent white, blinding me.

"You've just landed on the moon," he said.

17

Gasping, I looked around at the pale sandy surface pitted with craters, the pitch blackness of space lying just beyond the horizon. It all seemed so real that for a second I was afraid there might not be any oxygen. It was as if I had been beamed up from earth and onto the surface of the moon. I was so amazed that for a moment I forgot to be afraid.

"What is this place?" I whispered.

"It was used by the Apollo astronauts to train for the moon landing, to help adjust them to what the moon would be like. It's fantastic, isn't it? Barren and at the same time full." He put his finger to his lips. "Shhh."

We stood listening. The room was utterly silent.

"You can hear your heart beat," Lestat said quietly. "They warn us in training that the silence in space takes getting used to. The absence of any normal, natural sounds bothers some people. It's never bothered me."

"This is so incredible," I muttered as I glanced around.

"But it can't come close to the real experience," Lestat said. "The feeling of being in space is indescribable."

I looked at him. "I understand now why you were throwing things. I went to Foster's meeting. I know the mission was canceled. It must have been a disappointment."

He put his hand on my arm. "That's why I had to talk to you," he said urgently. "Please don't tell anyone what you saw today. My throwing things. It was a stupid reaction. I went crazy for a minute."

In the virtual moon's glow I could see the white-hot intensity in his face, and it flashed into my head again that I shouldn't be alone with him. The room was soundproofed. It had no windows. I wasn't even sure any longer where the door was.

"You don't have to worry," I told him shakily, backing away a few inches. "Your emotional ups and downs make no difference to me." I tried to make the words sound casual. Lestat had been right, you could hear your heart beat—and mine was going as fast as a bird's. I was afraid he would hear it.

He took a step toward me. "You see, I don't believe that. I think you're interested in everything that goes on around here. That's why I want to be up front with you. I was angry about the mission being canceled, and I needed to blow off some steam. But it has to be private. Do you understand?"

"Because astronauts are supposed to be nonemotional thinking machines and you blew a circuit?"

"I guess I did. Look, it doesn't mean anything. But if certain people found out that I had lost control like that, they'd question my stability. We're all under microscopes here. It could ruin my chances."

I wondered how often he lost control and what damage it could lead to.

"I didn't see anything to tell anyone about," I told him. "Besides, what you do in a private moment is your business, right? I mean as long as it's legal."

He turned in a half circle, casting his eyes over the moon's surface. "To be an astronaut, to command the space shuttle has been my dream. It's the reason I joined the Air Force, the reason I've worked so hard, the reason I never had time for a wife and kids. And now that's being taken away from me."

"There'll be other missions," I said.

His eyes came back to me. "Will there? The police are questioning me about Garza. Just because I was around the building last night, they're on my back."

"It's more than that and you know it. You called Garza. You said you wanted to meet with him and you sounded pretty irate."

His eyes narrowed. "How could you possibly—"

"Garza's voice-mail messages are all stored on the computer. You should know that. If anything, that's your best claim to innocence. Anyone who was going to kill him probably wouldn't arrange the meeting with a recorded message."

Lestat's hand closed around my wrist. "I didn't kill him."

I looked into his eyes and I could see the titanium gears spinning behind them. Part of me wanted to run; the other part needed to know what was in his head. I pulled my wrist out of his grip.

"What was it you needed to talk to Garza about? What made you so angry?"

"Okay, I was angry," he said. "Mad as hell. But not mad enough to kill him."

"Then what was it about?"

He hesitated, sighing. "It doesn't matter anymore who I tell."

"So tell."

"Garza was in trouble," he said after several moments.

"With who?"

"Nobody yet, except with me. But it was going to explode. He had done . . . unscheduled experiments on the last shuttle mission."

"What kind?"

"Unauthorized tissue cultures. Cultures that weren't scheduled until the SM–15. I saw him with the culture containers, these small jars filled with pink liquid. I knew what they were because I was briefed on them in training a year ago. And I knew they weren't supposed to be on board. At first I didn't say anything, but it bothered me, and later I asked him about it."

"And what did he tell you?"

"That I was mistaken. That the cultures were scheduled. But when we were back on the ground, I checked the paperwork. He was lying."

"Did you tell anyone else?"

"No, I couldn't. I had too much respect for Garza. I wanted to settle it with him directly. When he denied it I went into the flight-plan records to see what culture work was planned for later missions, and I found what I was looking for. I confronted him with what I suspected, and he confirmed it."

"You're talking about the cultures where they grow cells into organs? Michael explained some of it to me."

He nodded. "I'm no bioscientist, but I do know that a successful project like that would be worth a hell of a lot of money. At first I couldn't believe Garza would do it, but there wasn't another explanation. He did the experiments so he could sell the results."

"Did he admit it?"

"It's strange, but he did. He said he had debts and creditors closing in, that the money pressure got to him. But he's no white-collar criminal."

It crossed my mind that "space-suit criminal" was a more appropriate term.

"Garza admitted everything," Lestat continued. "I think the deceit had gotten to him. He wasn't really that kind of man, you know. He was a hero to me. He wanted to tell Foster what he had done. I asked him not to."

"Why would you care?"

"Because if he told, there was a good chance the scandal would delay the SM–15 mission, if not get it canceled completely. I asked him to wait until after the mission. Then he could spill his guts, confess his sins."

"So you would get to be second-in-command," I said quietly.

"Yes, so I would get the chance to fly a damn shuttle instead of just being a passenger. To be in control," he said, his tone impassioned. "Do you know what it's like to want one thing so badly? You work for it, you sweat for it. You make sure you're the best. You beat out everyone. Then finally your chance comes and you lose it over a stupid thing like that. It wouldn't have been fair. Garza agreed. He said he would wait."

"So why the angry phone call? Sounds to me like Garza had agreed to your terms. What happened?"

"*You* happened. When Margo announced she was hiring someone to investigate the computer hacking the crew was okay with it. Finding the hacker meant less chance of a mission delay. But then you and your partner walked into the conference room and said you would be investigating people as well as machines. I saw the look on Garza's face. I knew he was afraid he'd be caught before he had the chance to confess."

"Did he think that if he confessed he'd be dealt with differently?"

"He told me that he hadn't sold the results of his work and that he wasn't going to. So all he'd really done was perform an unauthorized experiment. He thought—worst case—he'd get suspended from the astronaut program, but not kicked out of NASA."

"But Ben, if you figured out he was going to sell the results, other people would reason it out the same way." I felt a gnawing in my insides. The more I learned about this case, the more uneasy I felt. Lestat's face reflected my own sentiments.

"They couldn't prove anything, you see? Besides, Garza could claim it was scientific zeal or something that made him do it."

"Overcome by his thirst for knowledge," I said sarcastically. "Or maybe he just couldn't wait to grow a liver for some deserving soul."

"Don't joke about it. It would be a big deal. The experiment was originally slated for that mission anyway. It got put off because of some political thing. A senator from the midwest wanted an experiment with soybeans instead."

"So let me see if I'm getting this right. After Paoli and I showed up, you were afraid Garza would confess and get the SM–15 mission grounded to a halt. That's what you were so angry about in your voice-mail message?"

"Yeah." He ran his hand through his hair. "I met Garza outside the WET-F. We exchanged words. When I left him, he was alive."

"What was he doing at the WET-F in the first place?"

"He thought there was a problem with the new WET-F suits, that the breathing modules cut in and out."

I turned it over in my mind and tried to envision Lestat as a killer. He had thrown that pen set against the wall, but he had waited until he could go downstairs and close himself off in a room where nobody could hear him. That didn't seem like the behavior of a guy who had uncontrolled fits of rage.

On the other hand, Lestat had a more than adequate motive for wanting Garza dead. Garza's desire to purge his soul was standing between Lestat and his dream.

"I think you've got a problem with the police," I told him. "You admit you met with Garza and that you argued. It's awfully convenient that he died just before he was about to lay out his sins to Foster."

"But that's it, you see," Lestat said earnestly. "He had already told Foster everything that afternoon."

18

When I got back to the office and told Paoli what had happened, he sprang out of his chair and stomped around the tiny room, looking like one of those cartoon characters with steam coming out of their ears. But when I was finally able to recount what Lestat had told me, Paoli was too interested to stay mad.

"Do you believe him?" he asked after he cooled off and settled down into his chair.

I closed the door to our office, leaning my back against it. "It doesn't make sense to me that Lestat killed Garza. According to Lestat, Garza had already told Foster about the experiments earlier that day. So what was Lestat's motive?"

Paoli frowned. "Easy. When Lestat found out that Garza had gone back on his promise and wrecked Lestat's chances of being second-in-command, Lestat followed Garza into the WET-F. They quarreled and he shoved Garza into the pool and let him drown. Simple as that."

I shook my head. "I'm not convinced."

Leaning back in his chair, he put his feet on the desk. "You're too hardheaded to deal with sometimes. Okay then, let's switch gears. It seems to me that Lisa Foster's got as good a motive as anybody for murdering Garza."

I went over to the desk and politely pushed his feet off, then sat on the edge. "Explain."

"Well, you said yourself that Foster was more concerned about her career than anything else," Paoli said, energy building up behind his words. "What if her dream of making her director position permanent was at risk? That's an excellent motive to kill someone."

"I see your point, but Foster doesn't seem like an icy killer."

Paoli turned up his palms. "But that's the real point I'm trying to make. Haven't you learned anything since you've been an investigator?"

Sure. I'd learned how to get three meals a day out of vending machines, how to put off bill collectors, and how to elbow out the Asian girls at the petite racks at end-of-the-season clearance sales.

He got out of his chair and began pacing the room again. "Your average killers are not cold. Far from it. They're passionate. Desperate. Pushed to the wall. Out of options."

I crossed my arms, eyeing him. "You'll have to connect this to Foster for me."

Paoli put his hands on the desk on either side of me, his face a few inches from mine. When he gets that close it's hard for me to concentrate.

"Easy. The technology for growing organs would be worth a fortune in the marketplace. NASA wanted to take credit for it themselves. They need the win. But not only do the higher-ups think Foster has no control over her employees, they also figure she'd screwed up a moneymaking opportunity for NASA at a time when the agency badly needs the cash."

"But why is it Foster's screwup? She can't control the astronauts' behavior," I said.

He pointed a finger at me. "But she's supposed to control the mission. The buck stops with her. There's a big snafu, she's responsible. By getting rid of Garza she could cover it up. In my book that's a motive *el grande.*"

I had to agree with him. As far as Garza's murder was concerned, Lestat and Foster both had decent motives and opportunity to do the deed. Of course, Margo had motive and opportunity as well, but I didn't say that. There was no point in getting Paoli more worked up than he already was. I could handle the Margo angle on my own.

We worked all afternoon. Paoli was still testing the system for weaknesses by trying to hack into it and I borrowed Michael's laptop, logged onto the Internet and researched hackers' bulletin boards to see if anyone had ever hacked successfully into NASA's computers in the past.

Most companies and government agencies have only begun to realize that their computer systems are getting hacked into all the time. They just hadn't known about it because the hackers slip quietly in and quietly out. In most cases hackers only do it to prove they can; they don't want to destroy anything. They do it for the bragging rights, and hackers are notorious braggers.

The Internet is an excellent source for this kind of data. Hackers boast about what computers they broke into all the time on the Net. But after hours of searching I didn't find any references to successful NASA infiltrations.

I called Dave Kane and left him a message, asking him again about the Olander case, this time with more urgency, and whether a suicide note had been found. Then I called the police and did the same thing, only I got to give my message to an actual living, breathing person. I impressed upon this person how important it was that the police determine whether or not the note existed. I got about as much reaction as I had from the machine.

By six-thirty I had a cramp in my neck and badly needed a break, so I went to the vending machine and purchased a nutritious meal of Cokes and pretzels.

"Take a look at this," Paoli said when I returned, pointing to the screen. I pulled up my chair. His finger was beside a line of programming code.

I peered at it. "That means zilch to me."

"That's because you're the looks and I'm the brains in this operation." I chuckled at that one; in my mind it's more the other way around. "That block of programming is a coding connection to a satellite," Paoli said.

"So what? I'm sure NASA gets communications from lots of different satellites."

"This satellite connection doesn't belong here. I've checked it three times. I got the idea for checking all the satellite connections when we saw the satellite dish on the TV van. This is definitely an outlaw satellite connection."

"But how would a hacker get access to a satellite dish?"

"Ever heard of cable television?" Paoli asked.

"Would a cable dish handle computer data?"

"If you knew how to reconfigure it."

My adrenaline surged. This could be the answer to finding our hacker. I could have kissed Paoli right then and there, but since it was working hours, I just gave him a couple of highly affectionate shoulder squeezes. But then a thought crossed my mind.

"You realize finding this satellite connection may crush McKenzie's alien-trying-to-communicate theory?"

"I know. I have mixed feelings. But we still don't know anything for sure."

He was right. We didn't know where the satellite was or who owned it, but still, it was great progress.

Paoli started to pack up his briefcase.

I checked my watch, but it wasn't on my wrist, having drowned in the WET-F pool. "What time is it?" I asked Paoli.

"Close to seven."

"We can't leave yet. We can get a couple of hours in still." I noticed that Paoli had that grave look he gets when he's about to say something that could cause an argument.

"Listen, Julie, Lindstrom called earlier to set up a meeting at some restaurant. He wants to talk."

"About what?"

"Didn't say."

I grabbed my purse. "I guess we'll find out when we get there."

He took my purse from me and put it back on the desk. "You're not going."

"Of course I'm going."

"Julie, there have been two deaths around here and I don't feel comfortable with this Lindstrom meeting. He wants to meet in some town half an hour from here. I'm going to see him alone. So let's not bicker, okay?"

But of course we bickered. It was the same running argument we've had over and over about dangerous situations and how I should stay out of them. The only thing different about this argument was that for the first time Paoli won. I'm not exactly sure why. Maybe because I was beginning to realize how great it was that he cared about me. Maybe because being alone on the moon with Lestat had frightened me more than I realized. Maybe because I thought Paoli should win an argument now and then.

After Garza's murder I wasn't interested in hanging around NASA at night by myself, so I called Max at the motel and told her what was up and that I needed a ride home. Paoli drove me out to the main gate and waited with me until she arrived. Then he took off.

I got in Max's car, a rented red convertible. She was wearing a long denim skirt, a crisp white shirt, a red baseball cap with DKNY written across it and lots of gold jewelry.

"Thanks for the ride. I appreciate it," I said.

"You're *going* to appreciate it." She put on large sunglasses and drove off after Paoli.

"The motel's the other way," I said distractedly, rubbing my aching neck.

"I know. We're not going to the motel."

"Where are we going?"

"We're following Vic."

That got my attention. "What for?"

She tossed me her "you're-such-an-idiot" look. "You mean you fell for that story that he was going to meet someone about the case?"

Up until that moment it hadn't occurred to me to think otherwise. "Where else would he be going?" I asked innocently. Max hit the gas. The car accelerated and wind whipped through our hair.

"To a tryst with Margo the Mannequin, that's where."

A lump formed in my throat. "Paoli would never do that. He loves me," I said with a lot more fervor than I felt.

"Then we'll prove it, won't we?" Her expression softened. "Listen, Jules, I'm not trying to cause trouble or make you unhappy. I just want what's best for you."

"Your problem is that you're so mad at Wayne that you don't trust men in general."

"There's probably some truth to that. On the other hand, I don't trust this Margo person, and I'm not sure that Vic has the strength to withstand the type of subtle sexual maneuvering a woman like that is capable of. Few men do."

I watched the Chevy, which was a few cars in front of us, and wondered if Paoli would ever lie to me. "Following him is dishonest, Max."

"Yes, well, so is going through the express lane at the grocery store with more than ten items, but we all do it, don't we?"

"I never do."

She scowled at me. "So what else is there to do tonight? Sit on our tushes in the Bates Motel and watch the cockroaches? This will be fun. And admit it," she said, her voice turned throaty. "Deep down you want to, don't you? You want to know where he's going."

She had me there. Still, my finer nature, or what was left of it, knew that spying on Paoli was wrong. I knew I shouldn't do it, that I should tell Max to turn the car around. I even opened my mouth to say it, but the words never came out. Max had planted the evil seed in my head and now, fertilized by my own suspicions, that little seed was blooming into a rose garden. I slid down in the seat, got out my Maalox and took a fortifying gulp.

Max pushed a button and put up the top of the convertible, staying a discreet distance from Paoli. We followed him through a couple of traffic lights and three turns and finally down Farm Road 371, which cut across a landscape as flat as a countertop and so barren that the cement roadway actually improved it. But what the terrain lacked the sky made up for. The sunset was a masterpiece of golds, pinks and purples, stretching across the horizon with such grandeur you felt as if you were driving into heaven.

As it turned out, we weren't.

The gorgeous sunset had faded to deep twilight by the time Paoli pulled off 371 and onto the main street of a suburb called Hillview. We drove past sleazy motels and shabby apartments. *Confrontation* announced the marquee of an old movie theater that had been converted into a church. We paid no heed.

At the far end of the street Paoli turned right. Rounding the corner we saw him pull into the parking lot of a small, sad-looking Mexican cafe. Max slowed her car as we passed it. Its neon sign flashed a red "El Toro Loco" into the fresh night, intermittently illuminating the peeling stucco façade. Max pulled the car around the back and we parked.

"This place looks disgusting," Max said. "I guess Vic and Margo are into a low-life sex thing. Sorry," she added quickly, seeing the expression on my face.

"It's more likely that Lindstrom wanted to be sure he wouldn't be seen with Paoli. Max, I don't feel right about this. Let's get out of here."

Her eyes squinted and her mouth dropped open. "Are you nuts? After we drove all the way through the boonies? We're past the point of no return, toots. We have to see this thing through."

Filled with misgivings, I knew the right thing was to drive away, have a stiff drink and forget it ever happened. That was the right thing. I did the wrong thing.

"Well, we can't see anything from here," I said.

Max smiled deviously and rubbed her hands together. "Come, *caballera*, let's ride," she said.

We got out of the car, inhaling the aroma of enchiladas and *carne asada* mixed with the faint smell of sulfur from the oil refineries. Mexican mariachi music floated out from the jukebox inside. We walked around the side of the restaurant and peeked through a filthy window. The room was lined with booths, and a few tables were scattered in the center. Only a couple were filled. To my relief, there was no Margo. On the other hand, there was no Lindstrom either.

"Paoli hasn't come in yet," Max said.

We walked toward the front, staying close to the building, and peered around the corner. Paoli was still in his car, his head down, probably looking for his wallet.

The faint sound of the music blended with the song of the crickets in the adjacent field. A little Hispanic girl, ten or eleven maybe, stood in the restaurant's front door, one hand on her hip. She gave us a hard stare.

I reached into my purse for my Maalox bottle, unscrewed the top and tried to take a swig, but all I got were the dried flakes around the rim. Running out of Maalox was a bad omen, right up there with black cats and sets of three sixes. I felt a tug on my sleeve.

"His car door is opening," Max whispered excitedly. "I don't see flowers. That's a good sign."

Paoli got out of the car and started across the parking lot in our direction.

"We've got to get out of here before he sees us," I whispered frantically.

"No way. Now is when we go for the kill. We wait for Margo to show up. We confront them—"

I gestured for her to be quiet as three men emerged from the shadows on the other side, the third one rather largish, all of them wearing insolent expressions. I saw Paoli cast a wary glance their way. One of them grabbed his elbow as he tried to go by them. Paoli let out a "Hey!" and spun around. All my nerve endings started tingling.

"Where you going?" one of the smaller men said to Paoli in a heavy Texas accent. He was wearing blue jeans, cowboy boots and a stained long-sleeved T-shirt that said "Save The Whales." A redneck environmentalist thug. Go figure. The larger guy, who was wearing a baseball cap, stood to one side watching. Maybe he had a nonviolence policy.

"I'm just going in the restaurant, fellas," Paoli said. "Is there some sort of problem here? Am I parked incorrectly? One of my wheels touching the white line?"

I mouthed a silent *no*, squeezing my eyes shut. When I opened them the three men were closing in menacingly. The big one stepped in front of Paoli. I was sure I had seen him at NASA's gates with C-CINS.

"You're not going anywhere. We're here to tell you something," he said to Paoli.

"Don't mess with C-CINS," said the third one, the shortest. He was wearing long baggy shorts and a cotton shirt with a button-down collar.

"What are you talking about?" Paoli said.

Shorty stepped up to him. "I'm talking about you poking your nose where it don't belong. Nobody at C-CINS is breaking into anybody's computers."

Lindstrom's spy at NASA had been busy. I made a move toward Paoli. Max grabbed my arm but I shook her off.

"Excuse me, but we're being paid to find out who's hacking into NASA," I said loudly, marching up to them. "If C-CINS is a suspect, then we have a right to investigate them."

"Julie, what are you *doing* here?" Paoli asked with surprised annoyance.

I ignored him. "Intimidation is pointless," I told the short guy, directing my finger at him. "I insist that you leave this man alone."

Shorty pushed me, shouting something derogatory. That is, I assume it was derogatory. I didn't actually hear the words because as soon as he laid his hand on me Paoli shoved him backward and he lost his balance and fell down.

And that's when all hell broke loose.

19

The big guy came flying, his fist landing on Paoli's jaw. Paoli let out a groan and fell backward.

Something in me snapped. All my normal analytical processes ceased functioning. It didn't matter to me that Big Boy was colossal and that I had no hope of as much as rearranging his hair. I ran at him, throwing my fists wildly. At first he looked at me like I was crazy—I *was* crazy, but I didn't care. Most of my punches missed and the ones that connected were little more than love pats. But I was scoring high in the effort category.

Large hands grabbed my waist, pulling me off him. I saw Big Boy's huge bear paw cock backward as Paoli started to get up. I jerked free of whichever of the other two had grabbed me and lunged at Big Boy. Due to lack of brawling experience, or bad luck, or both, I somehow ended up clinging to his back.

I'm not sure of everything that happened next. I only remember being on the man's back, shouting at him, holding onto his tree-stump neck with one hand and pounding him with the other. His shoulder felt like stone beneath my puny fist, but at least I had distracted him.

The next thing I knew Max ran up in her high heels, hurling unflattering adjectives at the guy and smacking him in the head with her handbag over and over. Knowing all the stuff Max keeps in there, I'm sure it hurt.

Paoli watched us, horrified, his mouth dropping open. But he couldn't have been any more surprised than I was to find myself wrapped around a perfect stranger, engaged in a bizarre mambo, so close to him I could smell his cheap aftershave, and Max pummeling him with her best Gucci.

Paoli got to his feet. The two other guys went for him, but he hit one in the face and tossed the other onto his back, putting both at least temporarily out of action.

"Get off me!" Big Boy yelled, his thick voice now whiny. Believe me, every inch of me yearned to dismount, but his huge body lurched around so erratically it was impossible. Max now had one of her shoes off and was giving the short guy the business end of her Charles Jourdan. Big Boy chose that moment to toss a particularly ugly insult at me, and the situation took, if possible, a turn for the worse.

Paoli's fist shot forward, but Big Boy dodged him, me still on his back. Paoli stumbled. Big Boy went for Paoli. I wasn't sure what to do, but hitting him in the neck and shoulder area was having no effect, so I jerked his hat down over his eyes and wrapped my right arm around his head.

Big Boy howled with rage. Reaching up, he jerked my arm away, ripping the sleeve of my blouse, but I put my arm back, which irked him further. He was trying to shake me off now, and I knew I wouldn't last much longer.

"Hit him!" Max yelled to Paoli.

"I can't hit him now. He can't see anything. Julie, let him go!" he said.

I started to debate the point, but Max was behind me,

pulling me to the ground. As soon as Big Boy was able to see, Paoli hit him, his fist connecting squarely with his chin. Big Boy reeled backward and fell hard, his skull meeting the pavement with a disturbing thud. I ran over to see if he was hurt. He lay on the ground motionless.

"My God, are you okay? Can you hear me?" I asked him.

At that moment a black-and-white squad car pulled onto the gravel, raising a cloud of dust that glowed pink in the neon light. Two officers leapt out and ran toward us, nightsticks in their hands.

"What's going on here?" one of them yelled. Our two other attackers made a run for it. One officer ran after them, while the other stayed with Paoli, Big Boy, Max and me.

"These thugs attacked us," Max said indignantly as she put on her shoe.

Big Boy was sitting up, rubbing his head, looking no worse for wear. "No way," he protested. "It's the other way around, officer. I swear it. You saw them. They were on top of me."

Paoli stepped threateningly toward him. "You son of a—"

"Now cut it out," the policeman said, moving in front of Paoli. His name badge read "Pinsky." He looked in my direction. "Lady," he said. "I saw you on his back. What the heck were you doing?"

I straightened my blouse, attempting to regain some dignity. "Protecting myself and my friends. We have a right to self-defense, don't we?"

Pinsky narrowed his eyes. "How much have you folks had to drink?"

"Nothing," I answered, offended, although at that moment a cocktail sounded tempting.

Paoli cocked a thumb in Big Boy's direction. "This guy and his two buddies jumped me as I was walking into this restaurant."

"He's lying," Big Boy said defiantly.

"That's absurd," I said, then Paoli joined me in insulting him, with Big Boy giving as good as he got. The patrolman shouted and waved his stick at us as the other officer emerged from the darkness. He was pencil thin with a large head that bobbed forward like a turtle's.

"They got away," he said sheepishly.

Pinsky scowled. "Damn it, Digby. Go get us some backup." Looking downcast, Digby slinked away to the squad car.

"What exactly is happening here?" I asked.

"What's happening is that I'm taking all of you in," Officer Pinsky said.

I held up a hand. "Excuse me, officer, but you're making a mistake. We were here to meet Harvey Lindstrom. He's the one you should be questioning. I'm sure he's in there waiting for us right now. These men who attacked us work for him."

Pinsky eyed me, sizing me up. He crooked his finger for Digby, who came trotting. "Digby, go see if there's a Lindstrom inside and, if there is, bring him out."

Digby nodded and went inside.

"Thank you," I said. "I'm sure we'll get this cleared up."

"I'm not so sure," I heard Paoli mutter under his breath. I turned to him.

"What do you mean?" I asked.

"I don't think Lindstrom's in there," he said.

"So why did you come here?" I asked. Max raised an eyebrow.

Just then Digby came out. "No Lindstrom inside," he said.

"Don't you see? I was set up," Paoli said. "Lindstrom never wanted to talk to me. He arranged this meeting so his C-CINS goons could threaten us off the case."

I turned to Max. "See? He wasn't here to meet Margo."

"That's why you followed me?" Paoli asked in disbelief.

But we were prevented from further discussion by the arrival of a second squad car. Big Boy started to run, but Pinsky grabbed him. The reinforcement leapt to Pinsky's aid, since Big Boy was doing a pretty good job of resisting arrest, while Digby dealt with Paoli, Max and me. I supposed that this was because Digby was the smallest of them, and we seemed to be less of a challenge, but I wasn't sure if that was an insult or a compliment.

With Big Boy subdued, Pinsky came back for Paoli and left Max and me with Digby, who was pulling handcuffs off his belt. I felt my stomach turn inside out. We were actually going to be arrested? I looked over at Paoli, who was being handcuffed by Pinsky. They both laughed at something Paoli said. My boyfriend can make friends anywhere.

By this time a few El Toro Loco patrons had come out to watch the show. I was filled with shame to have strangers staring at me while I was being handcuffed. I would have cried, but I was too irate. Paoli was right. Lindstrom had set him up. It was just a trick to get him away from NASA so Big Boy and his hoodlums could beat him senseless.

"We work for NASA," I said over my shoulder as Digby cuffed my hands behind my back. I could feel him pause at the word *NASA*, but then the cuffs locked shut. Then he cuffed Max, who seemed to be enjoying herself.

"If you're going to do a cavity search you have to buy me dinner first," she told Digby, and he blushed.

"You gals wait here," Digby said, waving a scolding finger, like we were going to race off with our hands behind us. He went over to talk to Pinsky for a minute.

Digby put Paoli, Max and me in the back of the first police car, politely saying, "Watch your noggin," as we got in. Pinsky and Digby got in the front seat and then Pinsky started the car and we drove off. I was angry, embarrassed, insulted and afraid. On the other hand Paoli and Max seemed to be taking the situation in stride, which I didn't understand at all.

"Where are we going?" I asked.

Digby turned around and gave me a sardonic look.

"Disney World," he said, and he and Pinsky chuckled. Max looked at me and mouthed *How amusing.*

"I don't want to take you in. You look like nice, clean people. Maybe something happened. Maybe it got out of hand," Pinsky said as he drove. "But truth is, I've got no choice. There've been a lot of fights outside the Loco the past couple of months. I don't know why."

"Maybe it's the hot sauce," Digby said, chortling.

Pinsky chortled back. "But Maria, the owner, wrote a letter to the *Hillview Sentinel* saying we weren't policing right, and now I've got the high-ups breathing down my neck. I've got to start making arrests. You were having quite a squabble back there and Maria called in a complaint. So there you see, I've got no choice."

"No choice," Digby echoed.

I leaned forward in the seat. "Of course you have a choice," I said churlishly. "It was not a 'squabble.' We were defending ourselves."

"About bail—do you take American Express?" Max asked. "I have a platinum card."

Digby turned around to look at us again. "Only Master-Card and Visa. You all better be quiet now."

"It's okay, Julie. I'll call Margo as soon as we get to the station and she'll get us out," Paoli said reassuringly.

"No need," Max said. "I'll call Wayne. He'll have us out in an hour."

"Wayne's in California. It may not be that easy," Paoli told her. "We're better off calling Margo."

I exhaled with exasperation. "Margo, Margo, Margo," I whispered through gritted teeth.

"Now don't be whispering back there," Pinsky said as he stopped at a red light. I could see his eyes in the rearview mirror. "If you have to talk, okay, but no whispering."

"Margo, Margo, Margo, is what I said," I said loudly. "I don't want you calling her," I told Paoli. "It's her fault we're in this mess. She got us into this stupid case."

He looked hurt. "This is a great case."

"It's a labyrinth," I said.

Digby turned around in his seat. "No cussin' back there, either. You kids be quiet."

Once again I leaned forward, putting my face up close to the wire mesh between the front and back seats.

"I refuse to be quiet when I have committed no crime."

Digby snorted. "Lady, you were on that guy's back like a dog on a burrito. You can't go around beating up on people."

"It's not her fault," Max said. "She's premenstrual."

Paoli winced.

"I wasn't beating him up," I said to Digby. "I'm five feet three and weigh a hundred pounds."

"Hundred and five at least," Max said.

I ignored the remark. "Do you know any anatomy?" I demanded of Digby. "Do you know any physics? I couldn't have beat up that steroid victim if I knew karate."

"Don't sell yourself short, Jules. Under the right conditions you could have done some real damage, I'm sure of it," Max said encouragingly.

"Could you stay out of this for one minute?" I snapped.

Max gave me a superior look. "If you weren't premenstrual I'd be offended by that."

Paoli slid down into his seat. "I think we all better be quiet."

"That's one hell of an idea," Pinsky said.

"No cussin'," Digby said petulantly. We sat silently for a moment. Pinsky took a call on the radio. Digby contemplated the sins of foul language; I contemplated how on earth I had sunk to my current level of degradation.

I whispered an apology to Max. Paoli affectionately rubbed my foot with his.

"This will all be okay," he whispered with a smile. "It'll be a great story to tell our friends. Speaking of which, are any of yours lawyers?"

"We don't need a lawyer," I said stubbornly. "We didn't do anything wrong. We were assaulted and we protected ourselves."

What had I done to get myself into this humiliating predicament? Was it a karma thing? Had I been cruel to animals, or mean to my mother in a past life?

"There's the bayou that got Fred Harris," Digby said to Pinsky, looking out his window.

Pinsky craned his neck. "Sad thing. Sucked him right in is the way I heard it," he said.

Max leaned forward. "Excuse me. A bayou sucked some-body in?"

Digby twisted his head around. "Sure did. There are a couple of bayous around here so thick with weeds and mud that if you get stuck in one you can't get out. You just sink like it's quicksand."

"That one back there got Fred," Pinsky added.

As we pulled into the parking lot in front of the county sheriff's office, I whispered to Paoli, "We each get a phone call, right?"

He shrugged. "Beats me. I'm new at this."

"Excuse me," I said through the wire mesh. "We each get a phone call, right?"

"Sure do," Pinsky said.

"I'll call Wayne and get us a lawyer," Max said.

"Then I'll call Dalton," Paoli added, obviously having rethought the Margo option. "He might be able to help us."

Frank Dalton was a Silicon Valley policeman whom we had befriended during a couple of cases. I was praying that there was some sort of brotherhood among police types and that he could make a call and get us out of this mess.

Pinsky helped me out of the car and, holding me by the arm, steered me toward the police station. I turned to look back at Paoli and Max. It bothered me that we were being separated, and scenes from *Dr. Zhivago* popped into my head. I felt shamed and degraded as Pinsky walked me through the double doors.

I didn't deserve this. I'd been framed.

20

I like to think of myself as an optimistic person, the type who always looks at the bright side of any situation. But at this particular juncture in the time/space continuum, as the jaws of the penal system stretched wide to devour me, I couldn't manage to find any bright side.

Pinsky led me handcuffed into the harsh fluorescent glare of the police station. I expected to be photographed and fingerprinted, but he just wrote down some information and turned me over to a female officer. To my humiliation she patted me down—for weapons, I assume, unless she was checking my body fat percentage. She took my purse and earrings, recorded the transaction on a form, and led me to a cell.

"What's happening with my friends?" I asked her.

"Don't you worry about them," she answered.

"Do I get a phone call?"

She gave me a sympathetic smile. "Sure, honey. Right here, but make it quick." She led me to a desk with a phone and took off my handcuffs.

Since Paoli was calling Dalton and Max was calling Wayne, I decided I'd better call my mother, or she might make good on her threat to file a missing persons report. I was certain that police departments across the country have their computers networked, and even the smallest chance that my mother could find out I was in the slammer sent chills up my spine.

She picked up on the third ring. We exchanged the usual information and I told her as much as I dared about my work in Houston, which meant I left out the corpses, the street fight and the fact that I was about to be thrown into a cell.

"Will you and that sweet Vic be talking marriage soon?"

I didn't have the heart to tell her that in the immediate future we'd be too busy talking bail.

"Not yet, Mom."

"That's too bad, baby. You should work on it. You're in your thirties." She paused so I could contemplate the math. "By the way, I'm coming to visit next month."

I told her how delighted I was, and we said our good-byes and I hung up, the prospect of a jail term looking a little better to me.

The officer led me to a cell and bent to unlock the door. Seeing my apprehension, she patted my shoulder with a nurturing sympathy I couldn't remember ever getting from Mom.

"Now, don't worry, honey. I'm putting you in with Cherie. She's a lamb."

The door closed behind me with an ominous clang. I, Julie Blake, former vice president of the largest computer company in the world, president of the National Association of Women in Business, winner of the coveted TriCounty Science Prize at Lee High, was now in the slammer.

The cell smelled awful. My cellmate was sitting on a metal

bench bolted to the wall. She was overweight with tan skin that looked like she scrubbed it with Brillo Pads and she sat slumped over, her fiery red dyed hair hanging. She raised her head and looked up at me.

I admit that I was a little scared. Maybe more than a little. To me, the woman I faced looked more like a tigress than a lamb. Would she attack me? I wondered, pressing my back against the cell door.

"Hi there," she said, her voice thick and rough. "You ought to sit. It's probably gonna be a while."

So I sat, and after a few awkward moments we began talking. It turned out she had been arrested for petty theft in a convenience store. She was completely innocent, she assured me, although she anticipated difficulties, since she had some prior offenses on her record.

I told her my story and she was completely empathetic since she too had been undeservedly incarcerated. She explained that I was in a holding cell and at this point had not been officially charged with a crime. According to Cherie I had an excellent chance of avoiding conviction if I could just talk to a particular judge, whose name she had unluckily forgotten.

I'm not sure how long I was in the cell since I no longer had my watch. Cherie and I finally started discussing our jobs. She was a masseuse, although, when I asked, she seemed to be confused on whether she specialized in Shiatsu or Swedish. The conversation inevitably turned to men. I told her about how the moment I saw Paoli get hit, I instinctively pounced on his attacker.

"That's natural," Cherie said. "That scumwad hurt your man. You can't stand around doing nothing with a deal like that. A woman's got to take action."

My sentiments exactly. It turned out that Cherie was involved in a relationship with a man named Goldy. She was hoping that Goldy would be coming through with bail money, but after she gave me Goldy's history I had some doubts that he could be relied upon.

"Got any babies?" she asked. I shook my head. "Too bad. I have three. All no bigger than that." She raised her hand about waist high off the floor, then she contemplated me, her eyes sad.

"You ought to have babies, you know," she told me. "You know what a womb is with no babies ever in it? An empty purse. Nothing more than an empty purse."

With that Cherie curled up into a fetal position on the metal bench and fell quickly into a deep sleep. I rested my head against the cement wall and wondered how Paoli and Max were faring. Talking to Cherie had improved my outlook. It was funny that, bottom line, people weren't very different from each other.

I guess it was about an hour later when the female police officer came and unlocked the cell, motioning me out. Cherie was still sleeping, an amazing feat, considering how hard the bench was. I didn't want to wake her, so I left without saying good-bye.

"Where are you taking me?" I asked.

"You're out of here, honey."

I didn't want to jinx it, so I kept my mouth shut. She gave me back my belongings, I signed a receipt for them, then I was taken to a waiting room.

Happily, Paoli was standing there all in one piece. Unhappily, standing next to him was Margo, the last person I wanted to see. It was humiliating enough to be a jailbird, but my last good outfit was torn, my hair was messy and I smelled funny. Margo, of course, was looking casually elegant in jeans and a sweater, with every blond hair perfectly in place.

"There's a reasonable explanation," I said to her.

"It's okay, Julie," Paoli interrupted. "I already explained things."

"Where's Max?" I asked.

"She'll be here in a minute."

Margo put a reassuring hand on my shoulder, but getting a whiff of me, she removed it.

"It's completely terrible what those C-CINS people did to you. They're animals, and I feel some responsibility for what happened. I want to do something."

"You've done plenty. You got us out," I said.

"Think of it as NASA getting you out," she said as Max walked in.

"You look like something that should be bagged up and left at the curb," she said to me.

"Thanks. You look great yourself," I said with a smile.

"Don't complain," Paoli chimed in. "My jaw hurts and I have puke in my loafers."

Max smiled broadly. "They may file charges against us later."

"I'm glad you're so happy about it," I said.

"Of course I'm happy. Wayne will be furious."

I turned back to Margo. "I'm grateful for your help," I told her. "I'd also appreciate it if no one at NASA knew about this little episode. At least the jail part."

"I need to tell Foster that the C-CINS people threatened you, but I think I can leave out the rest," she said, and I thanked her.

Our cars were still at El Toro Loco, so Margo dropped us

off, and Max and Paoli and I all headed back to the motel, me riding with Paoli this time.

During the first ten minutes of the drive Paoli and I engaged in a jail story competition, which Paoli won with his tale about a guy wearing a bra.

I didn't smell great, but I was Chanel No. 5 compared to Paoli, so we rolled down the windows and enjoyed the balmy Texas night air. It was after midnight.

"Did you see me go after that guy, Julie? Jab, jab, uppercut to the kisser," he said contentedly, punching at the air with one hand.

"You were impressive," I said.

"You're a scrappy fighter yourself. If this business of ours doesn't work out, I think you have a future in mud wrestling."

"How can you joke? We may have charges filed against us."

"Oh, don't worry so much. Wayne Hansen's lawyer will get us out of this."

"Hansen's lawyer is corporate," I replied.

"Then Max will have Wayne buy the town," Paoli joked.

I sighed and rested my head against the seat. "I like this case less and less."

"On the contrary, I think we're finally getting somewhere with it," Paoli said. "At least we found the outlaw satellite connection."

Maybe he was right, but I didn't like the way the violence was escalating—especially now that it had been directed at us.

21

As soon as I fell out of bed the next morning, I got out my notebook and wrote down the vitals for day three: "Billable hours"—*Twenty*. "Progress"—*Traced hacking to outlaw satellite.* Misc.—*Jailed for assault and battery.*

I didn't regret what I'd done the night before. The only problem was the physical reminders. I'm not used to leaping upon the backs of foul-mouthed Goliaths; I was sore all over, and a pulled muscle on the inside of one thigh made me limp. Paoli had a bruise under his eye.

To top things off, we hadn't gotten enough sleep. Max called early and said she was spending the day at a spa. She came to our room to loan me a fresh blouse and skirt and promised that, between her facial and her pedicure, she'd make some calls and find us a lawyer just in case charges were filed against us.

As soon as I was dressed I called the jail and asked about Cherie. Goldy hadn't come through with any cash, so I arranged bail for her. It maxed out my credit card, but we female jailbirds have to stick together.

Day four. Paoli and I arrived at the office and were working on nailing down a location for the hacker's satellite when the call came from Foster. She wanted to see us right away, but Paoli was too absorbed in his computer to take a break. He gets like that occasionally: eyes glazed over, nose close to the screen, only incoherent mumbles escaping his lips. As with a sleepwalker, it's best not to disturb him, so I made the trip to Foster's office alone.

She was sitting at her desk punching numbers on a calculator, wearing a silk blouse in a vivid green that made her skin look yellow.

"Where's Vic?" she snapped when I came in. Lately it seemed women were always wanting Paoli. I made a mental note to toss out his aftershave. Foster's elephant eyes drilled holes in me.

"Working," I answered, my tone snippy. It's funny how a little jail time can leave you cranky.

Her lips twisted into a tiny fist. "I spoke with Margo this morning. Let me extend my apologies about last night. That never should have happened, and NASA feels obligated to provide some legal assistance should that become necessary," she said primly. "But I'm sure you agree that NASA has no responsibility here. If you were attacked on NASA property, that would be one thing. But when you go driving thirty miles away, well, we can't be held liable."

She spit it out pretty casually, but I could see she was nervous.

"Don't worry. We won't be suing you."

She relaxed, one threat to her career out of the way. Putting her calculator in a drawer, she tidied the papers on her desk.

"I hope you won't use this incident as an excuse not to

meet your deadline," she said, trying to regain the upper hand.

"We won't."

"I'm glad to hear that. We can't have some idiot messing with the software for every mission."

I stared at her in surprise. "I wasn't aware the hacker had interfered with anything but the software for the SM–15."

She stopped fiddling with the things on her desk and looked directly at me. "But now that SM–15 is canceled, there's no telling what this hacker will do. If he got into one set of software, he can get into another. He's a criminal and should be arrested."

"Have the SM–15 experiments been rescheduled for SM–16?"

She shook her head. "No. It's a completely different payload. We'll reschedule the SM–15 work later. Right now I think you should step up your investigation of C-CINS. The men who attacked you are C-CINS members. The police caught one of them and he admitted it."

So Big Boy cracked under questioning. All brawn and no backbone. The mere thought of him made my muscles ache.

"Obviously C-CINS has plenty to be worried about," Foster continued. "Not only are they suspects in the hacking, but everyone knows that Garza and Lindstrom hated each other. Lindstrom's bound to be a suspect for Garza's murder."

"But how could Lindstrom have gotten onto NASA premises?" I asked.

She opened her mouth to answer, but nothing came out, and she just gaped at me a second. "Well, of course he couldn't," she finally said. "But maybe Garza let him into the WET-F himself. Maybe Garza wanted to talk things out with him to see if he could get the lawsuit dropped." She was reaching and she knew it. "I don't know. But no one at NASA could have done it. Lindstrom and his people are the only logical choices."

"Hardly the only logical choices," I told her.

She took in a quick breath and held it a second. "Why do you say that?"

I considered what I was about to say. After my experience the night before, the last thing I needed was a battle with Foster. But I was weary and irritable, not to mention that I was retaining water and felt as puffed up as a blowfish. I was in no mood to be subtle.

"If Garza had made it public that he had done the cell cultures on the last shuttle mission it wouldn't say much for your management skills. That kind of screwup doesn't get you a promotion."

I watched her face turn all the colors of the Mexican flag as it dawned on her that I knew the secret she most wanted to hide. Some people back down when faced with hard truths, but not Foster. She stood up slowly, every inch of her ready for a fight. If my career stayed on this path I was going to have to sign up for judo lessons.

"I could fire you right now," she said, her voice low and hoarse.

I tried to appear nonchalant, even though my skin prickled. "You won't accomplish anything except to make it look like you're afraid of what we might turn up."

A shudder ran through her, and her hand, as she flung it toward the door, was trembling. "Get out!" she snarled.

I obliged, glad to get away from her. Lestat wasn't the only one at NASA with a very nasty temper—maybe even the temper of a murderer.

Women are complex creatures. Within them are deep oceans of thought, a rich and varying landscape of emotion and spirit. Men are so simple in comparison.

At least that's my theory. Sure it's sexist. Sure it's not exactly scientific, but I'm basing it on years of observation and anecdotal evidence going all the way back to my first biology course. I was thirteen and flipping through the textbook when I came across a fuzzy black-and-white photo of male and female chromosomes. The two X chromosomes of the female looked so robust and competent compared to the X and Y chromosomes of the male; the poor Y chromosome looked crippled, as if it had lost a leg or something.

When Lisa Foster ordered me out of her office I'd seen ten conflicting emotions on her face, like hungry dogs all fighting over the same bone. I was standing at the elevator pondering it when I felt a warm breath behind my ear.

"You're in danger."

My heart froze. I spun around to find myself facing McKenzie.

"You startled me," I said, pressing my hand to my chest.

"We have to talk. We can go to my office."

"What's going on?"

"Just come talk with me."

So I did. His office looked as spare and neat as it had that first night, which seemed a month ago now. He ushered me in, closing the door behind us. Neither of us sat and he didn't waste any time getting to the point.

"The police are saying someone pushed Garza into the

WET-F. That he was deliberately drowned."

"What proof do they have?" I asked.

"They found no medical condition, no evidence of a coronary or seizure."

"What about an accident?"

"There was trauma to his head, but they've determined that it wasn't from hitting it on the edge of the pool. Someone hit him. From the position of the wound they think he was struck after he was in the water. Dave Kane said you're the one who first realized it," McKenzie said.

Sometimes it doesn't feel good to be right. The disturbing pictures ran through my head once more. Garza went to the WET-F to check out the suits. He pulled on the torso section of one. Before he put on his helmet, someone lured him to the edge of the pool and pushed him in. When he tried to save himself, the murderer brutally kicked him in the head and let him drown.

"The killer entered the WET-F with Garza. It was someone Garza knew, possibly someone he trusted," I said.

McKenzie ran his hand over his head, pressing it against his skull as if to keep the thoughts from escaping.

"There are lots of people who could have followed him to the WET-F. That's what's so troubling." He sat down, swiveling slightly in his chair from side to side, his fingers tapping nervously against his leg. He had lost some of his usual Zen demeanor. "I'm worried about you. Whoever did this is a desperate person. And your investigation is going too far beyond computers for the killer's comfort. You've been talking to quite a few people around here. You're becoming very visible."

He said the words with difficulty and I could tell his concern was real. That's what bothered me. Of all the people I had met at NASA, it was his judgment I trusted most.

"I appreciate what you're saying, but Paoli and I can take care of ourselves." I tried to say it forcefully, but it came out somewhat less than that.

He gave me a long, assessing look. "Is any job worth risking your life for?" he asked. The man was a mind reader.

"Listen, I've got to go," I told him. "Thanks for the advice. We'll be careful." Fumbling with the doorknob, I left quickly, not wanting to give him time to reason with me.

I walked down the hall to the ladies' room, went into a stall and closed the door. Sometimes a rest room stall is the only place you can be alone, and just then I needed to get my thoughts together. After all, Paoli and I were on the periphery of this case, I told myself. We weren't really a threat because we didn't know anything of importance. We had only bits and pieces. On the other hand, I wondered how many weird ways there were to kill someone at NASA.

When I walked into our office Paoli was leaning back in his chair with his feet on the desk, shooting rubber bands at some spot on the wall, looking as nonchalant as I felt worked up.

"Working hard?" I asked, closing the door.

"I'm thinking."

"Don't strain anything you may need later."

He fired a rubber band at me, and it whizzed past my ear, bouncing off the wall. "I could have hit you right between the eyes, my aim's so perfect, but you're already in such a bad mood I decided it wasn't worth it."

I sat down. "You're wrong about your aim, right about my mood. I just spoke with McKenzie. He thinks we're in danger."

That got Paoli's attention. He put down his rubber bands. "What did he say?"

"Garza was definitely murdered. My theory about his head wound was right. McKenzie thinks whoever killed Garza might come after us."

Paoli scrunched up his nose. "Just because we're conducting a hacking investigation? Seems far-fetched."

"McKenzie doesn't think so."

"That's because Space Monk is being overprotective," he said, swinging his feet to the floor. "He has a crush on you, Julie."

I swiveled my chair in his direction. "Don't be absurd."

"I can tell by the way he looks at you. His eyes get all mushy."

I rolled my eyes. "Sure they do."

"Trust me. McKenzie's got a rocket in his pocket he wants to show you in the worst way."

"Don't be crude."

"He wants to land his lunar probe in your love crater."

"Are you older than twelve?"

"He wants to get your engines fired up and ready for thrust."

I crumpled up some paper and threw it at him.

He laughed. "I don't know why it bothers you. You should be flattered."

At the present moment I was much less interested in McKenzie than I was in the fact that someone around NASA perhaps wanted to use us for rocket fuel. I was worried, and I knew Paoli well enough to suspect that, despite his jokes, he was worried, too.

The phone rang and I picked it up.

"This is Harvey Lindstrom," said the voice at the other

end of the line. I mouthed the name to Paoli and he rolled his chair over and put his ear near the receiver. "We need to talk," Lindstrom said. "Can we meet somewhere?"

Paoli and I exchanged a look of disbelief.

"I don't think so. Our last meeting didn't turn out so well," I said dryly.

"But that's just it," Lindstrom said with energy. "I never arranged a meeting. I swear it. Whoever set up the meeting was pretending to be me."

"How do you even know a meeting was set up in the first place?" I asked.

There was a pause. "I'll explain when I meet you."

Paoli shook his head and made an obscene gesture, but I considered Lindstrom's statement.

"Where and when?" I asked him. Paoli threw up his hands. "It has to be someplace public with lots of people. And in broad daylight."

Lindstrom suggested a nearby Denny's restaurant and gave us directions.

When I hung up Paoli jumped out of his chair. "Are you trying to get us into another free-for-all?"

"But we performed so well last night. So the big guy got in a couple of lucky punches. You could have taken him if I'd kept his eyes covered."

"Don't kid around about this. And for your information you can't hit a man when he's blinded. It's bad form."

"I didn't realize there was an etiquette to street brawls."

"It's not in Miss Manners. And I'm not interested in a re-match."

"There won't be one. No one would bother us during the day at a Denny's. And can you be sure the voice on the voice-mail message yesterday matched the voice you just heard on the phone?" I asked. He admitted he couldn't and reluctantly agreed to meet Lindstrom.

Lindstrom had asked us to meet him in one hour. We pulled into the parking lot twenty minutes early, just in case he brought his henchmen along, but at the appointed time Lindstrom's battered Honda drove up and he walked into the restaurant alone.

Feeling reasonably safe from assault, we went inside and found him at a booth by the window where he busily examined the menu, running his finger down the margin. When we slid into the booth, he looked up at us with a dazed expression.

"You came. Thank you." His voice had lost all the previous cockiness. He took a good look at Paoli and winced. "Your eye. I'm so sorry."

Paoli frowned. "That makes two of us."

Lindstrom leaned forward, his elbows on the table, his palms pressed together in front of him as if he were praying.

"I know you're investigating the hacking at NASA. That much I admit to. But I promise you, I had nothing to do with what happened last night," he said. "I don't approve of violence in any form."

"How do you know about last night? For that matter, how do you know we're investigating the hacking?" I asked.

He smiled slightly. "I told you before, I know a lot of what goes on at NASA. The point is, I didn't have you attacked by anyone. I told those men what I knew about you, that I admit, but they decided on their own to try and scare you off."

"But they were C-CINS members. The police confirmed it," I told him.

Lindstrom nodded. "I'm not denying that. I talked to Louis. He's the one who was going to press assault charges against you. He won't be doing that now."

Paoli leaned back and stretched his arm along the back of the seat. "That makes me feel so much better about those guys trying to rearrange our faces. But it doesn't change the facts. Someone who knew we were investigating you told those jerks to come after us. Who could that be except you?"

"But it wasn't me. They did it on their own. I'm not a violent man. I have to convince everyone of that." He sounded frantic.

"Who's everyone?" I asked.

Just then the waitress came up and asked for our order. Paoli and I ordered coffee. His voice strained with anxiety, Lindstrom asked the waitress to point out all the vegetarian items for him, which she did grudgingly. He finally ordered pasta with tomato sauce, garlic bread and a chocolate shake.

"I'm stress eating," he said apologetically as he handed his menu to the waitress. His fingers danced on the tabletop. After she left, he leaned forward and whispered, "What with the police and everything." He saw the puzzled looks on our faces. "I guess you don't know. The police are questioning me about Garza's murder. You know, where I was at the time and all that."

"Because the two of you had some problems in the past?" I asked.

Lindstrom shifted uncomfortably in his seat. He took a packet of sugar out of its metal rack and turned it over in his fingers.

"It's more than that. The police found out that Garza played golf with Jeb Willis a couple of weeks ago. Willis is my boss, you see."

I didn't see. Lindstrom looked down at the packet of sugar intently, as if it were talking to him.

"What kind of work do you do?" I asked him. "You must have flexible hours. You've been at NASA almost every day we've been there."

He raised his eyes up to me. "I do contract bookkeeping for a small software consulting firm. Willis owns it. He lets me do most of my work at home. I'm raising my kids on my own. I have a baby-sitter most days so I can do my C-CINS work in the mornings."

"Raising kids, holding down a job and being an activist sounds like a full schedule," I said.

He nodded. "It is."

Paoli turned up a palm. "I still don't get the connection between your boss, golf, and Garza's murder."

Lindstrom shrunk into his seat. "Garza bad-mouthed me to my boss. They belong to the same country club. Garza sought Willis out. He played golf with him and used the opportunity to tell Willis I was unstable."

"But that doesn't necessarily mean your boss believed it," I told him.

"Garza's an astronaut," Lindstrom said, his voice turning sour. "A hero, at least to some people. Willis believed it, all right. He called me into his office two weeks ago and told me what he thought about my C-CINS work. He said it was anti-American, which is a lot of bunk. My contract is up in a month, and if it doesn't get renewed it'll be Garza's fault."

The waitress, who arrived at that moment with our coffees and Lindstrom's shake, looked at him with raised eyebrows. As soon as the shake was in front of him, he sucked half of it down like it was his only source of oxygen. Some guys prefer martinis.

Paoli eyed Lindstrom making like a Hoover. "But why do they suspect you of his murder? How could you have possibly gotten into NASA?"

Lindstrom put the shake down. "They found my fingerprints in Garza's office."

We stopped our questioning while we absorbed this last piece of information.

"How did they get there?" I asked.

He stared at us a moment, deciding what to tell us. "Let's just say someone sympathetic to C-CINS let me in. I was looking for files relating to the SM–15 mission. I'd heard they were having personnel problems with Gary Olander and I wanted to find out what they were. As mission commander, Garza would have documented all of it."

I sat up straighter. So Lindstrom was able to get inside NASA. And if he was able to get inside Garza's office, why not the WET-F?

"And did you find anything?" I asked him. I also wanted to find out about anything pertaining to Olander.

Lindstrom shook his head.

"So why are you telling us this?" Paoli asked.

"Because I'm sure you think I'm a suspect in the hacking. I didn't feel like I should give you any help before. But now . . ."

"But now what?" I pressed.

"Now I need to clear my name. I want to give you and the police whatever information I have."

I put both my hands on the table. "Do you know who's been doing the hacking?"

Lindstrom shook his head. "I only have suspicions." He glanced around him then tipped his head forward. "C-CINS has a spy in NASA," he said, his voice conspiratorial.

"And it was your spy who got you into Garza's office," I said.

He nodded.

"So who is it?" I asked.

Lindstrom looked pained. "Michael Jaep," he said, spitting out the name like he was coughing up a hairball.

22

"Michael's your spy?" I asked with skepticism.

Lindstrom looked put out. "Why's that so hard to believe? There are all kinds of people sympathetic to our cause."

"I'm sure there are, but Michael doesn't seem the activist type."

"He came to our side about six months ago."

"Did you recruit him?" Paoli asked.

"We're a protest group, not the KGB," he said irritably. "Michael came to us. He'd seen us every day outside the gates, and he became interested in our cause. Then he started giving us information about what projects were being planned, what the projected costs were. Critical information. It gives us a chance to get moving early, so we can tell the people of the United States how much money will be wasted."

Paoli looked unimpressed. "But if Michael is so valuable to C-CINS, why are you exposing him?"

"Because I think he could very well be the hacker. He certainly has the computer skills to do it. And to be honest," Lindstrom said, taking a good breath, "Michael was very zealous about his work with C-CINS." Lindstrom leaned even closer. "*Very* zealous."

"Zealous enough to kill Garza?" I asked.

Lindstrom sat back in his seat. "It's possible. That's why I want all this public. Michael was very upset about the trouble Garza was causing C-CINS. When I told Michael that Garza was trying to get me fired, trying to ruin my life, he became very disturbed."

"Why not tell the police about it?" I asked.

"I intend to. But I wanted to tell you, too, since you're working on the hacking. The police are only investigating the murder."

The waitress brought Lindstrom's vegetarian pasta and he dug into it with enthusiasm, apparently unconcerned that a tomato had died for the dish.

Paoli and I asked him a dozen more questions trying to find out if he had any real information linking Michael to the hacking or to Garza's murder, but all Lindstrom had was supposition and innuendo, which was as much as anyone else had given us so far. I paid the bill since he had a family to feed and was in danger of losing his job, making a mental note to add it to our expenses. We thanked him and left.

"That was disgusting," I told Paoli when we got in the car.

"No kidding. Did you hear those sucking sounds he made when he ate?"

"I don't mean that. I mean that he was willing to rat on Michael."

"Sounds normal to me," Paoli said. He started the car and pulled out of the parking lot.

"It may be, but I expected more from Lindstrom. He's self-righteous about so many things, so concerned about ethics. Michael risked his job to give C-CINS information, and now Lindstrom turns on him."

"Listen, Julie, this is a murder case. Lindstrom doesn't want to go to jail just to protect Michael. If Michael did the dirty deed, he's the one who's got to pay for it."

"I don't like either one of them."

We decided on the drive back to NASA to confront Michael as soon as possible with Lindstrom's accusation. When we walked into his cubicle we found him sitting at his desk thumbing through a fresh copy of *Wired* magazine, a slick and opinionated publication aimed at computer dweebs. He was sucking on a long licorice whip, the red rope variety, and it looked like an alien tongue hanging out of his mouth.

His feet were pulled up onto his chair, and he had the magazine propped against his knees. He looked quietly absorbed and content. When we walked in he quickly dropped his feet to the floor and removed the licorice from his mouth, which widened into its usual smile, only dyed red.

"Oh, hi. I was taking a little breather." He closed the magazine and held it up so we could see the cover. "Ever read this?"

"Sometimes," Paoli said. In fact he consumes *Wired* from cover to cover every month, including letters to the editor, but I guess he didn't want to reveal such personal information to a possible hacker/murderer.

"This month there's a really neat article on high-speed networking."

"Sounds interesting. We'd like to talk to you a few minutes," I said.

His head bobbed agreeably. "Sure. But can we do it later? I have a report due."

"It can't wait," I said firmly.

Michael's eyebrows rose, giving him a look of childish innocence which seemed a little incongruous considering that at the very least he was handing confidential information to the enemy behind his employer's back.

Paoli took a step toward him. "Harvey Lindstrom just gave us some fascinating information about you."

Michael opened his mouth to speak, then closed it again. "Maybe we should talk someplace else," he said abruptly.

We followed him out of the building and onto the quadrangle, where the three of us sat on one of the benches near the duck pond, Michael in the middle.

"We know you've been giving NASA information to C-CINS," Paoli said. The words came out rough, and I knew Paoli wasn't feeling kindly toward Michael. Neither was I.

Michael hugged himself. He looked sick.

"I believe in what C-CINS is trying to accomplish. Is that so terrible? This country needs money for social programs, not esoteric space research. It was the right thing to do," he said petulantly.

"It wasn't the right thing to do," I said.

His eyes turned venomous. "How can you pass judgment? You don't understand the issues."

"I understand that you signed your name to a document when you started working here, just like Paoli and I did, promising you wouldn't disclose confidential information to outsiders. Maybe I'm a stickler for formalities, but I think promises mean something."

"Sometimes rules must be broken."

It crossed my mind that whether his motives were right or wrong, he was still a spineless twerp.

"The point is, you have the knowledge and the motive to be doing the hacking," I told him.

His fingers plucked at the fabric of his shirt, twisting it. "I'm not the hacker. I promise you."

"And your promises mean a lot to us, but we still want your ID and password so we can go through all your computer files," Paoli said sarcastically. "By the way, you also have a viable motive for killing Garza."

At this Michael's face turned ugly. "Why would I want to kill him?"

"Because he was bad-mouthing C-CINS. He was also doing a number on your fearless leader," Paoli said.

"Don't refer to Harvey that way. You can say whatever you want to about me, but it's not going to matter because I didn't do it."

Paoli smirked. "Tell it to the police."

That wasn't what Michael wanted to hear. His fingertips traveled from his shirt to his mouth, where they tapped his lips nervously while he calculated his next move. It took him a few seconds to figure it out, but when he did he sat up straighter and put his hands in his lap, holding them tightly together.

"I wasn't going to tell you this, but now I guess I have to," he said, his voice shrill.

"Are we going to find this interesting?" Paoli asked.

Michael's lips curled up just slightly. "I think so. You see, Margo had as good a reason to kill Garza as anybody does."

Paoli went rigid. I thought for a second he might pick Michael up by the windpipe.

"We know Margo was dating Garza," I said quickly. "She hasn't tried to hide that."

Michael turned to me. "She was more than just dating him. Margo's pregnant with Garza's baby." He looked from one to the other of us. "Surely you've noticed how green she looks?" he said, seeing our surprise. "She's throwing up half the time."

"Maybe it's something she ate," Paoli said grimly.

"I have it on good authority. I'm good friends with Eileen, one of the secretaries. She overheard one of Margo's calls to Garza. She's pregnant all right, and Garza dumped her when he found out. Margo was hysterical. Crazy. Out of her mind with rage. She threatened him. What do you think about that?" he asked, his tone disgustingly smug.

I took a deep breath and let it out in a rush. I thought it was a motive for murder.

23

A few days earlier I would have been quietly delighted to learn that Margo Miller could be a killer, but now faced with it, I found the concept depressing, although not quite as depressing as Paoli did.

He and I stood in the Texas heat, our arms crossed, and watched Michael Jaep walk away from us. His step was jaunty, which made me like him even less.

"He's lying about Margo. She would never threaten anyone. I'd like to pick him up and shake him until his eyes fall out," Paoli said, his face flushed.

I wasn't as confident about Margo's innocence as he was. Of course, I'd never slept with her, but I knew we all have some capacity for violence if the motive is strong enough, and being rudely dumped by your lover was plenty of motive for a pregnant woman by my reckoning. But if I brought up the point with Paoli without firm evidence, he would assume I was still jealous of her. Which, in truth, I was.

Paoli stood there heating up until he looked like he was ready to chase Michael down and throttle him. I took his arm and tugged him in the other direction.

"Michael will pay for his sins soon enough. We have to

tell the police about his C-CINS activities. After that I doubt he'll have his NASA job for long," I said.

Paoli's eyes remained on Michael until he disappeared around a corner. "Yeah, well, it's a great day for a drive to the police station. Let's tell the cops in person. I'd love to see that little creep in trouble."

"Sounds tempting, but we shouldn't go quite yet."

"Why?"

"Because I think we should talk to Margo first."

Paoli looked at me with disbelief. "You don't believe Michael, do you? Trust me, Julie. I know Margo. She's no murderer."

"We have to clear her name, don't we? When the police question Michael he's going to point the finger at her. Let's get her side of the story."

Paoli reluctantly agreed, and we went back to the office and called, but Margo wasn't in. It could have been my imagination, but Paoli seemed relieved, and I thought perhaps deep down he had the same suspicions I did and didn't want to confront her with them.

Our tiny office seemed oppressive, the walls closing in on me, but there was no place to go since the heat outside was just as bad.

I tried to get my mind off of it while Paoli called Bart, the NSA code breaker, and asked how he was doing with the string of numbers we had given him. I couldn't hear what Bart was saying, but I watched Paoli nodding, throwing in a "Yes" and a "Really?" now and then.

"What did he say?" I asked eagerly before Paoli had even time to hang up.

He looked perplexed. "Bart said they've run the numbers through their computers and they can't figure it out. They've tried to trace the code to different numbering systems, ancient languages, all the normal stuff. Nothing works."

"Maybe the numbers are random and mean nothing." That's me, always the pragmatist.

Paoli shook his head. "Bart doesn't think so. He says the grouping and repeated patterns indicate a definite code. He's going to try running it through their networked Crays. It could take until tomorrow."

Crays are mammoth supercomputers the government uses to crunch huge amounts of data. Think of a personal computer as a toy soldier. Think of a Cray as a fleet of tanks.

"Julie," Paoli said, his voice tentative, "what if McKenzie's theory is correct and the numbers *are* a message from some higher intelligence?"

"If this intelligence is so intelligent," I whispered confidentially, "why does it use a code? Why doesn't it simply say 'Howdy, ya'll drop on by?' "

He leaned back in his chair. "Cute. But it's generally accepted that if some being from another solar system wanted to communicate with the earth it would use numbers. Math is the universal language. I thought you'd know that."

I did know it. I just couldn't believe McKenzie's theory. I was banking on the satellite connection. We agreed to shelve the discussion until the Crays finished crunching.

Paoli and I had both been spooked by the previous night's run-in with C-CINS as well as McKenzie's warning. As a result we decided to work as a pair as much as possible, even if double-teaming slowed us down. At least we'd be in one piece. So when I told Paoli I wanted to interview Lanie Rogers, he said he was coming along. Lanie was the only person on the SM–15 mission we hadn't interviewed, so we had to question her.

We started back across the quadrangle, passing by the pond. Paoli, still upset about Margo, shoved his hands in his pockets and stomped threateningly toward a couple of ducks. Instinctive creatures, the ducks recognized his basic harmlessness. They quacked and waddled toward the pond just to make him feel manly, but they didn't seem overly perturbed.

Lanie wasn't in her office, but there was a computer printout of her schedule sitting on her desk, right on top for all the world to see, so I didn't think it was wrong of me to take a look at it. Printed at the top was SM–15 and since the mission had gone the way of the unicorn, I assumed the schedule had also. Searching the halls we found two women sitting in adjacent cubicles at the end.

"They must be administrative help. Maybe they'll know where Lanie is," I said, and we started in their direction.

"Why would you assume that when you see two women sitting together that they're secretaries? Isn't that sexist?" Paoli asked.

"Sexist or not, that's the reality. I don't make the world. I just live in it."

It turned out they were secretaries, and one of them informed us that Lanie was currently scheduled for the workout room and gave us directions.

It was on the first floor, on the opposite side of the building from where I had seen Lestat throw his tantrum. The workout area was much smaller than I expected. Attached to the medical facility, the gym was about fifteen feet square, with a couple of treadmills, a StairMaster, and a rack of free weights. A window along one wall looked out at some trees.

Dressed in black stretchy shorts and a NASA T-shirt, Lanie was on one of the treadmills doing a moderate walk.

She was so lost in thought she didn't notice us at first.

"Lanie?" I said. She looked up, her expression grim.

"Hi," she said, forcing a smile.

"Can we talk to you?"

"What about?"

"We're interviewing everyone associated with the SM–15 mission," I told her.

She responded with a quick shrug. "But it's been canceled."

"We still have a hacker on our hands, and we're still going to find him."

"Yeah, okay," she said, giving her curls a little shake.

We asked her the usual questions: Did she know of anyone at NASA who would have a motive for hacking into the computer? Had she given her ID and password to anyone outside the organization? Would anyone have had a chance to get her ID and password without her knowing? She gave us a solid no to every question, her breathing becoming more rapid as she increased the treadmill's speed. She gazed mostly out the window, seeming distracted.

"Have your investigations into the hacking given you any leads on who killed Garza?" she asked. Grabbing a bottle of water that hung off the handrail, she took a swallow.

"At this point it looks like Garza had a way of making people mad. It seems as if everyone had some sort of motive," I said.

"Except for you," Paoli added. He said it good-naturedly, but she didn't take it that way. She glared at him, but then caught herself. She increased the treadmill's speed until she was jogging.

"That's where you're wrong," Lanie said, breathing harder. "I had as good a motive as anyone."

Lanie pressed a button to raise the base of the treadmill to an angle so that she was running uphill.

"You'd find out sooner or later. Not that many people know, but some do, and one of them would tell you. Or they'd tell the police." There was a slight smile on her face now, but her voice was bitter. "Garza wrecked my brother's chances in the space program."

I looked at Paoli. "How?" I asked.

Lanie again pressed the treadmill's speed button. She was running full out now, sweat sprouting on her forehead. She didn't answer me. She just kept running, her arms pumping at her sides. She kept on that way for a full minute, grunting as her feet pounded the moving ramp, like she was angry at it. Then she stopped suddenly, jumping off the treadmill with a groan. Hanging onto the handrail as she looked at me, she gasped for air.

"I'm not telling you anything else. This room is off-limits to outsiders. You better leave. I have things to do."

Paoli and I didn't budge, more out of surprise than obstinance. She stared at us, her eyes burning. Then she pushed past us, closing the door after her with an emphatic clunk.

24

"Seems like only last night," Paoli said as we pulled the car into a parking space marked *Visitor.*

I was less than thrilled with the idea of seeing the inside of the police station again. It was one of those places a person doesn't want to visit twice, but I've learned during my months as an investigator that when you need to talk to the police it's best to do it in person.

"Just walking up to it makes me nauseated," I said. I could have used a swig of Maalox, but if I indulged myself in front of Paoli he'd wax on about how I had to relax more and about that island in the Caribbean where we could both be bartenders.

He gave me a one-armed hug. "Look at it this way. At least we're walking in of our own free will."

"It's walking *out* of your own free will that's the trick," I said.

The place looked different to me. For one thing it was broad daylight and we were entering through the front door, the one favored by the guests who weren't handcuffed. But everything inside was the same dull, pale brown. We gave our names to a uniformed officer sitting at a desk behind bullet-proof glass and asked to see the police chief. Initially he was reluctant, but we explained that we had information regarding the NASA murder and parked ourselves on two metal chairs. While he was making some calls, I was praying we wouldn't see Pinsky or Digby, but I guess I'm going to have to start going to church because, ten minutes later, Pinsky appeared.

He put his hands on his hips. "You two are managing to stay out of jail. That's good," he said, his manner friendly.

"Nice to meet you under better circumstances," Paoli said cheerfully, never the type to hold a grudge. He and Pinsky grinned at each other like old drinking buddies.

"No charges are being filed against you, I hear," Pinsky said. "You two have some pretty good friends at NASA."

"There was never any reason to file charges in the first place," I told him.

He smirked. "You were riding that boy's back like you were in the rodeo. When we drove up I half expected you to dig your heels in his side and yell 'yahoo.' "

Paoli tried not to laugh but couldn't help himself.

"We're here to see the police chief," I said, my manner cool. It would be a couple of weeks before I could laugh about that night.

"He's not here. Bob said you have information on the astronaut case. You can give it to me. I'm working it now."

We followed him into a small dingy office with a dirty window looking out on the street. Pinsky sat behind a dusty gray metal desk covered with old coffee rings, and Paoli and I sat in two hard wooden chairs facing him. We answered some questions about how we came to be hired at NASA, and then he asked to see our California investigator's licenses. Paoli had his handy, but it was the first time anyone had wanted to see them and I had to dig through my wallet to find mine.

"We've worked with the Santa Clara Sheriff's Department in California," I told him. After putting on reading glasses, Pinsky inspected both cards closely, running his thumb over the photos. Although I knew our licenses were in order, the scrutiny made me nervous.

"So they've got computer detectives now," he said, handing them back. "That's really something. You don't mind if I call NASA and check you out?"

I assured him we didn't. He made the call, asking for personnel, and spoke for several minutes. Then he hung up, leaned back in his chair, laced his fingers across his stomach and asked, "So what can I do you for?"

Paoli and I told him about Michael's involvement with C-CINS, and Pinsky squinted at the ceiling while he digested the information. "Can you substantiate it?"

Just then the door opened and a fiftyish woman stuck her head in.

"Oops," she said, her hand going to her mouth. "I didn't know you were with someone. Just wanted to tell you there's birthday cake in the interrogation room." She whispered the last part like it was naughty. Pinsky nodded and waved her away.

"If you want substantiation, talk to Harvey Lindstrom," Paoli said. "He said he was going to give you the details himself, but we thought we should go ahead and tell you in case he changed his mind."

"I appreciate it," Pinsky said.

"We also know something else," I said, shifting in my seat

and recrossing my legs. "Something more to do with the murder."

Pinsky lowered his chin and looked at me over the top of his glasses. "And that is?"

I glanced at Paoli, who tipped his head forward to let me know that he knew what I was going to say and that he thought it was a good idea. A lot of information for a simple tipping of the head, but that's how well you get to know someone when you sleep as well as work with him. "Garza did some experiments on his last shuttle mission that weren't supposed to be done."

I expected more of a reaction, but all Pinsky said was, "That's kind of interesting."

"And although as far as we know he didn't sell the results, we think that was his original intention." I waited, but still nothing percolated in him. "You don't seem to think it's important," I said.

"Oh, it's important," he replied. "It's just not new news. We found some kind of weird jars of stuff at Garza's house when they searched it. We confirmed this morning what they were."

"How?" I asked.

"With help from NASA. They were some sort of biological thing, like they were growing something. People acted real surprised he had them."

With a grunt, Pinsky stood up and thanked us for our help. He obviously wanted to get rid of us, but Paoli and I stayed seated. Pinsky's piece of birthday cake would have to wait.

"Now we need some information from you," I said.

His expression turned guarded. "Like what?" he asked. He hadn't expected the relationship to be two-way.

"Do you know about the association between Garza and Lanie Rogers's brother?" I asked him.

Pinsky sat back down, the chair squeaking under his weight. "Why would you be interested in that? That's pertinent to the murder investigation, maybe, but not to your computer stuff."

"If Lanie Rogers was angry at Garza, she could have been angry at NASA, too. Angry enough to mess with their computers, or get someone else to do it," I said.

He mulled it over a moment. "I'll tell you this much about it, since you're working for NASA and NASA's the biggest employer in the county. Besides, we're halfway friends, aren't we?" he said with a wink. "We know that Ms. Rogers' brother Jim was in the Air Force. Three years ago he made the short list for the astronaut program. Garza got him kicked off it."

"Why?" Paoli asked.

"Apparently he didn't like the fact that Rogers had some kind of official reprimand on his military record. It was just a prank he and some other guys played his first year, but Garza didn't like it. Thought he was unreliable."

"Is Jim Rogers a suspect in Garza's murder?" I asked him.

"Not at this point. He's on the East Coast and has been for months. But it gives his sister a motive. Apparently Jim Rogers took it hard that he wasn't going to get a shot at the space program. He left the Air Force and hasn't got his life back on track."

"Do you have any evidence against her?" Paoli asked.

Pinsky frowned. "I haven't said we have any evidence against Ms. Rogers, and I haven't said that we don't. I'm just giving you some background information because you've tried to give us some help. That's all."

"What about Gary Olander's suicide?" I asked quickly.

My question surprised Pinsky. "What about it?" he asked.

"I've called here a couple of times to find out if a suicide note was ever found and I've never gotten an answer."

"Well, I know something about that, and for your information there was no note," Pinsky said. "Now I've got to go."

Pressing his hands against his knees, he stood up and we followed suit.

"Listen, I think you need to look into Olander's death more. I called in and told one of your officers that there was a broken drawer handle in the lab in the shuttle trainer where Olander killed himself."

"And what does that have to do with anything?" Pinsky asked.

"I just think it's possible he didn't kill himself, that there was a struggle. The fact that there's no suicide note makes that more likely, don't you think?"

"I think you better leave the police work to us," Pinsky said, but I could tell he was interested. He went to the door, but turned toward us before opening it.

"There's one more thing you might want to know about," he said. "Somebody tore up Garza's place. They were looking for something. Looking hard."

"Could they have been searching for one of the jars you talked about finding? Or maybe some documentation on them?" I asked.

"Could be. Whatever it was, I don't think they found it, because they kept looking and looking," Pinsky said. "If you figure it out, let me be the first to know."

He said it like he didn't think we'd be figuring it out any time soon.

When we got back to NASA, I checked our messages. There was a call from Max saying that Cosmos was barking too much to be left in the motel room and that she was leaving to meet one of Hansen's relatives for dinner, so could she leave Cosmos with me at NASA? I called her back and told her I'd meet her outside the gate.

The second call was from Foster. She wanted a written report detailing our progress to date and she wanted it on her desk by the next morning. Then there was a third call, by far the most interesting.

"Paoli, I think we may have another job," I said when I hung up.

He swung his feet off the desk. "What kind?" The way he said it implied that we had so many offers we could pick and choose. We didn't.

"The paying kind. Some software company wants us to review their security system and make enhancements. But the man who called," I said, looking at my notes, "said he wants one of us to call at three, West Coast time. They're having a systems meeting and it's an agenda item. He said we should schedule an hour."

Paoli checked his watch. "So it's five-thirty now. Two-thirty on the West Coast. We can do the call from here."

But a few minutes later we heard a loud racket outside our office door. Apparently the air-conditioning ducts needed adjustment and the two men assigned to the job insisted that they had to do their hammering and drilling at that precise time.

I can work in the middle of the freeway, but the sound of the drilling came right through our closed office door, which would make a conference call impossible. Paoli and I flipped a coin. He won. I insisted on two out of three. He still won, which meant he took a cab back to our motel to make the call while I stayed in the office and worked on Foster's report with the drilling as accompaniment.

Paoli had been gone five minutes when I remembered that Max was coming with Cosmos. I kicked myself for forgetting, since Paoli could have baby-sat Cosmos at the motel, but it was too late to rearrange things. I met Max outside the gate, then after some cajoling, I left Cosmos in the guardhouse with Zack. Turned out he was a dog lover. Max had brought along Cosmos' favorite chew toy, so once I had gotten him a bowl of water I felt he'd be happy with Zack for an hour. Zack assured me the guard on the next shift would pick up the dog-sitting duties.

At seven Paoli called to tell me we got the job and could start when we returned to California. He said it hadn't hurt when he dropped the fact that we were currently working for NASA.

He told me he'd wait until I got back to have dinner. By eight forty-five I had finished and I went and slipped the report under Foster's door. As I headed for the parking lot, I saw Margo putting her briefcase in the backseat of her Mercedes. We exchanged good nights and I got in the car, picked up Cosmos and started for home.

Cosmos insisted on being in the front seat with me, which was difficult, since he liked to jump around a lot. After about five minutes I got him to lie down with his head in my lap.

Paoli usually does most of the driving when we're together, which means I always have to adjust the mirrors down to my height when I drive alone. The third time I fiddled with the rearview mirror I realized the car behind was following me.

25

The car was dangerously close, no more than a few yards behind. Its brights came on and their reflection in the rearview mirror blinded me.

I told myself to be calm, but a lump of fear lodged in my stomach. I took my foot off the gas pedal, praying the car would pass. But it didn't pass. It stayed there, coming even closer.

Had C-CINS decided to finish what they'd started? I strained to make out the driver, but it was impossible, the night too dark and the car's headlights too bright for me to see anything clearly.

I slammed my foot down on the accelerator and tried to pull away, but the car speeded up. It was a light-colored sedan, but I couldn't tell the make or model.

There was no doubt the driver intended to frighten me, and it was working. I frantically considered my options. Then my headlights lit up a sign. There was a side street ahead. I took a deep breath and peeled out, careening around the corner onto a narrow two-laned road. Cosmos raised his head from my lap, his ears at attention, sensing my nervousness.

There were no other cars and no streetlights. I hadn't any idea where the road led, but it didn't matter as long as I was alone and safe. But peace would be brief.

Suddenly I saw headlights growing larger in the rearview mirror and my breath left me in a rush. The car closed in. I heard its engine racing as the driver accelerated. Within seconds it was right behind me. Its front bumper tapped my rear one, and I cried out. Cosmos started yapping, jumping crazily around the front seat.

Again the car hit my bumper, this time harder. I floored the gas pedal, trying to get away, but the car stayed on my tail.

The car pulled up alongside, speeding down the wrong side of the road. It sideswiped me and I let out a yell. I tried reducing my speed, then increasing it, but my attacker stayed with me, his car dancing with mine. Sick with fear, I realized the driver wasn't trying to scare me. He was trying to kill me. He swerved again, ramming into me much harder this time.

I careened to the right, tires crunching gravel, the sound like thunder. Clutching at the steering wheel, I struggled to keep the car on the road, but it veered out of control, flying off on the shoulder, then off the road entirely. My car hit the water with a bang, as if it had struck cement. Everything in front of me exploded into white.

I felt like I'd been punched in the face. I had this weird disoriented feeling; everything was happening in slow motion, the car sinking inch by inch. My head hurt like hell. There was this lifeless white thing in front of me like a bunched-up pillowcase and I realized it was the airbag hanging out of the steering wheel. It was Cosmos' whimpering that brought me to full consciousness.

I said his name and felt his nose on my neck. He had his

foot through my purse strap, and when I got him untangled I flung my purse out the window toward the bank, realizing as I did it how crazy it was to be worrying about it now. It landed a foot short.

Looking out the window after it, I realized with sickening clarity what was happening. I fumbled with my seat belt, pulled myself halfway out the car window and fell into the thick sludge. The weeds and mud pulled me downward as surely as hands wrapped around my ankles.

My breath was coming in gasps, my fingers clutching at the edge of the window. I remembered Digby and Pinsky talking in the squad car about the bayou and how it had sucked someone in, and I felt the first flutterings of absolute panic. Cosmos had his front paws out the window, ready to jump after me.

"Stay!" I yelled. He must have known how much trouble we were in because for the very first time he minded me.

I pulled myself up onto the hood and then onto the roof of the car. It sank a few more inches. The only way to survive was to jump and take my chances in the sludge. The bank wasn't very far away, not more than a few yards, and there was a thin tree at the edge. If I could jump far enough, I might be able to reach it, but I couldn't leave Cosmos, and he would never be able to make it through the thick muck on his own.

"It's okay, boy. Stay," I said to him. He looked up at me fretfully. I knew just how he felt. The car sunk a few inches further and my insides clenched up. I didn't want to die this way. I didn't want to die at all. I yelled for help, and to my amazement, I heard a frantic voice respond.

"Julie, is that you?" It was Margo. She appeared from out of the bushes, looking as scared as me.

"Margo, I need your help!"

She dropped to her knees and extended her arm to me, but her hand was at least three yards away.

"I have a phone in the car. I'll call for help," she said. As she stood up, my car dropped suddenly at least six inches.

"Don't leave!" I shouted.

Her hands went to her mouth and her eyes widened. "I . . . I don't know what to do."

She sounded so frenzied I wasn't sure she would be any use, but she was all I had. Cosmos was terrified now and I had to calm him. I was on the roof of the car, he was halfway out the window, so I kept my hand firmly on his head, telling him things were okay. If he understood the words, I'm certain he was smart enough not to believe them.

"Is there a branch or something you could hold out to me?" I said to Margo.

She spun around and searched for a few seconds. "No, there's nothing here. Julie, I have to get help."

Help would be too late. I tried desperately to think of something else.

"Do you have your shoulder bag with you?" I asked her.

"It's in the car."

"Go get it," I told her. "Fast."

She looked at me blankly at first, but then scrambled up the bank. When she disappeared it occurred to me that I shouldn't have told her to go. What if she took the time to call for help? What if she didn't come back at all? But in a matter of seconds she returned with her purse in hand.

I had longingly examined Dooney and Bourke handbags at Nordstrom's enough times to know it had a sturdy strap with a working buckle.

"Okay, Margo. Listen to me carefully. I want you to unfasten the buckle on the strap. That will make the strap longer. I'm going to jump off the car as far as I can. After I do, I want you to hold onto the strap of your purse and throw the bag to me. I'll grab it, then you pull me in."

"But what if you drag me in with you?" she asked, her voice rising hysterically.

"Just hold on to that tree beside you. If you start to get pulled in, then just let go of the strap," I said as calmly as I could. "Now wait until I jump, then throw me the purse like I told you and hold on to the tree. Can you do it?"

There were a few seconds of silence that scared the hell out me.

"I can do it," she finally answered.

I didn't trust her. Not only didn't I trust her in a crisis, but it also flashed through my mind that she might have been the one who drove me off the road. But beggars can't be choosers.

"Get my purse before it sinks," I said. "It's right in front of you." Margo bent over and pulled it in with two fingers, letting out a disturbed "Oh" when mud got on her dress. This was the woman upon whom my life depended. I took a fortifying breath and jumped off the car without any splash.

"Come, Cosmos. Come on, boy," I called.

Cosmos leapt into the sludge and began trying to swim, struggling wildly against the weeds and mud. I got him by the scruff of the neck and pulled him toward me, firmly wrapping my left arm around him. I could feel the poor dog shivering.

Margo hooked her elbow around the tree and swung her purse at me, holding on to the end of the strap. It landed a couple of feet away. Pushing myself through the marsh I strained to reach it. The thick muck was up to my shoulders and I could feel myself sinking. With both arms free I could have gotten out on my own, but with one arm wrapped around Cosmos I was crippled. I strained farther, pushing myself forward, stretching my fingers until I reached the purse.

The purse was slick with mud and my fingers slipped off. I cried out in frustration and fear. The sludge was up to my neck and Cosmos could barely keep his head above it. I managed to get my fingers around the handbag's strap and I felt Margo pulling.

"Don't pull yet!" I shouted, afraid she would wrench it out of my hand. I wrapped my fingers around the purse strap more firmly. "Now," I told her.

She pulled me toward the bank, inch by inch, with me frog-kicking through the mud. When I was close enough she let go of the tree and, with a sob, used both hands to pull Cosmos and me onto the bank.

"Are you all right?" she asked, crying as she wiped mud and grass off my face.

"I think so," I barely managed to whisper. Cosmos was still shivering but seemed okay. I stroked his head murmuring wordless reassurances in his ear. He licked my face and I kissed his nose in return, feeling giddy with relief. I was shaking myself and it took me about five minutes to recover enough to talk.

"Julie, I saw that car run you off the road," Margo said.

I looked at her. "Why were you there?"

"We left the office at the same time. We saw each other in the parking lot, remember? I was right behind you when you left the gate."

"You go home the same way I do?" I asked, trying to keep the suspicion out of my voice.

"Yes, I . . . No, but after I saw you leave the office I decided I wanted to talk to you. So I turned to drive to your motel."

"How do you know where we're staying?"

"I asked Vic yesterday and he told me. I was a few cars behind you. At first I just thought it was a bad driver or a kid giving you a hard time. Then you turned so fast and the other car came screeching after you. It worried me, with everything that's been going on, so I followed."

I studied her face. Her expression was urgent, concerned. I wondered if I could believe in it.

"Did you see the other driver?"

She shook her head. "I just saw the car. I think it was light-colored. I'm sorry. It's so dark out here."

"What did you want to talk to me about?" A pain shot through my temple and my hand moved to my head.

"Are you sure you're okay?" Margo asked.

After a few seconds the pain passed. "I think so. But I don't think your Dooney and Bourke will ever be the same."

Margo looked down at her handbag, which was completely covered with mud. She laughed out loud, and for the first time, I really liked her.

26

*E*very inch of me dripping with primordial ooze, I stood up with Margo's help and did a quick assessment of the obvious body parts.

"Everything seems functional," I said, hugely relieved to be alive and in working order. "I have a headache, but other than that I'm fine."

"Cosmos seems okay," Margo said. Cosmos was on his feet shaking water and mud off of himself and onto me. Not that you could tell, I was so filthy.

"I just need to go back to the hotel, take a hot bath and—" My head began to swim. My knees buckled and Margo caught me.

"I'm taking you to the emergency room," she said with newfound authority. "We'll call Vic from the car. He can meet us."

I protested that I was fine, but Margo was insistent. She picked up my purse, which was in just as bad shape as hers, and helped me up the bank and through the bushes, Cosmos following, a trip made easier by the wide swath my car had mowed en route to the bayou.

Her Mercedes was parked on the shoulder. Trying my

best to be stealthy, I checked out the right side of it for scrapes. I was grateful to the woman, but there was no need to be stupid about it. The car looked clean.

"You're sure you want me to sit in your car like this?" I asked her, looking down at my mud-covered body. "And what about Cosmos? He's grungy."

"I've got a raincoat in the trunk. I'll put it over the seat," she said. Trying to touch as little as possible, I sat on her coat and held Cosmos in my lap while she drove to the hospital. She called Paoli, who responded with gratifying panic and said he was on his way to meet us. Then she called the police. An officer would meet us in the emergency room.

My head throbbed, but it hurt less if I leaned it against the window. I closed my eyes and the sound of the road beneath the wheels cut painfully into my skull. Opening my eyes again, I examined Margo's perfect profile while she drove. Was she friend or foe? I wondered what secrets lay deep in her heart.

"Thanks for saving Cosmos and me."

"You saved yourselves," she said softly as she turned onto the main road. "You told me what to do. I would have just stood there and watched you drown."

"You would have thought of something."

A small shudder ran through her. "I'm not so sure. I'm not like you. You're strong and capable. You stay in control. Me, I fall apart. Lately it seems I react so emotionally to anything that happens."

"Your hormones could be acting crazy because you're preg—" I said before I could stop myself.

She darted a quick sideways glance at me, and I cursed myself for blurting it out. On the other hand, I wanted to confront her about her relationship with Garza and now was as good a time as any, if you ignored the fact that I had a splitting headache and was muddier than the Creature from the Black Lagoon.

"I'm sorry, Margo. I heard a rumor. Then I remembered you were sick the other morning. It added up."

The shining lights of the gas stations and convenience marts flickered into the darkness of the car. She stared straight ahead, her manicured hands gripping the steering wheel too tightly.

"It's okay, I guess," she said, sighing. "People are going to find out anyway. I should start showing soon."

I sensed she wanted to leave it at that, but I couldn't. "Is the baby Garza's?"

There was a short silence. "I guess everyone will know that, too."

"Does that bother you?"

Cosmos stirred in my lap and I stroked him. I could feel Margo's agony and it made me wonder for the two thousand and fifty-fifth time why women let men use their hearts for doormats. Not that I was any different.

"It's what I wanted to talk to you about tonight. You seem so levelheaded. I just wanted your perspective," she said. She sounded sincere.

"I don't know how much good I could do, but I'd be glad to talk about it." I waited a moment before asking, "Did Garza want the baby?"

She let out a cheerless laugh. "When I told him about it two weeks ago he went crazy. Said he wanted nothing to do with it. That he never wanted to see me again." Her face tightened up and tears sprang to her eyes.

"Something like that would have devastated me," I said.

"So was I devastated enough to kill him?" she asked bitterly.

"I'm sorry. I wasn't implying anything," I said, and meant it.

She sighed again. "It doesn't matter. I probably wanted to kill him, at least at first. I didn't want to get pregnant. It was an accident, but he didn't believe it. He thought I was trying to trap him."

"Did he want you to get an abortion?"

"He demanded it. But I couldn't do it. I just couldn't. I guess I thought he'd change, that once the pregnancy started showing and the idea of a baby became more real to him that he would have married me."

I didn't know what to say. I tried to imagine how I would feel in her situation, with a baby on the way and its father dead. It would feel lonely, I think, even with life growing inside me.

Margo turned up the ramp to the freeway. "He called me the day he died. He asked me if I could meet him in one of the conference rooms in building three."

"He wanted to talk about the baby?"

"That's what I thought at first. He was pestering me every day about an abortion. But that wasn't it. He sounded so worried. He said he wanted to play a tape for me."

I sat up and the sudden movement made my head hurt. I put my hand to my aching skull. "Why didn't you say anything about this before?"

"I suspected that John was in some sort of trouble. He had all kinds of debts. I thought maybe he had gone to some cheesy loan shark or something, but that it didn't have anything to do with the hacking. But when he was killed—" She didn't finish the sentence.

"What kind of tape was he talking about? From his tape recorder?"

"I don't know. When I went to the conference room that night he never showed up." She stopped and took a breath. "I guess he was already dead."

"Did you tell the police this?"

"Yes, but I don't know if they looked for the tape."

But somebody had. I remembered what Pinsky had said about someone tearing up Garza's house. I leaned my head back against the headrest.

Margo glanced at me again. "What are you thinking?"

I looked at her. "That the tape could be important. Garza didn't give you any idea what was on it?"

"No. He just said that something might happen and that he wanted me to hear it. I never found out what it was."

"We need to find it," I said.

"Maybe it's at his house."

"The police said somebody already looked."

"Who was it?" she asked.

"They don't know. But police don't think that whoever it was found anything."

"Maybe it's at his office then."

"It's the most likely place. Is his office usually locked?" I asked.

"At night it is. I could try to get a key. I could say I need a file or something."

"The tape might help us find his killer," I said.

"I'd do anything to find out who murdered him. He was the father of my child."

"Margo, I'll do whatever I can to help. If you hadn't turned up on that muddy bank, Cosmos and I would be six feet under."

She didn't look at me. "Just help me find out who killed him."

I watched her as she stared at the road, her pain filling the short distance between us. She seemed broken, the way my toys had looked when I was a kid, after I had abused them.

"You don't need a man, Margo," I told her. "I mean, I'm all for nuclear families with mommies and daddies, but if that option is taken away from you, then you can handle it on your own. You're strong enough."

She looked at me for a second, her eyes brimming with tears. After that we didn't talk anymore.

Minutes after we got to the emergency room Paoli and Max burst in, both wild-eyed and demented with worry. Paoli sat beside me, shooting a hundred questions at me, stopping only to frequently hug me, which really hurt my head.

As soon as Max knew I was all right, she looked in the phone book for a twenty-four-hour animal clinic and took Cosmos there to be checked out.

The police came and took my statement. While they were talking to Margo, I told Paoli what she had said about Garza's tape. By that time Margo looked worn out, and although it wasn't easy, I convinced her I'd be okay, so she went home.

When I finally saw a nurse an hour later, it took her almost another thirty minutes to clean me up enough so they could examine me. They took X-rays and the doctor told me nothing was broken but that I had a mild concussion, probably from the impact of the air bag, and that I should rest for a day.

When Paoli and I got back to the motel, Max was already there with Cosmos. Cosmos was in okay shape, but he was dirty, so we put down a couple of towels for him to sleep on. I threw my filthy clothes on some newspaper in the corner, took a shower and went straight to bed.

The next morning when I opened my eyes there was still a pain in my head. I lifted my upper body onto my elbows and moaned. I felt sore and groggy, but the urge to work was stronger. I was heading for the shower when Paoli came up from behind, picked me up and put me back on the bed. His hair was tousled from sleep, and he was in his underwear, which to my mind was his most attractive outfit.

"Hey, what are you doing?" I said.

"You're resting today."

I started to get up. "Forget it. The doctor was just making sure I can't sue him. I feel fine," I insisted.

Paoli held me down to the bed. "You don't look fine."

"Thanks a lot."

"The truth hurts. You're going nowhere."

"We have to find Garza's tape."

"Lie down. I'll worry about that. Are you thirsty, hungry, want aspirin?"

"You need my help."

"Believe it or not, sometimes I'm capable of functioning without your assistance."

"I only let you think that to build up your self-esteem." He didn't smile at my little joke. "And I don't need anything."

Pressing softly on my shoulders, he made me lie down with my head on a pillow.

"I have something to tell you," he said. "I think we may be able to locate the hacker's satellite."

I sat up. "How? Where is it?"

"If you don't stay still I won't tell you anything else."

I fell back against the pillows. "I'm still. Tell me."

"Turns out NASA has some software. It's a tracking system that traces satellite connections."

"How does it work?"

"I'm afraid if I give you that much information right now your brain will explode. Just accept that the software figures it out. It's already told us which NASA satellite the hacker's signals are bouncing off of. Now all it has to do is give us the location of the sending dish."

"And when will it do that?"

"Maybe today. I'm still working on it."

I was back up on my elbows. "But we don't have much time left. You have to let me help you."

"Sorry, Julie. Today I'm solo. I don't think you have any clean clothes left anyway. You've trashed two suits and the things you had on last night should be given a decent burial. I've got to shower now. Get out of bed again and I'll tie you up in front of the TV and force you to watch *Regis and Kathie Lee*."

To be honest, I didn't feel as good as I pretended. My head throbbed and my body felt like it had been used for a punching bag. I nestled back into the pillows and closed my eyes. When I opened them fifteen minutes later, Paoli had come back in looking handsome, dressed in slacks and a clean shirt, freshly shaved, his hair still wet and curly from the shower.

"Since you drowned our government-issue Chevy I'll have to take a cab into work," he said, buttoning his cuffs.

I pressed my hand to my forehead. "Jeezus, I didn't think about that until now. I hope it's insured."

"Of course it's insured. Don't worry so much. Listen, they don't have room service here, but I'll stop at the front desk and make them bring up coffee and some breakfast."

He sat on the edge of the bed next to me. "Max is going to bring you something for lunch. I told her not to call you before noon, so you can sleep. Need anything else?"

We went through a short verbal tussle about my wanting to go to work. If my head felt better I would have won, but it didn't, so I stayed in bed. I figured as soon as he left I'd call Max and talk her into letting me borrow her car.

On his way out the door, Paoli stopped and turned back to me. "By the way, I've already talked to Max. She won't take you anywhere and I've taken all the money and credit cards out of your purse so there's no way you can take a cab."

"You can't—"

"I can and did. If you need anything, call. Have a good rest," he said, and left. A few minutes later an older woman from the motel reception desk named Sweetie dropped off coffee and a muffin for me. I passed on the muffin but downed the coffee.

Cosmos and I spent the rest of the morning sleeping. Normally I hate sleeping when it's daylight, but in addition to being exhausted, it felt strange being in that old motel room all alone and sleeping was a great excuse to keep my eyes shut.

I'd spent hardly any time in the room during the day, and lying there in the bed I realized what a blessing that was. The place was exceptionally tacky, everything shabby and peeling. I felt restless and tired and lonely in there.

I would have let Cosmos on the bed with me just for the warm body, but he was still dirty from the previous night's dunk in the bayou, so he napped on the floor.

Around lunchtime Max came with a tuna sandwich, some aspirin, another set of clothes and a new purse. She bathed Cosmos—a major accomplishment—and dried him with my hair dryer. While I ate my sandwich we watched Martha Stewart whip up her own crème fraîche, while Max waxed on about how she thinks Martha Stewart is sexually repressed and that most of the domestic activities she demonstrates are thinly veiled sexual metaphors. I turned off the television, deciding I felt much better.

I called Paoli to get an update on his progress. There wasn't any, but he assured me his efforts were superhuman and would soon produce amazing results. Afterwards I asked Max if I could borrow her car, but she said no. I tried begging, but Paoli had brainwashed her too completely, so I finally told her I had a headache, which was true, and she left so I could sleep. She said she needed to go shopping anyway, since I was destroying both our clothes at such an alarming rate.

As soon as the door closed behind her, I called Margo. She answered on the second ring.

"Julie, I think I know something about John's tape," she said urgently. "I went into John's office and Lisa Foster was there."

"Doing what?"

"Looking through his desk drawer. The police looked through his office late this morning, but Foster got there before they did."

"Which drawer was she searching?"

There was a short pause. "Why is that important?"

"Because if she was looking for a document she would go through one of the file drawers. If she was looking for an object, like a tape or a little tape recorder, she would search a top drawer."

"It was a top drawer," she said excitedly. "You should have seen her face when I came in. She said she was looking for a report, but you're right, John wouldn't keep a report in his top desk drawer. I've seen it. It's full of pencils and pens."

"Did she have anything in her hand?" I asked.

"Not that I remember. But she had her purse with her. She could have taken something and put it in there."

"Then we've got to look through it. Listen Margo, my car's still at the bottom of the bayou. Which reminds me, that car was insured, right?"

"Of course it was."

"Good. But I still don't have a car. Could you pick me up?"

Another pause, a longer one. "Vic said you might ask me to do that. He said you're not supposed to leave the motel. The doctor told you to rest."

What was I, a prisoner?

"Okay, Margo. Then you have to look in Foster's purse yourself."

"How do I manage that?"

"Easy. Sneak into her office when she's not there. Hire a purse snatcher. Anything. But you have to do it. She could have Garza's tape."

She agreed, sounding eager to get the opportunity. Polite, well-behaved women are always titillated by the prospect of breaking a few rules. I know because I used to be one of them. It was almost two hours before she called me back.

"Julie, I did it," she said, excited and breathless. The guilty, elated enthusiasm that comes from peeking somewhere you shouldn't was audible in her voice. "I went into her office when she wasn't there. She had her purse stuck in the back of a file cabinet, but I found it and looked inside."

"Was the tape there?"

"Yes, I saw it. It was a little one from his tape recorder."

I raised my fist in the air. "Fantastic. Good work, Margo. Come get me right away. We'll find a tape recorder and listen to it."

There was an uncomfortable few seconds of dead air on the other end of the line. "Well, I didn't take it with me."

My mouth fell open as I absorbed this. "Why not?" I asked.

"Well, what if it wasn't John's tape? I can't go around stealing things out of people's purses."

Maybe my values had gone down the toilet, but I personally thought stealing the tape an excellent thing to do. Still, I remembered that I used to have the same sort of Girl Scout scruples that currently hampered poor Margo. It's so easy to have them when you've got a regular paycheck, a 401K and health benefits.

I gently chided her, not enough to make her feel really bad, but enough so she agreed to try to steal the tape from Foster's purse. I figured it would be good for her self-esteem. At four she called and told me with disappointment that Foster hadn't left her office and didn't have anything on her schedule that would require her to leave for the rest of the day.

After some prodding on my part, Margo felt understandably guilty about her inappropriate display of honesty, guilty enough to agree to get me another NASA fleet car and pick me up within the hour.

"But what's the point? If I couldn't get at her purse how are you going to?" she asked.

It was a reasonable question. "I'll figure it out," I told her.

"And what if it *was* John's tape that I saw? Lisa has probably gotten rid of it by now. Thrown it in the trash or something."

"I don't think so. If I had something in my possession that I didn't want anyone to see, the last place I would get rid of it would be at NASA. I'd dump it someplace else," I told her. "Besides, we won't know until we check it out."

So Margo picked me up, and on the way back to NASA she and I developed a plan. Or at least I developed a plan, and Margo agreed to participate. We went straight to Margo's office, where she called her administrative assistant. She told her to call Gerald and have him tell Foster that she was needed right away in Building Six to talk to a reporter about the SM–15 cancellation. Margo was going to keep Gerald occupied while I slipped into Foster's office and looked through her purse. Unfortunately we saw Foster walking across the quadrangle, her purse on her arm. Margo called her assistant again and told her to call Gerald back and say that the reporter had to leave suddenly and that the meeting was no longer necessary.

Paoli was upset when he saw me at NASA, but I assured him I was completely rested and had never felt better in my life, which wasn't true. At five forty-five he and I were in the NASA lot in a dark government-issue sedan parked across from Foster's white Toyota convertible. Even with the top up it was a sexy car; it looked like a bright white jelly bean. We'd been waiting fifteen minutes. I had taken off my shoes, and Paoli was slouched against the driver's door eating a bag of pretzel nuggets.

"So tell me again what we're doing," he said, sounding dubious as he tossed a pretzel into his mouth.

"Margo told me that Foster usually leaves the office

around six or six-thirty. If Foster comes out and Margo hasn't been able to get inside her purse, we're going to implement plan B."

At that moment I saw Foster come out of building three. She was wearing a prim suit and carrying a briefcase, and her hair was pulled into a low ponytail. My eyes zeroed in on the black shoulder bag hanging off her arm.

It's intriguing how multidimensional a woman's handbag can be. The contents of each one are unique, an assortment of lipsticks, scraps of paper, photos and house keys, a banal collection of everyday items. Yet you put them all together and like a puzzle they form a picture of that woman, give you a little glimpse into her soul. When the previous night I thought I was in danger of drowning, it had been my instinctive reaction to try and save my handbag, and as if to reward my sensitivity to their sect, Margo's handbag had saved me in return.

And now Foster's bag hung on her shoulder, a temptress in black leather, swinging back and forth, enticing me, luring me to plumb its depths.

I knew that tape was in there, and somehow I was going to get it.

27

Get down! Slide down so she can't see us," I said to Paoli, tugging his arm.

He groaned as he slid down in the driver's seat of our new government fleet car. "This is so stupid. If she looks our way she'll think we're trying to hide."

"We *are* trying to hide. But she won't see us if you scrunch down a little more."

Gripping the dashboard, I peeked over it. Foster approached her car with Margo about five yards behind her. Margo made a face and gave us a thumbs-down. She hadn't been able to get at Foster's purse, which meant we had to implement plan B.

Foster got into her car and pulled out of the parking lot. Paoli and I scrambled up in our seats, and he started the engine and pulled out after her keeping a safe distance behind.

"Okay, now explain this plan B," he said as he turned out of the main gate and onto the road.

"We follow Foster home, ring her doorbell and tell her we want to discuss the hacking," I said, craning my neck to keep an eye on Foster's car in front of us. "We talk a few minutes, then I make some excuse about how I have to use the bathroom or I need a drink of water or whatever it takes so I can be alone with Foster's purse. Then I take the tape before she has a chance to get rid of it."

Out of the corner of my eye I saw Paoli grimace. "This isn't exactly well thought out, is it, Julie? What are we supposed to say to her about the hacking if and when she lets us in her house? And what if she has her purse in the living room with her?"

"Don't be so negative. If it's in the living room you simply think of some excuse to get her into the kitchen." His expression remained skeptical. "Okay, maybe it's not a great plan, but it's the best I could do on short notice and with an intermittent throbbing in my skull," I said, bristling.

He gave me a worried look. "I knew it. You should be in bed."

"I'm fine. This is a two-person job."

"I told you, Margo and I could have handled it."

My jaw clenched—if we didn't wrap up this case soon I was going to crack a tooth. "She doesn't have the necessary skills," I said through gritted teeth, hoping my voice didn't sound as tight to him as it did to me.

Foster stopped at a red light. Paoli pulled into the next lane behind three cars so we wouldn't be right in back of her. She took off again when the light turned green and pulled onto the freeway.

"I don't get this. Margo said Foster only lived a few miles from NASA," I said after we had passed three exits.

Paoli exhaled loudly. "Great. That means she's not going home. Now what?"

"We keep following her and improvise."

He lifted his hands from the steering wheel for a second

to perform one of his Italian gestures of dismay. "And do what, Julie? Mug her?"

"If we have to."

"You're kidding, right?"

"I'm not sure. We have to get that tape."

"Listen, I've been in jail once this week and I'm not—"

"Concentrate on what you're doing! She's pulling off. We're going to lose her!" I shouted, pointing to Foster's car, and Paoli had to swerve to make the exit. A car behind us honked punitively.

We followed her several blocks into a run-down suburb of shabby old tract housing with broken fences. After two right turns and a left, Foster pulled her car into a crowded parking lot in front of a large warehouse. A big painted sign across the top of the building said SADDLEHORSE. We parked at the far end of the lot.

"Where the hell are we?" Paoli asked after he turned off the engine.

"I hear music. Must be a restaurant or a bar or something."

"So why doesn't she get out of the car? Do you think she knows we're following her?"

I gave him a *who-knows?* shrug.

We sat there for at least ten minutes, our eyes glued to Foster's car, before she finally exited, and when she did, I realized what had taken so long.

Paoli let out a long wolf whistle as Foster picked her way across the parking lot. Her hair was loose around her shoulders, her prim suit replaced with a low-cut black top and skin-tight black pants that had to have been hell to squeeze into inside that tiny sports car. On her feet she wore black patent stiletto heels. The same black handbag hung off her shoulder. She disappeared into the doorway of the Saddle-horse.

I put my shoes back on. "Okay, let's go."

"Go and do what?" Paoli asked.

I looked at him. "Whatever we have to."

A fat cowboy with his shirt unbuttoned halfway to his belt sat inside the front door. He eyed us languidly, pointing a greasy finger to a sign on the wall behind him that said $10 COVER. Paoli got out his wallet, paid the twenty dollars, and we passed through the portals of the Saddlehorse.

The bar itself was large and smoky but brightly lit, the walls a vivid red, the floor rough brown planks strewn with popcorn. Bowls of the stuff sat on every table. A country band swayed on a small stage at the front of the huge room, blasting a song about a love affair gone lousy at earsplitting volume. In the center of the dance floor was a statue of a cowboy riding a bucking bronco. I saw people taking their mugs to it and filling them, and I realized that the horse's penis was a beer tap. The whole thing sat in a big tub to catch the drips. At least fifteen couples moved in a slow circle around the dance floor, but most people huddled at the bar or around the beer tap.

"There she is," Paoli said, pointing to the far end of the bar.

At first I couldn't find her, but then I saw Foster holding a beer in a frosty mug, leaning against the bar. With her hip jutting out sexily, she leaned forward, her cleavage gaping as she chatted up a man perched on the stool beside her. Cautiously we moved toward the other end of the long bar.

"Why, she's hotter than a sidewalk in August," Paoli said in a mock Texas accent. "You could fry an egg on her."

"A woman can't stay in a business suit all the time," I said, always ready to defend a member of my sex. I could see Foster's reflection in the huge mirror behind the bar.

"*You* do."

I gave him a look. "But I take it off when it counts, don't I?"

Paoli placed his hands on my waist and pulled me to him. "Speaking of which, how about tonight we play Space Invader Meets the Vixen From Mars, okay?" he joked. "We can go to the store and get some tin foil, and then—"

"Right now let's concentrate on Foster."

Paoli rested his elbow on the bar. "My idea is less of a fantasy than the one you're cooking up right now. What are we doing here, Julie?"

Assuming the question was rhetorical, I kept my eyes on Foster. She seemed absorbed in the man beside her. "I don't quite see how we're going to separate her from that handbag," I admitted.

"Lucid point, my love," Paoli said, "unless we follow Foster home, and from the looks of her, she'll be going home with a cowboy. In fact, she may be going home with a couple of cowboys. As long as we're standing here, you want a drink?"

I could have used some anesthetizing liquid, but ordered a Coke because of my headache.

"She's revved up and ready to race," Paoli said when he came back with my Coke and his beer, nodding in Foster's direction.

She had left the bar and moved out onto the dance floor, her hips swaying as she made her way through the crowd. Several people greeted her warmly, and she smiled and slid her hand over one man's hip as she passed, although her eyes remained fixed straight ahead. It wasn't the first time she'd been to the Saddlehorse.

"She looks so sensual," I said to Paoli. "So different from the stiff person she is at the office."

She was heading toward a young man in a gray T-shirt and tight black jeans who was standing with two other men near the bronco beer tap. Nice choice, I said to myself.

He couldn't have been more than twenty-five. His skin was tan, his hair a deep black, and he had a goatee and a mustache. His arms were well-muscled, his waist narrow and taut. He stood there oozing sexual confidence as he lifted a mug of beer to his lips and listened to whatever his friend was telling him. As Foster approached, his lips curved into a knowing smile and he set his beer down on a nearby table. A force like the gravitational pull between celestial bodies drew them together and Foster stood on her tiptoes, wound her arms around his neck and planted a slow, lingering kiss on his mouth.

"Whew. Beauty's in the eye of the beer holder. Foster's old enough to be that guy's mother," Paoli said.

"She's not *that* much older," I said, even though I was thinking the same thing. "Who knows? Maybe their relationship is strictly sexual."

Paoli smirked. "For her it's sex. For him it's more like an archeological dig."

The statement bugged me. "How come it's okay for a man to date or even marry someone twenty years younger but if a woman does it everybody thinks it's so awful?" I asked, but I had to admit they made an odd couple. Then again, some people think Paoli and I make an odd couple. I put down my Coke. "Listen, I have to make a move here. Foster will be hanging off guys all night."

"What kind of move are you talking about?" he asked warily.

"I'm going to ask her about the tape."

"You're crazy. She'll only deny having it."

"I can't just stand here. I have to take some initiative."

Paoli downed his beer and set the mug down. "All right then, I'll come with you."

I pressed my hand against his chest. "Let me go alone. She might open up if it's just me. You know, woman to woman."

Paoli could never argue with that line of reasoning. I pushed through the crowd until I reached Foster, who was now dancing with the young man, hanging on to him like he was a life preserver and she was adrift in the ocean. Her head was against his chest, her eyes half-closed. I tapped her shoulder and she gave me a sleepy look, but then her eyes snapped open.

"What are you doing here?" Foster asked.

Her boyfriend laughed and pulled me to him with an arm that felt hard as steel against my waist. "Honey, there's plenty of room here," he said, swaying me to the music.

"Sorry, I'm not here to dance," I told him, and pulled away. "Lisa, I want to talk to you."

Foster stopped moving. "About what?" she asked nastily.

"You have a tape in your purse. I'd like to have it."

Her eyes flashed and her whole body tensed.

"I don't have any tape. Now get out of here. I mean now."

Her boyfriend watched me with amusement. "Lisa's claws are showing. You better watch it, girlie. Lisa's a tough one."

"Let's go somewhere and talk, Lisa. Please," I said in a placating tone meant to make up for my previous abruptness.

But she wasn't having any of it. "Get out," she said.

"You need me to help?" her boyfriend asked her.

Lisa smiled slightly. "Yeah, Seth. Why don't you help me out here."

The next thing I knew, I was airborne. The crowd made hooting sounds of encouragement as Seth carried me across the room in the direction of the beer-peeing bronco.

"Put me down immediately," I said in a commanding tone. He complied with my wishes, dropping me between the bronco's rear legs. Before I could protest, he turned on the tap and beer spouted out of the bronco's penis.

28

It wasn't my finest moment. I reached over my head and turned off the beer tap, but my blouse and my hair were drenched, and I was sitting in about two inches of the stuff. Beer had splashed onto people nearby and not all of them accepted it gracefully. Some cheered, but others cursed.

Foster's boyfriend just stood there, one hand on his blue-jeaned hip, laughing at me. The band was playing a slow romantic song, and when the sight of me dripping beer ceased to amuse him, he walked back over to Foster and pulled her onto the dance floor, pressing her hard against him as if tossing women around made his testosterone surge.

My posterior was planted in the tub beneath the tap and I was struggling unsuccessfully to get out of it when I saw Paoli pushing through the crowd looking panicked. "Jeezus, what happened?" he said. "I took my eyes off you for two seconds, and the next thing I know you're—"

"Please, just help me up."

I held my hand out to him and he pulled me to my feet. I didn't want to discuss the particulars, because one,

I didn't want him picking a fight with Foster's boyfriend, and two, I was too busy being horribly embarrassed.

Everyone was staring at me, many laughing and pointing, reviving memories of every mortification I'd suffered in my childhood. I said half a dozen "sorrys" and "excuse mes" as I hastily crossed the dance floor. The band swung into some fast-paced, line-dancing music and the crowd soon lost interest in me, moving closer to the stage and forming themselves into two lines.

I ducked into the ladies' room, where I combed my hair and blotted as much beer as I could out of my blouse. Looking at my wrecked self in the mirror, part of me wanted to cry and part of me wanted to laugh. What was left was wondering, as it often did, why I had ever left the nice, safe corporate world to start my own business. Sure, my corporate job was hopelessly bureaucratic and often boring, but I never once got baptized in beer.

As soon as I exited the ladies' room Paoli fell in step behind me, harping at me as I slunk back to the bar.

"I want to know what happened," he demanded.

"It was a freak accident."

"Don't kid around, Julie. What did you think you were doing messing around with Foster anyway?"

"I was taking some initiative."

"It went well," he said sarcastically. "By the way, you have initiative dripping off your butt."

"Oh, shut up," I said, brushing it off.

Paoli leaned his elbow on the bar and eyed me. "Should I order another beer or just suck on your hair?"

"So funny," I replied coldly as I watched Foster move around the dance floor. The purse on her shoulder swayed on its strap, contemptuous of me.

I felt a tug on my arm. "Come on. Let's go home," Paoli said.

"I'm not leaving yet." I was staring at Foster. Paoli took my chin in his hand and made me face him.

"Julie, listen to me." He articulated the words carefully like I was deaf and had to lip-read. "You struck out with Foster, you're soaked with beer and you're going to smell like a skid-row flophouse."

"I'm not leaving until I get that purse."

He closed his eyes, taking a moment to collect himself. "Julie, okay, I'm sorry about the way I spoke to you before," he said in a tone I've heard people use with children. "I was out of line. But there's a time when you have to give up on something."

"I'm not giving up."

"Here we go," he muttered, slapping his hand on his forehead. He flagged down the bartender and ordered a tequila.

I watched Foster dance while I considered my next move. She was line dancing with the others, but she didn't look happy. No brilliant ideas hit me, so I bided my time in hopes that inspiration would suddenly strike. It didn't. Annoyed and anxious to get out of the Saddlehorse, Paoli badgered me every few minutes about how we could be at NASA working on fixing the satellite location, but I ignored him, tossing back another Coke.

Foster's reaction when I'd asked for the tape had left me more convinced than ever that she had it and that there was information on it vital to the case. Even if there wasn't, if Foster thought a mere beer dunking was going to frighten me away I'd show her how wrong she was.

Paoli and I sat at the bar, Paoli glaring at me, me glaring at Foster, and Foster keeping her eyes glued to her boyfriend.

Paoli had definitely been right about one thing: as the beer on me dried I was pretty fragrant and it was getting worse.

A few songs later the band stopped. Foster gave her boyfriend a deep kiss and walked away.

"Wonder where she's going," Paoli said, showing only a glimmer of interest.

I slammed my glass onto the bar. "The ladies' room," I said excitedly. "She's going to the ladies' room and I'm going with her."

"Unh-uh. No way," Paoli said. "*Not* a good idea."

But I didn't take the time to argue. I slid off my stool and went quickly after Foster. I could hear Paoli calling my name. He grabbed me from behind about ten yards from the door to the ladies' room.

"I'm telling you, Julie. Leave it alone."

But I jerked away before he could stop me and rushed inside where I was safe from him. Deep down Paoli thought of ladies' rest rooms as a mysterious places of secret female rites, like we're in there chanting and stirring dead frogs into cauldrons, and if a man so much as cracks the door open a swarm of Tampax would fly out and pummel him.

There were three stalls. I looked under the doors. Two were empty, but under the third I saw Foster's black patent spike-heeled shoes. Only they were facing the wrong way. I heard her rummaging through her purse, and then there was a snipping sound, followed by a flush.

"No!" I yelled, and pulled on the door. After two yanks it flew open. Foster was standing there, completely clothed with nail scissors and a long strand of tape in her hand, looking astonished. I pushed her aside and looked into the toilet bowl where I saw a small plastic case and small bits of tape swirling in the water. Without stopping to think about it, I thrust my hand in and scooped out as many of the bits of tape as I could and then wrenched the rest that she held away from her.

Just then two women walked in, talking and laughing, but they stopped abruptly when they saw Foster and me together in the stall, both of us looking crazed, me holding the tape in my dripping hand. After one good look they left.

I locked eyes with Foster. Her lips were drawn tight and she seemed as if she was ready to shove me into the toilet along with the tape. I kept a close eye on the nail scissors still in her hand.

"It's no good to you now," she said defiantly. "It's ruined."

She had a point. All I had was a wad of wet, chopped-up tape. My brain churned for a few seconds.

"Hardly. Once the pieces are dry it'll only take a couple of hours to do enough splicing so that we can compile the tracks and get most of the data reconfigured." This was complete nonsense, but being a computer expert has some of the same advantages as being a doctor—you can spout technical jargon to a layperson and they'll probably accept it.

Foster's face fell. For extra effect I quickly put the tape in my purse and zipped it closed. After that she just stared at my handbag like I had put her soul in there. All the feistiness had left her and she seemed to shrink in front of me.

"You stole this tape," I said. She didn't respond. "You might as well tell me. It's all going to be out in the open tomorrow." I was bluffing, but she fell for it.

"I didn't steal it. Garza gave it to me."

That surprised me. "Then what were you searching Garza's office for?"

"The copies. He told me—threatened me—that he had copies."

"Did you find them?"

"No."

"So he was blackmailing you?"

She didn't say anything, but the anger in her eyes was all the answer I needed.

"Listen, I've made some mistakes, but I didn't kill anybody," she said rigidly. "Are you going to give the tape to the police?"

"I don't even know what's on it yet."

"Nothing that implicates me in anything criminal."

"Then you have nothing to worry about."

I meant what I said, but she laughed bitterly at me. "I've got plenty to worry about."

"So tell me about it. Maybe I can help. What's on the tape?" I asked more urgently than I intended to.

She looked at me with suspicion. "I'm not telling you anything else. You can just reconfigure the tracks or whatever. You could be bluffing. And if not, nothing matters anymore anyway."

There was a resignation in her voice that made me feel sorry for her. I opened my mouth to tell her I was willing to talk things out, that although I would never hide any evidence, I would try to put things in the best light with NASA and the police, but before I could say a word, she turned and walked out.

I followed her into the crowd to press more information out of her, but she walked into the waiting arms of her boyfriend. He looked at me threateningly and I knew he wouldn't let me near her. One beer bath was enough for an evening.

29

I told Paoli I was ready to go, and we wasted no time hustling out of the Saddlehorse. But before we left I looked around, searching for Foster. She was standing at the bar, tossing back a drink. Her eyes caught mine. She raised her glass to me, her face solemn.

"How'd it get wet?" Paoli asked when, once we were in the car, I showed him the tape.

"You don't want to hear. Let's go."

We drove straight back to the motel, and on the way I told Paoli what had happened with Foster. I filled him in on all the details, even the part about the tape in the toilet, finishing as we walked into our motel room. I turned on the light and threw my purse and briefcase on the bed.

The dreary room was almost starting to feel like home to me. The place had been cleaned and someone had left cellophane-wrapped candies on our pillows. Not quite Godiva chocolates, but the thought was there.

"The tape is too damaged to put back together again. Besides, some of it went down the toilet. We've got to find one of Garza's copies," I said to Paoli, who had immediately started stripping.

He raised his shoulders as he unbuttoned his shirt. "Why don't we just tell the police we suspect that Garza was blackmailing Foster and let them do the dirty work?"

The idea made sense, yet I didn't like it one bit. "We'll tell them, of course," I said, stammering. "But we have to stay involved. We can't—"

He stopped unbuttoning, put his hands on my shoulders and looked into my eyes as if trying to see the inside of my brain.

"This isn't another Margo thing, is it? You're not so irrationally jealous of her you're determined to prove that you're better than her, that you can run faster and jump higher?"

"Don't be ridiculous." I pulled away from him. "This is our first really big case and I want us to solve it. Is that so hard to understand?" I sat down on the bed, put my feet up and leaned back against the headboard. "You talk like we're in high school."

He chuckled. "Haven't you figured it out yet? Life *is* high school. We're all acting out the same stupid insecurities we had in eleventh grade. I'm still the class clown and you're still . . . what's that name they called you in school?"

I squeezed my eyes shut. "Gearhead."

"See, it still hurts even to say it." I opened my eyes and watched him toss his shirt on a chair. "I'm taking a shower," he said. "You should, too. You're really starting to stink."

Admittedly, the odor of stale beer emanating from me was developing increasing pungency. He gave me a quick kiss, stripped off his pants and walked into the bathroom muttering "Gearhead" and laughing.

I sat up, hugging my knees to my chest. I don't think Paoli realized his theory would be a mind-bending revelation to me, but it was. In high school it had hurt when the name "Gearhead" stuck, but the only way I knew how to fight back was to be smarter than everyone else.

So wasn't my situation with Margo just a replay of my high school torture? She was the beautiful popular blonde. I was the studious geek. She won the boys. I won the straight A's. Now we were fifteen years out of high school and I was still trying to prove to the Prom Queen that I was smarter, more capable, more independent.

But recognizing this was very different from changing it, and I was still determined to show the Prom Queen that the Gearhead could solve the NASA hacking.

I noticed the red light blinking on our phone, so I called the front desk. Max had left us a message saying she was shopping late and that Cosmos would need a walk, so, using the key she'd given me, I went into her room, took Cosmos out, then brought him back with me. As soon as Paoli was out of the shower I jumped in. When I was done I found Paoli and Cosmos lying on the bed watching *Cops* on television.

"We still have to find a copy of Garza's tape," I said as I towel-dried my hair. I was wearing one of Paoli's T-shirts and a pair of his gym socks. I love to wear his clothes.

He clicked off the television. Cosmos looked annoyed.

"You told me in the car that the tape in Foster's purse was the one Garza gave her," he said.

I sat down next to him on the bed. I picked up my brush from the nightstand and brushed the tangles.

"Yes. She admitted that she searched Garza's office but didn't find any copies. So Garza kept them someplace else."

"You missed a spot." Paoli took the brush from me and ran it through my hair. "Or it could mean that Foster just didn't find them," he said, handing the brush back to me.

"It would be tough for us to search Garza's office. We'd get caught."

"Then let's try his house."

"But Pinsky said someone else already searched it," I said.

"So what? There are a thousand places to hide something in a house. Just because someone else didn't find the tape doesn't mean we won't."

His reasoning had an optimistic sort of logic that appealed to me. Problem was, we didn't know where Garza lived and we didn't have a key. I thought of Margo. Convincing Paoli it would be better if I did the talking, I picked up the phone and called her.

I was still suspicious of Margo's innocence as well as her attentions to Paoli, especially now that she was pregnant and at least temporarily manless. But she was still our main conduit into NASA and I had no choice but to make as much use of her as I could. I gave her a rundown of what had happened with Foster, leaving out a few of the more embarrassing details, and I asked her about the key.

"Well, yes, I have a key to John's house . . . " she said hesitantly.

"But?" I asked her.

There was a brief silence. "No one knows I have it. John didn't even know. He would have been furious. He never let me stay at his place."

Nice relationship. And this guy was the father of her child? "So how did you get it?"

A few seconds of dead air.

"One night I took his spare set out of his car. I thought he was seeing someone else and I—I wanted to go through his things. I had copies made and put the keys back in his glove compartment before he ever missed them. I never used the keys I'd made, but if the police found out I had them . . . "

"Listen, Margo, I need to borrow them. I'll never tell anyone how I got them." There was no response. "It might help us find John's killer."

She reluctantly agreed. We didn't want to go into Garza's house at night when neighbors would see the lights, so we decided it would be safer to do it the next day.

The next morning was Saturday, and after getting the key and a suitable amount of coffee inside us, Paoli and I headed for Garza's, a forty-five-minute drive from NASA. His neighborhood turned out to be an upscale, walled development called Monterey Pines. It surrounded a golf course and country club, everything very upper class and very white.

After finding the address we cruised by the house a couple of times. It was contemporary and expensive looking with gray wood siding and lots of big geometric windows. Like the rest of the houses in the neighborhood, it had manicured landscaping in front and a garage with two spaces for cars and one for a golf cart. I wondered how much money astronauts made, and I remembered what Lestat had said about Garza having big debts.

We cruised by twice before deciding that our best option was to park in the driveway and walk right up to the front door. We didn't want anyone to see us, but on the other hand, if someone did, it would look as if we had a right to be there.

Inside the house was a wreck. Books and magazines had been tossed on the floor, furniture upended, and the drawers yanked out and overturned.

"This place makes your house look cozy," Paoli said as

we stepped into Garza's living room, but it wasn't the dis-array he was talking about. I've never had the time or incli-nation to do any decorating, and I refer to my decor as neo-Sears modern, but Garza's place had all the warmth of a dentist's office. A very expensive dentist's office. Everything was chrome, leather and glass.

"Although I've got to admire the guy's taste in art," Paoli said with a grin, cocking his thumb in the direction of a large oil painting of a nude woman. The painting was at least four by six feet and the model's position looked painful. All the paintings and photographs on the walls were of female nudes.

"This is revolting," I said.

"You bet it is," Paoli said while he studied a nude paint-ing. "And after about an hour I'm going to force myself to leave."

"Cute. So let's start looking for the tape," I said. "I want to spend as little time in here as possible."

He unbolted his eyes from the artwork. "If you insist. That room looks like a study," he said, looking into the ad-jacent room. "You start there. I'll take the bedroom. There might be things in it a girl like you shouldn't see." He gave me a wicked grin.

I made a face and went into the study. Garza's desk was a massive English antique, dark oak with a green leather sur-face. Its contents were spilled rudely on the floor. I sat down cross-legged on the carpet and started sifting through the stuff.

My heart soared when I saw a small tape recorder, but there was no tape inside. I wondered if whoever had searched the house before us had removed the tape. But if they had found the tape they were looking for, then why did they toss the rest of the house? Garza's desk had to have been the first place they looked. It made me think that they had found the tape recorder empty and had kept searching.

There were a lot of bills from places like Niemans and Lord and Taylor, a couple of sporting goods stores, and numerous credit card companies. Most were still in the envelopes with the part you send in with your check still attached, so they hadn't been paid. There was also quite a number of past-due notices, including a couple of threatening letters from collection companies. It looked like Garza had been in hock up to his ears, which was probably why he had gotten the idea to do the experiments and sell the results. Still, if what Lestat said was true, Garza had loved NASA so much that when it came down to it, he hadn't been able to go through with the plan.

The edge of a large photo was sticking out of the mess. I pulled it out, raising my eyebrows. It was an eight-by-ten black-and-white photograph of Margo. It looked professionally taken. She was lying on her side on a chaise lounge, stark naked, looking absolutely gorgeous.

The photo had been mixed up with all those bills, and I thought sadly that maybe that's what Margo had become to Garza with her pregnancy and her demands—just another obligation, another creditor on his back.

I opened my mouth to call Paoli, then realized what an incredibly stupid idea that was. I slipped the photo under a stack of papers and resumed my search.

Somebody had obviously looked under the rug, but I pulled it back anyway and then lay on my back and examined the underside of the desk. Nothing. Next I tried the kitchen. If I were going to hide something, that's the place I'd choose, but I checked the refrigerator and went through the stuff from the freezer and the drawers. Still zero.

I was standing there feeling frustrated when I heard Paoli calling me from the bedroom.

"I haven't found the tape, but take a look at this," he said, taking me inside a walk-in closet.

In front of me was a sophisticated computer setup as well as a minilibrary of computer manuals. Garza had every computer subject covered from programming to the Internet. But most interesting was the fact that the majority of books were on networking and operating systems.

Paoli sat down in front of Garza's computer, flipped the switch, and let it boot up while I watched over his shoulder. A screen appeared asking for a password. Breaking through the password on your average personal computer is child's play, but Garza had some additional security software loaded, and it took us an extra twenty minutes to get past it. We quickly found what we were looking for: the program Garza had written sending the string of numbers into NASA's software programs.

"That does it then," I said as Paoli scrolled through Garza's homegrown program. "Garza was our hacker. I'm guessing he did it to delay the SM–15 mission until he could sell the results of the experiments."

"Except that Lestat said Garza had decided not to sell them. So why keep up with the hacking?" Paoli asked.

"Maybe he was lying to Lestat and was going to sell his findings after all."

Paoli ran his fingers through his hair. "Still, there's something weird about this," he said, staring at the screen. "Our hacker is breaking into the NASA computers with a satellite. I'm sure of it. But this computer is networked with a standard phone line."

"There's something else I don't get. If Garza was the hacker, how did he get the numbers to float across the shuttle computers when they were powered off?" I asked.

He shook his head. "I don't know. I guess it's possible he could have done something to the shuttle computers to make it look like the power had shut down. Kind of a simulation effect. Although it would take some pretty heavy technical ability to fool the NASA computer staff."

Paoli and I looked at each other as the same thought crossed our minds.

"You think Michael was playing both sides of the fence?" I asked. "Giving C-CINS information on one side and helping Garza on the other?"

"How else could the computer work been done? And by helping Garza with the hacking, he would have been delaying the next shuttle mission, which was C-CINS' goal in the first place," Paoli said. He turned off Garza's computer and stood up. "We should get out of here."

"Ten more minutes. I still want that tape—now more than ever."

There were two more bedrooms and we each searched one, but by this time I was feeling the effects of all the coffee, so I went into the bathroom and shut the door.

There was a bookshelf behind the toilet, although all the books had been thrown on the floor. They were mostly sexual in nature—books of nude drawings, the pornography of Pompeii and the like. Moving some aside with my foot, I saw the Kama Sutra, a book I had always wanted to see but was too embarrassed to ask for at the bookstore, much less check out of the library. I picked it up and opened it, the pages falling open to page 105. Only part of the fascinating diagram remained, because an even more fascinating square hole about a quarter of an inch deep was cut in the pages. Inside it was a tape.

I yelled, "I found it!" and Paoli came running. I remembered seeing the tape recorder by Garza's desk. We went into the study, found it, and put in the tape.

It began with Garza giving the date, which was three weeks earlier. He admitted to doing the experiments on the shuttle, and that he was able to grow the cells in zero gravity with even more success than NASA had hoped. Garza recognized that the actual medical use of such technology was years off, but he had taken the first step.

"I realize fully the worth of such a breakthrough," Garza said, "And although I could have received millions for what I've done, I never tried to sell the research results. That is in my favor."

"All this we knew," I said with frustration.

Paoli shushed me. "Let's hear the whole thing."

Garza went on to say that he was able to complete the experiments because of Foster's negligence, and that she never had proper control of the mission. Garza then listed half a dozen aspects of the SM–13 project that Foster had mismanaged.

"What travesties could occur because of her ineptitude?" Garza asked. "I'm doing the government a favor by exposing her incompetence. If necessary, I will tell all that I know."

There was silence. I turned off the tape recorder.

"So that's it," I said. "Lestat said that Garza confessed everything to Foster the day he was murdered. He put it on the tape and handed it to her."

Paoli nodded. "He was afraid we'd find out about what

he'd done and report it to her before he got the chance to. It's nice to know our skills strike fear in the hearts of criminals."

"I wouldn't be so cocky. Remember, according to Lestat, Garza was going to tell Foster anyway. Our investigation only caused him to tell her a few weeks sooner than he had planned."

"So Foster knew about the experiments, but Garza must have been holding this tape over her head. If she tried to bounce Garza out of NASA he was going to take her with him. Nice murder motive."

"But you're forgetting something," I said.

"Which is?"

"Garza says on the tape that he has more to tell."

Paoli shrugged. "Probably just more dirt on Foster."

"Why hold back if it's dirt on Foster? He's already got enough on the tape to bury her. At least career-wise."

"What's your point?"

"I think it's dirt on somebody else. Maybe Foster wasn't the only one he wanted to take down with him, if it came to that."

"Who else?"

"I'm not sure. But we know that the hacking wasn't a virus, and we both saw the hacker's numbers on the computer screen after Garza was dead. That means only one thing. Garza had a partner."

30

We stopped off at the police department and gave Garza's tape to Pinsky and he seemed awfully glad to receive it, especially after we told him what was on it. We were purposefully vague about how it came into our possession, and Pinsky didn't press us too hard. He was up for promotion, he said, and solving the Garza case would really help his chances. With a promotion he wouldn't have to answer disturbance calls at El Toro Loco anymore, although he assured us that arresting us had been a pleasure.

"You came in real nice and easy," he said.

"If you really want to score some points," I told him, "check out every angle on the Olander suicide. I still have a feeling that was no suicide."

"Oh, I have," he said eagerly. "I've been all over it. Nothing too new yet, but I'm keeping after it."

Having done our civic duty we headed back to NASA, stopping on the way at a roadside barbecue place, our reward for finding Garza's tape. Besides, it was Saturday. Sitting outside at a picnic table, we ate barbecued chicken and sausage off sheets of white waxy paper and drank frosty Cokes out of those little bottles. There were a lot of things about Texas

I didn't much like, including the heat, the humidity and the way some of the males liked to toss people around, but the barbecue made up for about half of it.

When we got back to NASA we found things were much quieter than during the week. There were only a few cars in the parking lot and almost no one walking between buildings. The only traffic was blue trams carting tourists.

We got to work, and after about fifteen minutes Paoli raised his fist in the air and let out a joyful whoop.

"We got it!" he said, pointing to the computer screen.

"The satellite dish location?"

He gave me a huge grin and I hurried over.

"Where is it?" I asked, ecstatic, bending down and looking over his shoulder. The screen was crammed with information, but none of it meant anything to me.

"Right here. These numbers are the latitude and longitude of the dish."

"And now what do we do?"

"I found some software here that will interpret it down to a city block, but I'm going to have to work with it, and it'll take a while. Why don't you just sit quietly. I think you might have had a little too much beer last night."

"It could have happened to anybody," I muttered.

"Yeah, but somehow these things always happen to you."

I wanted to make a sarcastic retort, but since we were about to solve our case, decided against it.

Paoli hit a few keys and brought up some different software. He started typing with me looking over his shoulder, but we had problems figuring out the software. We cursed, put coffee on, drank coffee, bounced ideas off each other, tore out our hair. The computer crashed once, this event followed by more cursing and more coffee and a run to the vending machine for Twix. An hour and a half hour later Paoli got a printout and held it up like it was a winning lottery ticket.

"This is it! It gives us an intersection of two streets in Pasadena. There's a graphic and it looks to me like it's right by the ship channel."

"Let's go." I grabbed my purse and we were heading out when the phone rang. Paoli waited while I went back to answer it. "Foster wants to see us," I told Paoli, cringing as I hung up.

"She works on Saturday?"

"Apparently."

He gave me an encouraging slap on the back. "Don't worry, this will be fun. We have the hacker, don't we?"

I had to admit, it was going to feel good to tell Foster we had nailed Garza. Images of a glossy Data9000 brochure with a photo of NASA danced in my head like sugar plums.

Foster stood up as we came into her office. She was dressed casually in tight jeans and a scoop-necked T-shirt, but it was more than the Saturday clothes that made her seem different. She seemed relaxed. Happy even. She invited us to sit but remained standing behind her desk.

"Senator Halsey called me this morning from Washington," she said, like everyone in the world knew who he was. "He's heard about what's been going on here the past week and he's very concerned about morale."

I opened my mouth to say something, but she didn't give me the chance. "He wanted to know how I was going to fix the problems here. He wants my plan on his desk by Monday morning."

"The good news is that we know who the hacker is," I said before she could interrupt me. "It was Garza. We have the proof. We'll know exactly how he broke into your computer system by Monday morning."

"No, you won't," she said abruptly.

"Excuse me?" I said.

"You're fired. That's why I called you in here, why I came in today. I knew you'd be here. Please go straight to your office, pack your belongings and vacate the campus."

Paoli and I stared stupidly at her a moment, temporarily speechless. Paoli regained his faculties before I did.

"You can't fire us now," he said. "We're close to solving the case. You told us we had until Monday. We had a week, remember?"

"You'll be paid for your time and your expenses," Foster said.

I went to her desk and pressed my hands against its edge. "This is about the tape, isn't it? It's about last night."

At that her eyes shot off some sparks, but then they softened. She sat down in her chair and crossed her legs, looking up at me. "That's where you're wrong. I'm glad you got the tape. It's a relief not to have to hide anything. I told Senator Halsey about the tape and everything on it."

Paoli and I exchanged a glance. "What was his response?" I asked slowly.

She gave us a brittle smile. "Seems I may be leaving my job soon. To tell the truth, I don't mind so much. This goddamn place is a pressure cooker, and now that Seth and I are getting married, I don't want to be bringing the stress home." She blushed slightly.

"Who's Seth?" Paoli asked.

"I'll tell you later," I said to him, my eyes on Foster. "Congratulations. But I still don't understand why you're firing us. We've got your hacker, but it's just as important to find out how he was getting into your computers."

"That's very interesting, but—"

"We're also fairly certain Garza had an accomplice," I rushed on. "Someone here at NASA. That accomplice is the most likely suspect for Garza's murder."

"Go pack your things, Ms. Blake."

I threw up my hands. "I thought you were so determined to get results! We're offering you results and you still want to kick us out!"

To my amazement, she laughed. I had just told her that we had found the hacker and might be able to find Garza's murderer, and she just tossed her head back and laughed like it was all a joke.

"You don't understand yet how this place works, do you?" she said. "Results aren't important if they start interfering with funding. You can't send up rockets in space without money, and where do the dollars come from? Political pricks like Halsey. Halsey's not pissed off because two corpses have turned up here and that a mission's been canceled. He's worried about his committee seat. As a result he wants some heads to roll, so roll they will. We'll turn the hacking case over to the police. If it's really connected to Garza's murder, it's the right thing to do anyway."

I shook my head. "This is retribution against me. It has to be."

Foster gave me a patronizing smile. "Sweetheart, it wasn't even my idea to fire you. It was Margo Miller's."

When we got back to our office Margo was sitting at the desk. Wearing a blue cotton summery dress and sandals, she looked like she'd just stepped out of one of those douche ads full of blue skies and fields of flowers.

Paoli first stopped in the doorway and just glared at her. I slipped past him and went inside.

She shifted slightly in her seat, but her expression remained placid.

"I know you just met with Foster," she said. "I came by to say I'm sorry." She sounded as if she meant it.

"Foster said it was your idea to fire us. Is that true?" Paoli asked her, his voice amazingly calm, but I could tell by his face he was cocked and loaded.

She didn't flinch. "Senator Halsey is coming next week. We're under pressure and we had to show him we're taking some action."

"Why does the action have to be firing us?" he asked, this time the words coming out with some heat.

Margo bristled, fiddling with his calculator, avoiding his gaze.

"I know you didn't intend it, but you've stirred up things here. Halsey told Foster to make some changes, and she wanted my advice on who we could cut."

"And of course you recommended cutting us," he said.

"That's the only reason she asked me in the first place. She knew I'd have to recommend cutting you."

Moving from the doorway, Paoli stood next to her, looking down on her with disgust.

"So let me understand this. You're going to tell this Halsey guy that what's gone on around here this past week is our fault? We show up at NASA and people start committing suicide and murder?"

Her eyes flashed as they met his. "Don't be stupid. We can say you handled the investigation badly. That you put pressure on people, that you made the situation worse."

"It's a lie, Margo."

Sucking in her cheeks, her nostrils flared and her perfect skin turned pink. Up until then she had thought of Paoli as her lapdog, and now she didn't much relish him turning on her. It would force her to recalculate the strength of her charms, and she might not like the way the math came out.

"But you're only contractors," she said, an edge creeping into her silky voice. "You'd be gone in a few days anyway. Why get so heated up about it?"

"Because I don't like being screwed by a friend," he said.

Her eyes went back to the desk. "You won't be the only ones. We're firing Michael, too."

Paoli couldn't hold his temper any longer. He spun the chair so she faced him. "What about friendship and counting on each other and all that other garbage you laid on me when you thought your job was in trouble and you needed me to help you?"

"Things have changed," she answered quietly.

He put his hands on the arms of her chair and leaned close to her. They seemed to have forgotten I was in the room.

"This isn't because I wouldn't hop into the sack with you, is it?" he asked her. My eyes widened. He had *definitely* forgotten I was in the room. "You wanted to use me to step into your dead boyfriend's shoes. I wouldn't do it, so you're paying me back."

Margo pushed the chair back and stood up, looking at him coldly. "It's unfair to judge me like that. I was half out of my mind about John's death."

"You're good at making excuses for yourself," Paoli told her.

She stiffened, but she didn't crumble. "Grow up, Vic. I have a baby on the way. I can't afford to lose my job. I don't want to seem unfeeling, but if you're not out of here in fifteen minutes I'll have security escort you. I'm sorry."

She swept past Paoli toward the door, but then stopped, turning those blue eyes on me. "I admit I asked him to go to bed with me. I was feeling desperate about things, although it's no excuse. But he said he wasn't interested."

I didn't know what to say. She didn't seem to expect a response anyway. "Bye, Julie. I'm glad I met you," she said, and left.

Paoli and I packed in silence. He slammed things around on his desk and angrily shoved his belongings into his briefcase. I wasn't feeling that great myself. I wanted to know every last detail of what had gone on between him and Margo, but I couldn't bring myself to ask him. I was the one who finally broke the silence.

"Is this ours or NASA's?" I asked, holding up a new spiral notebook.

Paoli stopped what he was doing, knowing the real question I was asking.

"I hope you're not thinking that anything ever happened between Margo and me, because it didn't."

I closed my briefcase and set it on the desk with an impressive whack.

"She asked you to have sex with her. You could have told me about it."

"Right. You would have taken it well, I'm sure."

"It would have been better than finding out like this." I turned away from him. "Let's drop it."

I felt him close behind me. "I don't think we should, Julie," he said. "We need to talk about it." He put his hands on my arms. I pushed them away.

"I don't want to talk about it. Not now, anyway. There's

no time. Right now we have to find that damn satellite dish."

"Excuse me, but haven't we just been fired? We've already handed what we've got over to the police. So let's get back to California."

"We can't," I said, facing him. "We said we'd solve this case in one week, so let's solve it. We've got the satellite dish location. What's to keep us from finding it?"

Paoli tapped his knuckles on my forehead. "Julie? Hello in there, this is Vic. I know you're mad at Foster and at Margo and at me, and I can relate to that because I'm pretty ticked off myself. But someone has been murdered over this satellite thing. I didn't like risking my life when we were getting paid, but risking my life free of charge really lacks appeal."

I waved a hand dismissively. "So Margo and Foster tell us to leave and we immediately go scampering home?"

"Oh, I forgot. This is a competitive thing with you," he said.

"That's not the issue."

"Well, it's going to be a security issue soon because they're calling the guards if we don't get out of here."

"Fine, so we'll leave NASA, but we *have* to locate the satellite dish. It's a matter of honor. This is our project now. We need to show these NASA people that Data9000 Investigations handles a project start to finish."

There were a dozen things I wanted to say to him, but I couldn't manage to say any that really mattered. I went up to him, putting my hands on his chest.

"Just give me until tonight. If we don't find the satellite dish we go home tomorrow. We'll be back at the Hard Drive Cafe having coffee Monday morning. I'm only asking for a few hours."

He was looking past me toward the door. I was afraid he might be thinking about bolting through it, but I turned and saw Sally Olander there. She was wearing shorts, a halter top, tennis shoes and ankle socks, and she looked like a teenage girl. She stepped inside and tossed a folded piece of paper onto my desk.

"There. I hope you're happy now," she said bitterly. "I just dropped off the original with the police so they'd get off my back. Read it."

I picked up the paper and slowly unfolded it. It was a photocopy of a handwritten letter. The original had been written on a four-by-six memo pad with NASA and the emblem printed at the top. The words were crammed unevenly onto the page, front and back, some of them barely legible. But I could make out most of it.

It was Gary Olander's suicide note. In it he said that by leaving him, Sally had ruined his life, that she had wrecked his confidence, torn him apart. It was sad and vindictive, and it was hard to believe it had been written by the smiling man in the photograph I had seen our first day at NASA. I felt a dull gnawing in the pit of my stomach.

"Gary went nuts because I met somebody else. His ego couldn't take it. He started yelling and screaming at everybody," she said.

I handed the note to Paoli, remembering we had seen Olander storming out of the conference room. "And he was having trouble at work because of it?" I asked.

"That's putting it mildly," she said, sounding shaky. "They were kicking him off the shuttle crew. I guess that's what finally did it."

Our first day at NASA flashed through my mind: the arguments in the conference room, and later, the furtive conversation among Olander, Lanie and Lestat. They had supported Olander. That's why Lanie had been so upset at the meeting. It was Garza who had wanted to get rid of Olander, just like he had gotten rid of her brother.

"Did he give you any warning at all?" Paoli asked her.

"He told me he was going to kill himself, but I didn't believe him. I mean, guys don't kill themselves because their wives leave them, right?" she asked in a childish, defensive voice. "We'd only been married two years."

"I'm sorry," I said, but it was hopelessly inadequate.

Her face hardened. "You ought to be. You couldn't keep your nose out of it. I would have been able to keep the note a secret, but you stirred things up, and then the police started asking me about it, and that security guy from NASA."

"They were just—" Paoli started to say, trying to defend me.

"They were just digging it all up because she kept pestering them," Sally blurted. She turned her eyes back to me. "I figured they'd been talking to you, and they all admitted they had. Finally I had to show the note to them just to prove I wasn't a murder suspect. Now everybody's going to treat me like I murdered him anyway. You ought to mind your own damn business."

I couldn't think of anything to say that didn't sound self-serving or stupid. I had been so sure that Olander had been murdered. Now I had the proof that I'd been wrong, and I felt miserable and ashamed.

Sally looked at me, her eyes pools of misery. "It wasn't my fault, you see. Gary was never stable, not really. He—" Choking on the words, she walked quickly out of the room.

31

Don't be so hard on yourself, Jules. You thought it was a murder and it wasn't. A simple mistake," Max said consolingly from the backseat, waving a last french fry as she spoke. The car reeked of greasy potatoes. I had Paoli open all the windows halfway, and the road noise was loud enough that we had to raise our voices to talk.

We had stopped by the motel and picked up Max and Cosmos on our way to find the satellite dish. At first Paoli had objected, but I talked him into it. I hadn't seen her much the past two days, and when I told her on the phone where we were going she insisted on coming along, promising to wait in the car while we looked for the dish. I felt so bad about Sally Olander that I wanted Max with me.

As most good friends do, Max and I have this tacit agreement that no matter what lamebrained thing one of us does, the other will do her best to act as if it's completely understandable. Not that Max had been much help yet, since she spent the first fifteen minutes of the drive talking to Hansen on her cell phone, occasionally firing a french fry against the windshield when the argument got heated. She had hung up on him twice.

I sat with my arms crossed and staring gloomily out the window as we drove past forlorn-looking cows grazing fields of yellow grass. The black power lines overhead looked like whips strung across the landscape. *You ought to mind your own damn business,* Sally Olander said over and over in my head, even though I kept agreeing with her.

"Poor Sally. She looked so upset," Paoli said as he negotiated a lane change. "I'm not criticizing you, Julie, but you have to admit that sometimes you get an idea in your head and then you're glued to it. I told you that handle in the shuttle trainer could have been broken when they took Olander down. It was the most likely probability, but you—"

Max gave him a thump on the back of his head, and Cosmos, who was sitting next to her, started barking.

"Baboon. That was definitely criticism. Julie was only doing what she thought was right. God, you're just like Wayne," Max huffed, and collapsed against the back of the seat.

"You don't have to turn my dog against me," Paoli said sourly, rubbing his skull.

I pressed my fingers against my temples, hoping to relieve some of the pressure on my frontal lobes. The irritability level in the car had been escalating ever since we left the motel. We had already bickered over whether or not we should stop for food, over what food we should order, over directions, on how high to turn the air conditioner and at what angle the vents should be positioned.

I turned on the radio for the distraction, and as soon as I heard country music, I retuned it to jazz. Since the episode at the Saddlehorse, my appreciation of country music had waned.

"I think we're lost," Paoli said ten minutes later. Max

and I groaned, although it wasn't his fault, since we were the ones navigating from directions I had gotten at the Jack in the Box. We stopped at a gas station and spent twenty dollars on gas and two on a map of the Greater Houston Area.

After more quibbling and almost tearing the map into three pieces, we found the intersection of the two roads we were looking for. Even on paper it looked like the middle of nowhere. Using our map and the software printout as our guide, we backtracked and drove down the Pasadena Freeway in the direction of the ship channel.

The cracked and tarred freeway cut across flat bare land, its most distinguishing feature the hundreds of power lines held up by towering scaffolds that rose like huge futuristic robots conquering the earth. In front of us in the distance were the oil refineries, one after another, a thousand cement smokestacks belching black gas and fire. We exited the freeway, turning down Greenling Road.

"This is what I always imagined Purgatory would look like," Max said.

"You wouldn't want to put a pirate satellite dish in your back yard or on the roof of Saks Fifth Avenue," Paoli responded.

He pulled the car over to the side of the road and again asked for the map. After he took a long look, we started off again, turning onto a smaller road that ran behind a refinery. We passed a junkyard, then came to a cluster of small office buildings, all old, weathered and constructed out of cinder block.

Paoli pulled the car into a small unpaved parking lot across the road, and we sat staring at the buildings.

He drummed his fingers on the steering wheel. "Now

what? We have no idea which building it is. The software only told us where the roads intersected."

"If there's a satellite dish here, it's probably on one of these roofs," I told him.

"Brilliant analysis," he said.

Max reached forward to thump his head again, but I pushed her hand away. I looked at the buildings in front of us, deciding to concentrate on satellite dishes instead of my love life. The buildings were all four stories high, and from the outside a couple of them looked empty. Abandoned was more like it.

I pointed at the building on the corner. "Look, the lights on the third floor are turned on," I said.

Paoli shrugged. "So?"

"So that means that maybe someone is inside, right, Jules?" Max piped in.

"Which means the front door might be open," I told her. "We walk in, go up the elevator to the top floor and find the door to the roof. Then we can look around for the dish."

"Piece of cake," Paoli grumbled

"It'll be easy," I said, doing my best to be upbeat. "The buildings are all the same height. We can stand on the edge of one roof and see the others."

He sat up straight. "You make it sound so simple and there's this voice in my head telling me it's not going to be simple at all. And why? Because nothing's simple. Everything's complicated. Life's a maze with no cheese at the end. It's a labyrinth."

"No cussin'," I said with a smile, but Paoli's frown stayed put. "Listen, there's no point in just sitting here talking about it. Let's go," I said with all the enthusiasm I could muster.

Paoli started the car and pulled behind the buildings. When we got out Max came with us.

"You promised you'd wait in the car," I said to her.

She shook her hair. "No way, Jules. It's too eerie here."

"We don't know what we'll find. It could be dangerous."

"I'm a grown woman. I can make my own decisions."

Paoli decided to inject his manliness into the situation. "Get back in the car," he said to her, but Max wouldn't back down, and he finally gave up.

It was late in the day and the September air was starting to cool, so we left the windows partway open for Cosmos and set off across the muddy lot for the corner building.

The odor of sulfur filled my nostrils and I wrapped my arms around myself, struck by how desolate the place felt. The whole area seemed deserted.

A weathered sign on the door of one of the buildings read "B&K Refinery has moved." The new address was unreadable.

Parked behind the corner building was a small, dirty white sedan. The right headlight was broken and held together with duct tape. I went quickly over to it.

"This is it," I said to Paoli as he and Max came up behind me. "At least I think it could be it."

"Could be what?" Max asked.

"Look at this." I pointed to a streak of dark paint running inside a shallow dent along the right side of the sedan. "This could be the car that ran me off the road the other night. The car was light colored and look, the right headlight is out. And see here? The paint on the fender is the color of our loaner car."

Paoli stooped down and inspected it more closely. "This duct tape looks new. Okay, Julie," he said, standing up. "If this is the car that ran you off the road, we should get the hell out of here. There may be a murderer in one of these buildings, and I for one am not interested in confronting him. It's time to call the police."

I opened my mouth to argue, thought better of it and just nodded in agreement. We jotted down the car's license number and debated whether or not it was a legitimate 911 call, me being pro, Paoli being con. I won. We used Max's cell phone and the 911 dispatcher transferred me to the sheriff's department. A deputy told me he'd send someone out, but couldn't guarantee a time since it wasn't an emergency.

"I'm glad that's out of the way. I'm starved. Let's go eat," Paoli said.

"We just ate three orders of french fries," I said.

Max raised an eyebrow. "You call that food?"

"Listen, we'll eat, but not yet," I told them. "We have to find the satellite dish."

Paoli rolled his eyes upward. "Why?"

"Because if we don't, we won't be able to say we solved the case."

"I can live with that if it means we avoid tangling with a murderer," he said.

"But Data9000 Investigations needs NASA as a reference."

Paoli put his hands on my shoulders and gave me a penetrating look. "Julie, sweetheart, you attacked the NASA director in a public restroom and sunk a NASA car in a bayou, not to mention the fact that we were fired a few hours ago. I wouldn't set my heart on them giving us a glowing reference."

"The car was hardly Julie's fault," Max said.

"Listen, we're so close to solving the whole thing, this

isn't the time to back down," I told him. "Let's compromise. We'll go to the roof and take a quick look. If we find the satellite dish, we're home free. The police can track down the person who ran me off the road from the license number off that car. Whoever it is, is probably Garza's accomplice and possibly the person who murdered him. NASA will have to admit we solved the whole case. Big story in *Computerworld.* Color photo of NASA in our next brochure."

Paoli eyed me. "As soon as we find the satellite dish we go home?"

The brochure thing always got to him. We walked to the front door of the building where we had seen the lights. I grabbed the doorknob and gave it a twist. It was open.

"Voilá," I said.

"How do you say 'I don't like the smell of this' in French?" Max said, peering past me.

"We're going to find this satellite dish. You'll see," I told her.

"No, I mean I literally don't like the smell of this. What do they make here, manure?"

The inside of the building did have a foul odor, and I tried not to breathe as we went in. The lobby was small, with a cracked linoleum floor, yellowed walls and a heavy layer of dust. To one side was a long hallway piled with boxes. The sound of a gruff voice filtered through a closed door, but the voice was solitary, and came and went. Someone on the phone.

"There's the elevator," Paoli whispered. He tilted his head toward a battered door. "What do you say we take the stairs?"

I nodded. An exit sign near the hallway directed us to a door with STAIRS painted on it in peeling black letters. Taking my hand, Paoli opened the door and went through first, pulling me after him. Max followed us into a stairwell strewn with garbage.

I started for the dilapidated stairs but Paoli grabbed my arm.

"Let me go first," he said with aggravation. "Don't get me wrong, but since we started this business, I've noticed that your aggressiveness usually gets us both in trouble."

"Oh, right. Just because I'm not a prom queen like Margo means I'm overly aggressive," I said, following him up the stairs.

Paoli kicked at some garbage. "Don't drag Margo into this."

"No, not Margo," I said with mock horror. "Not every-hair-in-place Margo. The woman who got us fired."

"She saved your life. You said so."

"I was exaggerating wildly."

"I don't know why you're so jealous of her."

"You absolutely know why. You were considering sleeping with her. She said so right in front of me."

He turned around to face me. "That's not what she said. She said she asked me to sleep with her, but that I turned her down. Why are you so stuck on this Margo thing?"

"Hah. You think I'm stuck on it?"

"Like a suction cup."

"Now, now, children, let's play nice," Max said from behind me. "This little spat is very amusing, but we have to learn to get along with each other, to see things from the other person's perspective."

Max's phone rang. She dug it out of her purse.

"Stop bothering me, Wayne," she spat into it, and I held my finger to my lips, despite the fact that Paoli and I had been a lot louder. She reduced her voice to an enraged whisper. "Because I have things to do. Yes, Wayne. Important things. I'm breaking and entering an abandoned building with Vic and Julie. Yes, it's quite dangerous. Now buzz off and go play with your computer pals." Max disconnected the phone and put it back in her purse.

At the top of the stairs Paoli opened the door, and Max and I followed him through it and up a short flight of steps. Gravel crunched on the tar paper under our feet as we climbed up onto the roof.

It was getting dark, and dazzling pinks and golds swirled in the western sky. Surrounded by the tall towers of the refineries, we were stunned by the millions of lights outlining the towers as they all flickered on at once.

"It's really magical up here in a crazy sort of way," Max said softly. "All these lights. I feel like I'm in Oz."

Paoli turned in a slow circle, looking perplexed. "But there's no satellite dish up here. I must have input the data wrong."

I heard a car engine. We all hurried to the edge of the roof, looked down and saw the white sedan drive off.

"There's goes our suspect," I said.

"Good," Paoli answered. "At least we're safer. Let's take one more quick look around then get out of here."

"What about the next building?" I asked.

"There's nothing there either. Look." He pointed to the next roof.

"But we can't see behind that shed or whatever it is. The dish could be behind it," I told him.

We went over to that edge of the roof. There was a three-foot gap between the buildings, an easy jump, but the drop was an ominous four stories. I looked at some windows in the two facing walls. Nice view they had.

"We'll have to go back down and then—" Paoli began, but before he could finish I had jumped safely to the next building. I turned back to him and grinned. As a kid I had been the type with an agile mind but an awkward body; Gearhead was last to be chosen for any team, but my popularity usually skyrocketed just before test time.

"That was so stupid!" Paoli said.

"The urge to leap tall buildings overwhelmed me. It felt good."

"Falling four stories wouldn't have," Max said, sounding as annoyed as Paoli.

Paoli made the jump easily, looking rankled. It took a minute, but with our arms outstretched, Paoli and I coaxed Max over.

"I guess Margo would have gone back down and taken a cab," I joked to Max.

"She wouldn't have done anything stupid like jumping it without help," Paoli said.

"That's because she might snag her nylons," I said. I knew I was being childish, but I couldn't help myself.

But Paoli wasn't listening. He stared past my shoulder and then slowly raised his arm and pointed. I turned to look.

The shed we had seen housed a defunct-looking air-conditioning unit. Behind it was the satellite dish.

32

It sat perfectly still in the warm night, its concave face turned toward the heavens, beaming its messages into the blackness of space, oblivious of the pain and trouble it had caused. But it wasn't to blame. Humans initiate all the anguish and pain in the world. Machines are only silicon and circuitry, genius children innocently doing their parent's bidding.

We hurried over to the satellite dish. The sight of it made my heart thump. Paoli knelt down to inspect it.

"It looks like one of those television dishes that gets three gazillion stations," Max said, bending over, her hands on her knees.

I crouched next to Paoli. He fingered a cable leading from the dish to a connector that fed the cable through the roof.

"You're half right, Max," Paoli said. "This kind handles television or data signals. We know Garza was doing the hacking from his house, but he must have been transmitting the stuff by a phone line to this location."

"So there's a computer around here somewhere?" Max asked, straightening.

"There must be," I answered. "The hacker's numbers were being transmitted into NASA's computer even after

Garza died, and we know it wasn't a virus, so it had to be happening in real time. There's a computer somewhere in this building."

Max nodded, understanding. "And that computer sent the hacker's numbers to the satellite dish?"

"Right through that black cable," Paoli said. "Then this dish beamed the numbers to a satellite that was communicating to NASA."

We stayed like that a moment, looking down at the dish, Max standing, Paoli and me stooped down beside it, awed by the intricacies of the hacker's plan. Our trance was broken by the muffled ring of Max's cell phone. She reached inside her purse and pulled it out, mouthing *Wayne* to us after she answered it, as if we had any doubts. She resumed their argument, her voice rising until we shushed her again. Paoli and I studied the dish.

"Look," I said, pointing to a toolbox beneath it. I grabbed the dish's lower edge. "I can wiggle it, so it's definitely off its bolts. I think someone was trying to remove it."

"Why did they stop?" Paoli asked.

"Probably because they couldn't lift it on their own. It's awfully heavy. It would take two people to handle this thing."

Paoli looked at the satellite dish and then at me. "This proves Garza had an accomplice. He couldn't have gotten this up here himself."

"I suppose he could have tricked somebody into it. He could have said he wanted cable TV or something."

Paoli shook his head. "I don't think so. This isn't your ordinary cable dish. Any cable company would have been suspicious."

I sidled over to look at the back of the dish, and as I did

a beam of light shining upward caught my eye. I stood up and went towrd it.

It was reflecting off an old, dirty skylight, so grimy it was difficult to see through. There was a hole in the glass patched with the same type of duct tape we had just seen on the white sedan. I peeled up the tape, and looking through the hole, I inhaled sharply. It was a lab. Not the professional variety, but a homegrown one. Culture jars, a microscope and a piece of equipment I couldn't identify stood on a linoleum counter. A bright red jacket was thrown over the back of a chair.

I felt my insides knot up. "Paoli, come here," I whispered as loudly as I dared.

He came and knelt down beside me. Max hissed into her phone, unaware of us. I pointed to the hole. Side by side, we looked down into the laboratory.

"That equipment on the counter," Paoli said. "I don't know what it does exactly, but it's biomedical, I'm sure of it."

I touched his knee. "How do you know?"

"I saw one at the lab when we were working on the Biotech case. It would be nice if we knew what it was used for."

"I have a feeling it's used to grow cell cultures," I told him, straining to see the jars more closely.

The culture jars were lined up on a rack inside a machine that looked like an incubator. They contained a cloudy pink liquid and there was a milky mass floating in each one. My heart fluttered as I realized that the milkiness must be growing tissues.

I was transfixed by the sight of them, and by the fact that someone had taken the first steps toward actually growing human organs. I wondered how many lives would be saved because of this initial research, regardless of the circumstances surrounding it. And how long would it have taken to accomplish without the advantage of zero gravity, and how many lives lost in the meantime? I thought about C-CINS protesting the NASA shuttle program, and in spite of my previous sympathy, I found now that I couldn't agree with them.

Paoli's expression was troubled. "You think Garza was lying about not doing anything with the results from the shuttle experiments?"

I smiled at my boyfriend. Like me, he found solace in the fact that Garza had in the end chosen his life's work over greed.

"No, I don't think he did anything with them." I pressed my finger against the skylight. "But his partner did. That red jacket looks like the one McKenzie wears. Maybe Space Monk's not as Zen as he pretends to be."

"Lots of people have red jackets, Julie."

With a sick feeling I remembered what McKenzie had said to me that day in the shuttle trainer. He had said that the blackness within him was more frightening than the blackness of space.

"It's more than that. McKenzie was on the SM–13 mission with Garza. His kid's disabled and in an expensive school, so he's bound to need money. Maybe that whole Space Monk thing is a façade."

Paoli stared at the lab, turning things over in his mind. "Okay, so let's say Garza and McKenzie decided together to do the cell experiments. You think McKenzie murdered Garza so he could reap all the profits?"

I considered it. "I think the problem was that Garza decided his NASA career was worth more than money to him."

"Right. He wanted to come clean about it before any money was made."

"And that's why McKenzie killed him. It's starting to make sense to me," I said. "McKenzie and Garza did the hacking together. It confirms my theory that the whole green-light-numbers-on-the screen thing was a sham. McKenzie and Garza were the only ones who claimed to see the numbers when the computers were powered off. Remember? They could have turned off the shuttle power themselves for a few seconds." I saw the disappointment on Paoli's face. "Sorry. It doesn't mean there's no alien life. It just means there wasn't any on the shuttle." I looked back through the skylight. "If you don't count McKenzie."

I thought of the conversations I'd had with him. He had tried to frighten us into believing that the hacking was the work of some otherworldly force, and because of his hubris he expected us to believe it. After all, he was an astronaut. We were mere mortals, gullible nerds from California. But when his story didn't slow down our investigation, McKenzie tried another approach. He warned me that we were in danger. And when I didn't frighten off, he made the danger real by trying to kill me. The whole idea of it was loathsome.

Paoli stood up and dusted off his knees. "Max, get over here," he said. She spat, "I've got to go," into the phone, hung up and came over.

"Max, I want you to call the cops again and tell them to hurry," he said, and turned to me. "I'm going to check out the lab while we wait for the police. There's got to be a door on the roof that'll get me into the building."

He went to the air-conditioning unit, where a short flight of steps led down to a steel door. I followed him, watching him as he tried it, but it was locked. He muttered a curse.

"Okay," he said, "I'm going back the way we came in."

I put my hand on his arm. "I'm going with you."

"No, Julie. It's safest if you stay here," he said, running his fingers over mine, but his tone was adamant. "Whoever that was who just took off, we don't know how long he's going to be gone. I need you to stay here and call down to me if you hear him come back."

"Max can be the lookout. I don't think you should go poking around there alone."

"Believe me, the last thing I want is to go near McKenzie. That guy scares me. I just want to look around a little. You call down to me through the skylight if you hear anything."

Paoli picked up a large wrench from the toolbox, went down the steps to the door and jammed the wrench into a metal bracket intended for an outside lock.

"Now no one will be able to get up here," he said.

"I'm coming with you," I insisted.

"Which means I'm coming, too," Max said. I wished she hadn't.

"You're staying, both of you," Paoli told us, frowning.

He turned as if that settled the matter and went to the edge of the roof, jumping back to the corner building.

Max and I watched him disappear down the steps to the doorway.

She sighed. "You know, Vic really does have an attractive masculinity sometimes. I wish Wayne did. He just whines and throws money at everybody."

I figured Paoli had a good enough head start. "Call the police again, Max. I'm going after him."

Her brow furrowed. "And leave me here alone?"

"You're perfectly safe. Besides, I may need you here. If you hear anybody coming, I want you to yell like crazy."

I jumped across to the roof of the first building and went down the steps to the door, but when I tried to open it, it refused to budge. Knowing me better than I thought he did, Paoli had locked it from the inside. I uttered a "damn," kicking at the gravel, then went and leapt back to the other roof. I was getting good at it. If only those schoolyard kids could see old Gearhead now.

Max was sitting on top of the air-conditioning unit watching me. I told her what had happened.

"So now what?" she asked.

"We wait."

"I hate waiting."

"Be sure and tell me when you come up with an alternative."

Max arched an eyebrow. "No need to get snippy."

I patted her hand. "Sorry. It's just that I'm frustrated." My stomach growled. "I'm also hungry. You have anything to eat?"

She exhaled with aggravation. "Sure, now you want food when we're stuck on a rooftop with no way off."

I leaned my hip against the air conditioner. "I would have gotten a few more french fries if you hadn't flung them all over the car while you were having your little phone spat."

We looked at each other and laughed, and Max dug around in her purse and gave me her last two Tic Tacs. I went to the roof's edge to look for Paoli but didn't see him or anybody else, so I sat back down next to Max. I felt even hungrier after the Tic Tacs and decided to do some research on the nutritional properties of Maalox. I had just put the bottle to my lips when a car's engine rumbled in the distance.

I rushed to the edge of the roof, then shrank back so I wouldn't be seen.

"Oh, Jeezus," I muttered. I ran back to the skylight and crouched down next to it. Max followed me, looking scared.

"What was it?" she asked.

"The white sedan. It's back," I told her. "Paoli!" I said as loudly as I dared through the hole in the glass. After a couple of seconds he appeared below us.

"Julie, there's a PC down here networked to that satellite dish," he said, full of excitement. "And I found papers from some clinical research firm in Shanghai—"

"There's no time for that."

I felt Max's hand on my shoulder. "Jules, I heard the car door close," she said tensely.

Paoli was still looking up at me. "But it's proof that McKenzie was selling the results of the experiments. His name's on the letter."

"Listen to me. You've got to get out of there now! The white car is back!" I said.

Paoli passed a hand over his forehead. "Of all the crappy luck. I've got to get those papers first. They're made out to some company, and if we trace them we can find out—"

"You're going to find out plenty if you don't get the hell out of there. Get out now!"

Paoli looked up at me a second then dashed out of sight.

"I don't like this, Jules," Max said.

She started to say something else, but I hushed her, looking around the roof. My nerve endings froze. I heard voices, but at first I couldn't figure out where they were coming

317

from. Then I realized they were below me. I knelt beside the skylight, gravel digging into my knees, and brought my face close to it. I could see Paoli standing by the counter, but not whoever he was talking to.

Paoli took a step backward. The second person moved forward and I was looking at the top of McKenzie's bald head. There was a gun in his hand.

For a second I was unable to move, I was so terrified. There was no way I could get to Paoli. The roof door was locked.

"Dial nine-one-one, Max," I whispered frantically. "Tell them it's an emergency." She took her phone out, looking at me with frightened eyes, and punched the numbers. I put my ear close to the glass.

"Where's Julie?" McKenzie said.

"She's at the motel," Paoli answered. I couldn't make out McKenzie's response, but I heard Paoli say, "Then go look for her, if it'll make you feel better." McKenzie didn't make a move. Their voices sounded strangely calm. I, on the other hand, was shaking like crazy.

"You killed Garza, didn't you?" Paoli asked. I didn't wait to hear the answer, because I already knew it. Garza had been standing between McKenzie and money, and Garza wouldn't have hesitated to let McKenzie into the WET-F with him that night. All McKenzie had to do was wait until Garza got the WET-F suit on and then push him into the pool and watch him drown. A man that cold would kill Paoli without a second thought.

I couldn't let that happen. A half dozen thoughts bounced crazily through my head. I got up and went to the satellite dish, tried my best to lift it up. It was too heavy.

"Get over here and help me," I said to Max, who came running. Together we turned it onto its side and, with a lot of whispered swearing, rolled it to the skylight.

"What are we doing, trying to improve this guy's cable reception? We're in trouble here," Max said, nearly breathless with the effort and with panic.

I looked down through the hole in the skylight. I could hear Paoli's voice, but he was out of sight now. I could only see McKenzie directly below.

"Calm down and listen," I said to Max. "On the count of three we lift the dish over the skylight. When I say drop it, we drop it. Okay?"

Max screwed her face up, but nodded. I bent down and grabbed the dish from underneath, and Max did the same on her side. Taking a deep breath, I gritted my teeth, counted to three and then, groaning, we lifted it. It felt like it weighed a thousand pounds.

"This way," I said, my voice strained, and backed up a few steps until we were in position. "One, two, three—now!"

We jerked our hands away. There was a loud crash as it broke through the glass, followed by a second crash as the dish hit the lab floor. Then there were gunshots. Crying out, I fell to my knees.

A sound whizzed past me and I realized that McKenzie was shooting at Max and me, not at Paoli. I caught a glimpse of Paoli tackling McKenzie before I grabbed Max and tumbled both of us away from the skylight.

Then the shots stopped. I screamed out Paoli's name as I scrambled back on my hands and knees to look down into the lab. McKenzie was sprawled on the floor and Paoli stood over him, holding the gun.

"Julie, are you all right?" Paoli yelled. He took a couple of quick glances upward, afraid to take his eye off McKenzie, who was struggling to sit up.

"I'm okay." I turned and looked at Max. "Are you okay, Max?"

She stared at me open-mouthed, her eyes wide.

"What is it?" I asked her.

Her hand went up to her mouth. "You're bleeding!"

It was something to tell my grandchildren about, if I ever got around to having any. Shot in the ear. Just knicked, but the bandage was large, and I was sure that with some embellishment the story would really impress my friends back at the Hard Drive Cafe.

Paoli was sitting next to me in the back of the ambulance watching the half dozen police cars and the paramedics who were packing up to leave. They were in the process of loading Space Monk into an ambulance. Some of the glass had cut his face.

Max was talking on her cell phone to Wayne, exaggerating her role in the whole affair. I was just glad we were all alive.

"I hear multiple ear piercings are still in style," Paoli said to me. He was calm now, but when he had first saw me dripping blood he had acted like a nut case.

"The paramedic said I wouldn't have much of a scar. An earring will hide it."

Paoli looked at his watch. "It's ten-thirty. We solved the case with a whole day to spare. We're good, aren't we?"

"We're wonderful. But I doubt it will keep Foster from using us as a scapegoat."

"I meant you and me, Julie. We're a great team any way

you look at it." Paoli took my hand and held onto it. "Listen, what happened between me and Margo. There's something I want you to know about."

They had given me a painkiller and I was starting to feel pleasantly woozy. He could have said anything and it would have sounded like Mozart. "Which is?"

"I told her I was crazy about you. That there was no woman in the universe for me other than you."

"Is that why she got us fired?" I asked, yawning.

"I'm sure it didn't help." He reached over and stroked my hair. "But you know what she said afterwards? She said she wished she could be more like you."

"She did? I can't believe it." The fog was thickening in my head, but that amazed me. The Prom Queen wanted to be more like Gearhead?

"Why not? You're smart. Gorgeous." He pressed my hand to his lips. "Excellent at strip Scrabble. Sexy. A first-class computer geek when you want to be. Did I say sexy? And . . . "

I put my head on his shoulder. "And what?"

"And I always wanted a broad who'd take a bullet for me," he said. Then he kissed me.

33

From the beginning human beings have been driven to explore. It is our nature and our need. When a curious Neanderthal first wandered over a distant hill, an ancient Polynesian paddled out onto a seemingly endless ocean, or explorers crossed strange continents not knowing what dangers or wonders lay ahead, there were always skeptics who called them foolish, who cried out angrily that it was wiser to stay at home. But it is the law of life that growth means change.

I left NASA with the firm belief that exploration is one of life's necessities—not only of the space beyond us but of the space within. I had learned a lot about myself on the case.

I learned how badly I could misconstrue facts, how much I could mislead myself. By trying to paint Gary Olander's suicide as a homicide, I had caused poor Sally Olander a great deal of additional pain, and I would have to learn to live with that. I learned that I can trust Paoli and that I don't know as much as I sometimes think I do. I had learned a lot about my own weaknesses from this case, and I had come out stronger.

In other areas things also didn't turn out so badly. Worried out of his wits, Wayne Hansen had sent a Lear jet to Houston for Max and she went happily back to Silicon Valley, taking Cosmos with her so he wouldn't have to endure the humiliation of flying home in baggage.

The infamous hacker's numbers turned out to be McKenzie's Visa, Sears and American Express card numbers backwards. I called Senator Halsey and talked him into hiring Paoli and me to revamp NASA's shuttle computer security system. We were able to bill for an extra two weeks as a result.

Two weeks later, with our NASA job wrapped up, Paoli and I were sitting at the Countdown having a beer with Lanie and Lestat, a little going-away party before we headed home the next morning. Sister Teresa said it was the first time she had actually had astronauts in the Countdown, and she was so gratified she didn't overcharge us for the drinks.

"So McKenzie and Garza had done the tissue growth experiments on SM–13, but Garza had second thoughts about it afterward?" Lanie asked when she was halfway through her first and only beer.

I was on my second. "Garza wanted to back out, but McKenzie didn't. According to a document they found in his lab, McKenzie had a sale of the research already lined up. Garza was getting ready to ruin everything for him by telling the truth to NASA. So McKenzie killed him."

"Poor John," Lanie said, shaking her head sadly.

Paoli nodded. "Only we can't forget that Garza was hardly an innocent bystander. He was blackmailing Foster to keep himself at NASA."

Lestat raised his mug and drained it. "I know it doesn't hold a candle next to Garza's murder," he said, setting it back down. "But I'm still ticked off at McKenzie for screwing up the SM—15 on purpose and making us all look like fools."

Paoli cringed. "Yeah, I admit that I really fell for that alien code thing in the computer."

I couldn't help but rub it in a little. "And it went farther than that. Garza backed McKenzie up on this ridiculous story about a green light in the SM—13 cockpit, and all of you having the same weird dream about it."

I laughed and Paoli joined in. It took me a second to realize that Lanie and Lestat weren't exactly sharing our mirth.

"McKenzie and Garza told you about that?" Lanie asked.

Paoli turned up his palms. "Well, yes, but it was a made-up story, just like the hacker's numbers showing up on the computer screen. Dave Kane wants to interview us again about the case later and I thought we'd tell him—"

"No, please," Lanie pleaded. "You can't tell anyone about that."

"Why not?" I asked her.

"Because that part was true. It really happened," she said, her tone hushed. She stared into her beer a moment, then looked back up at us. "I had the dream again last night." Lanie saw me glance at Lestat. "So did Ben," she said.

Lanie went on to describe the green light that had filled the cockpit in space and pervaded her dreams on earth, and every detail matched the story we'd heard from McKenzie and Garza.

After that I switched to tequila.

That night, on the way back to the Seaview Lodge, Paoli and I pulled off onto the side of the road and sat on the hood of our government-fleet car, our arms around each other, just looking at the stars. I didn't think we'd ever view them quite the same way again.

When we got back in the car I took out my notebook, and under "Progress" I wrote, *Solved case* and under "Misc.," *Substantiated anecdotal evidence of alien life form. Still unconvinced.*

Months later something happened that struck me as even stranger than extraterrestials. When Margo had her baby girl, she named her Julie, after me.